T0265542

THE ONLY BLACK GIRL IN THE ROOM

THE ONLY BLACK GIRL IN THE ROOM

A Novel

ALEX TRAVIS

alcove
press

Published in the United States by Alcove Press, an imprint of The Quick Brown Fox & Company LLC.

Alcove Press and its logo are trademarks of The Quick Brown Fox & Company LLC.

Library of Congress Catalog-in-Publication data available upon request.

ISBN (hardcover): 978-1-63910-693-6
ISBN (ebook): 978-1-63910-694-3

Cover design by Stephanie Singleton

Printed in the United States.

www.alcovepress.com

Alcove Press
34 West 27th St., 10th Floor
New York, NY 10001

First Edition: February 2024

10 9 8 7 6 5 4 3 2 1

To all of the Black girls
who've kept me from being the only one in the room.

This is for you, and for us.

CHAPTER ONE

The casket is mahogany with platinum and diamond accents, and it costs more than most people will ever make in a year.

My boyfriend's sister nudges me. "It could feed a small African country," she whispers, shivering in her thigh-length black halter dress and pulling her silk shawl over her shoulders. It's a particularly rich comment coming from Joanna, who invested in a blood diamond company *after* it was in style. But can I really expect anything else from an heiress to a multimillionaire's estate? Her ankles, tanned and toned from her monthlong yoga retreat in Bali, look close to buckling, the worst peril of wearing six-inch stilettos to an event that requires hours of standing in the grass.

I'm not entirely sure whether the funeral attendees' tears are truly for Julian Landon, late CEO of the country's top alternative energy company, or for the millions of dollars they lost when the company's stock plummeted last week. If I've learned anything from dating Julian's son, Jude, it's that driving an electric car doesn't make you a good person. The same way having solar panels on your roof doesn't actually mean you care about the legacy you leave for your children.

Julian's wife Jackie wipes her glacial blue eyes, taking care not to get mascara on her pearl-white gloves. She caresses a yellow rose against her chest. Yellow, the color of death; it would be poetic if she hadn't chosen yellow because, and I quote, "Red washes Julian out."

Jude, my boyfriend of six years, has barely blinked for the entire ceremony. He just stares at his father's casket, as though the weight of his gaze can resurrect the dead. His gray suit jacket, slightly wrinkled from the thirty minutes he spent sobbing at the funeral home before we walked over to the cemetery, is unbuttoned, hanging forward as Jude wobbles toward the casket.

Jude and his father were always a matching set from different generations: similar build, the same sunset-red hair, an exact speaking cadence, with mostly opposite views on the role of their privileges. They both had stutters as children that were squeezed out, phoneme by phoneme, with daily speech therapy. Julian's never came back; Jude's does when he's upset or drunk. I haven't heard him get a single word out without having to pause to catch his breath in the last four days.

I squeeze his hand and he looks at me, blinking to pull back his tears, but one still leaks out, splattering onto his tie. I wrap my arm around his and lean my head against his shoulder. The burial ceremony has already lasted an hour and there are still at least fifteen people who want to speak. The speakers are a healthy mix of board members, employees, and Julian's former mentees. Several of them side-eye Jude and me, no doubt wondering why I'm with him. I've gotten used to it. Being one of a grand total of three Black people at this funeral is a pretty telling sign of the company the Landons keep.

Jude was supposed to give the eulogy, a touching tribute to his father and the company he stands to inherit. A testimonial on the lives Julian changed by providing them access to clean energy, the principles of strength, determination, and a recognition of the privileges inherent to being able to project your own environmental image onto the rest of the world. I know because I wrote it.

Jude gave me a thumbs-up when he read it, the most he could muster last night, but today when his mother tried to nudge him up to the front, he just shook his head. He hasn't looked at her since and she can't stop shooting him glares, as if we're not all standing around her husband's casket.

Jude shakes me off his shoulder and drops my hand. He takes a few steps away from me, and I reach out to pull him back. I've been pulling him back all week, just like he's pulled me back for the last year. Every time I get wrapped up in a story, in trying to write the article that will get me a *New York Times* internship without using Landon family connections, he pulls me back to the meal I skipped, the calculus assignment I forgot about, our friends' birthday parties.

So now, when he's the one sinking to the ground, I kneel beside him. I tug at his arm. "Babe, are you okay?"

"Y . . . Yeah . . . F . . . Fine . . . Y . . . Y . . . Yeah," he replies.

"Do you need to take a walk? Just for a minute? We can do those breathing exercises from therapy."

"No."

"What do you need? What can we do?" I catch a whiff of something then. "Is that vodka? Jude, did you—"

"S . . . stand up-p," he says.

"Huh?"

"Stand." He exhales, and the smell of alcohol rushes up my nostrils. "*Up.*"

I stand up, realizing that a hundred or so sets of eyes are now focused on us instead of Julian Landon's secretary from thirty years ago, who is reminiscing on the time they spent a lunch break building solar panel models from cafeteria spoons. I know he's drunk. I can tell by the consistent whiff of vodka and how he's slightly off-kilter on his knees. Last time he was this bad, he crashed a car. I wonder what he'll wreck this time.

"I'm standing," I say, gritting my teeth and trying to remain calm in front of our audience. "Do you need help getting up?"

Jude shakes his head. "No, I'm fine here." He takes another deep breath, and I watch his face start to lift, becoming the self-assured Jude I've seen in econ class instead of the Jude who got a phone call from his mom four days ago that upended his entire world, telling him that his previously healthy fifty-three-year-old father had died of late-stage pancreatic cancer that he'd never told Jude about. Maybe he's not as faded as I thought he was.

"Are you . . ."

He reaches into his pocket and pulls out a small black box. Someone behind him gasps, and it's then I realize he's kneeling. "Gen . . . Genevieve," he says.

"Jude . . ." My eyes zero in on the box in his hand. I can't make out the silver lettering adorning the top because my eyes are starting to well and my stomach has already begun to lurch.

"Genevieve . . . Elizabeth . . . Francis." He's projecting like a Shakespearean lead about to perform a monologue, and I'm forced to swallow my breakfast back down. I knew cinnamon waffles were the wrong choice.

I lean down so that we're face to face and no one else can hear me. I put my hands on his cheeks, like I do when I'm about to kiss him. "Jude Alexander Landon. Don't. You. Dare."

"Stand *up*," he repeats.

"Jude, please don't."

"Fine," he says. He makes his voice louder somehow. "Genevieve Elizabeth Francis. Will you marry me?" He flips open the black box and inside rests a three-carat cushion-cut diamond ring with a rose-gold band. I know it's three carats because it's the ring I drunkenly texted him a picture of when I stumbled through the jewelry district after a party downtown.

"Jude," I hiss. "This isn't the time or the place."

"It's what inspired me," he says. "When one marriage dies, another begins."

That's not a saying. No one has ever said that.

"It's your dream ring," he says. "You texted me."

I did. Four months ago. And I'm seriously regretting it right now. Four months ago, I was accepting the university's student journalism award, and Jude was the first student in university history to get a perfect score on the Econ II midterm. We wore coordinated outfits to his fraternity formal, and even though we stayed sober the whole night, I've never laughed as much with anyone since. Four months ago, we could each see all of our professional dreams start to form, and we knew how to grow them together. Four months ago, I sent him a ring. Today, I never would have.

His jaw clenches. "We've been together since freshman year of high school. Six good years. Well, five good ones, but we're working on the sixth."

Jesus Christ. Not here. Why is he admitting to everyone that we've been having problems? And anyway, they're mostly his fault. He and the Grey Goose he siphons from the family liquor cabinet have been picking fights with me for three months, ever since I told him he should take accountability for his DUI. My face feels like it's 100 degrees, despite the biting November air.

"I *know*, Jude. I know we've been together for six years. I know I texted you that ring, but not here. Not like this, please. I don't want this."

Our mutual best friend, Oliver, steps between us. His tuxedo hangs a little too big; it's his dad's and there's a jam stain on the lapel from the preserves he helped the Landon chef bottle this morning. Only Oliver would think that a funeral was black tie. The scar above his eye is just starting to fade, but not enough that I can forget Jude's the one who caused the accident. Some scars shine brighter on our darker skin, and this one has a special glow that always catches my eye.

Jude lied to me about it. He put Oliver at risk and expected me to never find out. As if I couldn't put the pieces together when Jude showed up the next day with a sprained wrist, reeking of cheap vodka, and Oliver had ten stitches lining his forehead. Jude never came clean with me. Oliver was the one who told me the full story—and then the Landons had him sign an NDA in exchange for his college tuition.

Jackie tried to get me to sign one too, but there was no way I was about to do that, even with $50K in student loan debt. I'm a journalist. Accepting a payoff would be career suicide before my career has even started. More importantly, I couldn't stomach it. I'd rather be in debt to the US government than Jackie Landon. My parents agreed—Jackie had offered to pay off their mortgage too—and that was that.

It was all so sordid, like something out of a TV drama I never asked to live.

Jude and I have been in therapy ever since. I want to forgive him, but it's hard, especially when all he seems to want is to go back to the way everything was before the DUI. He hasn't even really acknowledged the NDA. Anytime it comes up he just skirts past it, like it was a momentary lapse on his mother's part, instead of a concentrated effort to use her wealth for bribery.

Oliver grips my arm just as I'm about to pitch forward.

"Jude, I think we should just take a moment away from everyone to talk this out," Oliver says. "Maybe call Dr. . . . . someone to chat."

Oliver mouths *I'm sorry* to me. As if he's the one who revealed we're far less than perfect to an entire funeral full of people. But Oliver's been sorry ever since he told me Jude, at least three beers and two vodka cocktails in, was the one behind the wheel of the car when they crashed. Anyway, we probably *should* call our couple's therapist, or some kind of mental health professional. What would Dr. Givens say if she could see us right now? Did he tell her in one of their individual sessions that he was going to do this? No, she never would have condoned it. Not after basically telling us that we had a lot of work to do—together— to fix the relationship rupture caused by Jude's substance abuse.

Jude is still staring at me, moving his head just slightly so that he can't meet Oliver's gaze.

"I love you," Jude says.

"I love you too," I say. "Of course I do."

"So, put it on." He pushes the box toward me. "Say yes."

Maybe his mother can intervene, talk some sense into him. It's not like she's been particularly enthused at my continued presence over the years. When I first showed up, I was the first Black person introduced into the Landon social circle. Sure, there were Black employees at Landon Energy, Black security guards at the Landon estate, and even Oliver, but no one who actually sat at their dining room table. Jackie Landon and I have never really seen eye to eye. On Jude, on how to handle public prestige, and also on most world issues. Anytime we try to talk we end up in a debate, either over Jude's future career prospects or voting for fiscally conservative political candidates. Jackie wants to keep as much of the family money as possible with next to no restrictions, and also doesn't want to be forced to pay her housekeeper a living wage. Never mind that she didn't come from money and was working as a store clerk when she met Julian Landon. Twenty-year-old Jackie was a natural blonde, size 0, picture-perfect replica of a white movie star from the 1950s. She fit the image of the perfect CEO's wife, and molded herself into an iconic socialite. Julian was her identity, until she had children. That's never going to be me, and she hates that. I'm not enough of a team player—and I don't look the part.

She's focused on the other side of the cemetery, at far-off headstones of people she never knew.

Jude's sister leans into me, putting her arm around my shoulders. "Just say yes. We could be sisters—we *are* sisters—and we'll make it work with your career. You can have a long engagement. A job at whichever newspaper you want. Right, Jude?"

"She's right, it can be a long engagement. We can get married after graduation. You can take any job you want. Write whatever you want, and only come to the company functions you're interested in. Maybe even cover them," Jude says.

I shake my head. "I can't cover your events, that'd be . . . I want to focus on real . . . I'm figuring out what I want."

"The wedding will be beautiful, and huge, at Landon Farm—well, if you want huge. It can be normal. But beautiful. So beautiful. The farm is beautiful. Like you, Gen, like you. Like our relationship. Like our careers."

I've always wanted to get married at the Landon Farm. I have a whole Pinterest board of rustic décor and bushels of multicolored flowers. But I wanted to be at least twenty-seven. I wanted to be rising in my career. I wanted to not be clearing my husband's beer cans from his laundry basket. Of course I'll marry Jude—that's never been in question—but just *not now.*

"We're barely twenty-one," I say. "We have years of college left. Neither of us have jobs yet. We just . . . we don't have any business being engaged right now. I want to be a journalist and you want to get your MBA, and—"

"Age is just a number! And I can get a job at the company. You can finish school, do your internship. It can work. We're only twenty miles apart. We can delay kids."

"*Kids?* Oh my God, Jude, *we're* kids."

"It will work."

"If we just wait . . ."

He stands up and brushes a few blades of grass from his dirt-stained pant leg. Then he shoots me a wounded, anguished look I'm certain will live in my memory until my last breath. I've broken his heart. "Are you saying no?"

A tear plunks onto my necklace.

"Let's just talk later, please," I whisper. "Please, Jude. Please."

"You said I was your soulmate."

"I know. And you are. But we're so young. If we just wait another couple of years . . ."

"I don't want to wait another couple of years." He makes eye contact for the first time today. "It's now or no."

My stomach drops. I don't want to lose him, but I can't be with him like this. Our marriage can't start on an unfair ultimatum.

"Then it's no," I reply.

CHAPTER TWO

Four Years Later

The Chorus of Fates gathers around the coffee machine in the *Sykes-wood Tribune* staff kitchen, laughing about the YouTube link they sent to each other during the pitch meeting. Their voices blend together as they discuss the unfortunate dress the lead wore on the latest episode of their collective favorite reality show.

I glance at them while filling up my water bottle, pretending I'm examining the candy bowl next to the sugar container. The three of them have been missing in action from their cubicles, which surround mine, for at least twenty minutes.

"And did you see who liked her tweet about last night?" Clara asks.

"No, who?" Heather replies.

"Jude Landon. I can't believe he's even on the cesspool that is Twitter."

I'm the one who got him into reality television, and also Twitter. He must have forgotten to switch back to his personal account, given that his business account is exclusively focused on the perils of climate change. I, and three of our mutual friends, still follow his truly private Twitter, which he only uses to live-tweet his opinions on the *Bachelor* franchise and *Real Housewives of New York City*. I make sure to never like anything he posts, even if I agree. I hate that I usually agree.

"Maybe he knows her?" Heather says.

"Oh my God," Lucy says. "They'd be *perfection* together."

Jude would never date a reality star, unless he was trying to piss off his mother. For the CEO of a major company, he's kept a remarkably low public profile. Not that I've been checking.

"Right? Still hoping for my shot, though," Clara says. "You think he likes blondes?"

"Who wouldn't?" Heather replies.

I take a gulp of my water and grab a piece of candy from the bowl. Jude is neutral on blondes and, to my knowledge, hasn't been interested in a journalist since he dumped one over his father's casket. I can keep that fun fact to myself, though.

I don't know what kind of social media swipe we both did, but there isn't a single shred of evidence online that we ever had a relationship, beyond an occasional group shot from our high school's website. I sometimes wonder if he used his company resources to scrub the internet. As if it matters anyway—he could have any woman he wants. And meanwhile I haven't found anyone who gives me even half the butterflies he did.

My phone pings with a text from my mom in the family group chat. It's just five brown thumbs-up emojis. I hear a swoosh and

Dad jumps in with a *Have a great day changing the world via the free press. Love, Dad.*

I text back a smiley face. Before I can put my phone in my pocket, Mom sends back, *Chin up. You'll get a story soon. I can feel it.*

Dad replies with the phone number for the local NAACP chapter and a winking laughing emoji.

I text back a crying laughing emoji and head back to my cubicle.

Sykeswood, with a population of nearly 200,000, is the largest of our local towns, about four hours away from New York City. We have two claims to fame: that we were occupied by the British in the 1770s, and being the birthplace of Landon Energy, the New York City–based company that has revolutionized green energy. One of the Brits, Thomas Landon, founded the town and never left, dropping bits of generational wealth all the way down to Jude, who's using a not-insignificant amount to open a sizable offshoot of his father's company smack in the middle of downtown. The town square sits on the Hudson, and the most expensive restaurants and shops dot the boardwalk. Fellini's, a favorite of the richest of the rich, like the Landons, faces the river. Occasionally, a yacht will dock to whisk a local business owner down the river toward New York City. I'm always tempted to stow away on one of them, hoping to step out on the shores of Manhattan with a gnarly exposé for the *New York Times* or the *Wall Street Journal*. Maybe I'd even get a Pulitzer.

I keep a picture of my family from my college graduation on my desk, next to my first, and only, article for the *Tribune*. I "investigated" the local ice cream shop's new cinnamon-pumpkin ice cream last election day. All the other reporters were situated at local polling stations; we even had someone in DC. If I'm lucky, I might be able to nab a story about a toddler who learned to dial 911 the next time there's a world war.

Just kidding, *that* hard-hitting news story would probably go to the Fates—Lucy, Clara, and Heather—who have just emerged from the kitchen, loudly planning their lunch break excursion.

Clara breezes by my desk. "Panera, salads for *sure*!" she calls across the cubicles to the other two. Her infinite ponytail swipes the side of my desk and knocks over a small stack of papers. "Oh no!" she says. "Did I do that?" She slaps her hands as close to her cheeks as she can without messing up her contour. She looks like a hover-handed Kevin McCallister.

"It's no big deal," I reply, leaning forward to pick them up.

"Sorry!" she says. Her eyes flick between the papers on the floor and my desk. She stares at me for a few seconds before she goes back to her cubicle.

Days like today, I wonder if I should have taken a different job. Actually, I wonder that every day. I started here as an intern during college, and never left. My résumé has been in my Indeed drafts across an entire presidential term.

Heather sits on my desk and smiles at me. She thrusts her hand in my face. "Isn't it *gorgeous*?" "It" is her supersized heart-shaped engagement ring.

God, it's gaudy. But at least she has someone who'd get her a bauble that weighs her hand down as a sign of enduring love. A rising career *and* a stable relationship? Why do the people I can't stand get everything I want? Minus that ring. I do have *some* standards.

Finding someone to meet those standards when I can't even get to my own goals? Well, that's a touch more difficult.

"Wow! Con*grats*!" I say, trying to ignore how many octaves my voice is going up. College Gen never let her voice go up more than an octave in the newspaper office. College Gen also thought she'd be an editor at a national publication by twenty-five and married by twenty-seven. Instead, I'm here, a glorified copyeditor, single by a mix of choice and lack of personally acceptable options.

"I've got to go do some research for the medical racism series. Did you know that Black women die at like a *much* higher rate during childbirth? Page three!"

"Wow. Amazing," I reply. "And yes, I'm well-versed in the statistics."

"So crazy, right? You can totally sensitivity read for me. Your perspective is *invaluable*." She grins and flashes her hand at me one last time before heading back to her desk.

Yes, so invaluable that I can't write articles of my own. I'm the most valuable asset the paper has, but only to tell a group of white people that their articles are racist without actually using the "r" word. I might be the only person in Sykeswood who reads the paper cover to cover, at least twice, to make sure we won't end up trending on social media for the wrong reasons. Especially since last time we did, it led to our editor-in-chief of fifteen years getting ousted.

Once Heather's out of view I roll my eyes at my computer, then peek over the top of my cubicle—they've all gathered again around Heather's ring. She sits on one of their desks, leaning back practically against the computer, waving her hand back and forth. Our former editor-in-chief would have never allowed this kind of lackadaisical behavior, but he also did Blackface in his college year-book, so . . . guess you can't have it all.

I think I hear someone say, "Guess you can't do the dance when 'Single Ladies' comes on anymore," and I wait for the ground to swallow me into oblivion.

A *ping* sounds, and I glance at the email that has appeared in my inbox under Subject: Assignment.

Jennifer,

Caption this.

—Adam

Adam, the forty-five-year-old perennial bachelor who has run the *Tribune* for the last two years after a brief stint as assistant editor, remains convinced my name is Jennifer, because, as he once told me, my hair and face are a mildly similar shade of brown as a reporter who quit three years ago, Jennifer Warren. She was my mentor when I interned here, but she quit right around the time he came on board, so there's really nothing to tie me to her in his mind, except the obvious. It seems futile to try to correct him, even though all of my friends have repeatedly reminded me that the very least anyone can do is try to remember your name.

In the last two years, four Black employees have quit because of shit like this, and detailed it in their exit interviews. Nothing has ever been done, and they moved on to bigger and better things. As Black employees here there's a pervasive message: you're disposable, and your white coworkers are not. It doesn't matter how much you contribute, how hard you try, how good you are. Smile, keep your tone light. We're a team, as long as you don't step out of line.

I click the attachment and a Pekingese wearing a home-knit pink sweater, with a breast cancer ribbon knitted in the middle, fills my screen. I know it's for the "Cute" page on the second to last page of the newspaper. I know it brings people joy, after all the depressing sludge, but I can't pretend that it's what I thought I'd be doing with my college degree and six years of experience as an editor for both my high school and college newspapers. This dog and I have a lot in common, though. He's stuck in an itchy sweater that doesn't even match his complexion, and I'm stuck in a job that sounded incredible at first but doesn't match my five-year plan.

Fuck this sweater and fuck cancer, I type. I backspace until the page is blank again. I have to be cutesy, not mean. The hardest part of the workday is keeping my bitterness away from my blank document. I didn't believe the countless think pieces about how nothing turns out how you think it will after graduation. I'm not sure when the cynicism rotted me inside, but it was probably somewhere around the thirty-fifth time I was called "articulate" for catching basic grammatical errors in someone's piece. This caption is going to be the pinnacle of my professional success for the next month.

I reach for my coffee mug, nearly knocking it over onto my phone, and think of all the ways I could drown myself in it. I take a deep breath, and then take a large gulp. I don't actually want to drown myself with coffee. It would be a miserable way to go, and it's almost the weekend. I can go home, watch *Insecure*, and surround myself with people who don't make me feel like I can't belong in their circles for forty-eight blissful hours.

Take a pe(e)k at my new sweater! If I can support Breast Cancer Awareness Month, so can you!

Cheesy, barely passing for decent, and plugging our latest health awareness initiative. It checks all the boxes for the second to last page of the paper.

Clara appears at my side, reading the text on my computer over my shoulder. "Take a peek. *Cute*," she says.

"Thanks."

"Did you hear?" she asks. After I raise my eyebrows she adds, "Adam's going to pick someone to write a profile on a mystery CEO. Rumor has it he's going to pick a junior staff member," she says.

But that junior staff member would never be me. That's what her little smirk is telling me. The rumor has been that a major CEO has been circling the *Tribune* for months, offering exclusive access for a profile. But this is the first time it's actually materialized as a reality. After all the work he's put in, I'm shocked Adam would give it up. Why a junior staffer?

"Oh? We're all in the running?" I ask.

"I mean . . . *technically*. But some of us have already been on page three or four. Experience is everything for important pieces like this," she says.

Experience that I came into this paper with but haven't gotten since. College intern Gen made page four. Staff writer Gen has never been on a page that anyone actually reads. Which makes it more than a little difficult to actually be competitive for a position at any other paper. Despite all my past success, no one can see past my lack of published stories since graduation. If the paper that was willing to publish me when I was a college intern isn't willing to publish me when I've been a staff writer for almost three years, then it's hard to believe anyone else would. Adam's incredibly well respected in the field, even more so than Jennifer, or even our former editor Victor was, so if he doesn't see my potential, no one else will either. Victor wasn't particularly fond of me either, but my writing, and the power of someone else in senior leadership behind me, spoke for themselves. My portfolio is woefully outdated, and my former glory as a high school and college editor has faded into almost complete obscurity. I got stories when a more senior Black woman was here to advocate for me, and ever since she left, I've been stuck offering the "Black" perspective to white coworkers who can barely hide their disrespect for me.

Clara reaches out as if she's going to pat me on the shoulder but pulls her hand back once she's within an inch of me. "Not to, like, diminish your chances or anything. I'm sure we all have an equal shot."

"Oh, of course," I reply.

"You could apply for some affirmative action, maybe. Or is that gone now?"

If I could slam my head into the desk right now, I would. But then she'd be the one to write the story, and that would be a fate worse than death by blunt head trauma. "I'll let you figure that one out."

She smiles. "Enjoy your Pekingese."

"What's your assignment?" I ask, against my better judgment.

"The flooding of those low-income rent-controlled apartments downtown. Like tragic. But you get what you pay for, right?"

She heads back to her desk, awash in the glow of a page-four byline.

Adam's assistant, Regina, the only other Black woman in the office, whips by my desk and clips the side of my cubicle. "Ow!" she exclaims. "Darn corner." A couple of people glance up at her before going back to their articles.

"Are you okay?" I ask.

"I don't *think* my rib is broken," she says, rubbing her side.

"If the corner of my cubicle is sharp enough to break a rib, you have a killer lawsuit on your hands," I reply.

"Best believe I'd fight for every penny. And I'd never have to buy another triple shot almond milk latte with two and a quarter raw sugars."

"Say that three times fast," I reply, then lower my voice. "Care to spill about the mysterious CEO interview?"

She laughs. She can probably say it five times fast, given that she qualified for two free coffees this week already. It's Thursday, and she only drinks tea.

"I can confirm that it's true. I still don't know who the mystery CEO is, though, or who Adam plans to give it to. Except that it will be one of the junior staffers, per the CEO's request. He's under forty, and insists on giving the best junior staffer their shot. Don't sell yourself short, *we* both know who the best is."

I snort. "He doesn't know my *name*."

"I'll put in a word," she promises. "But first I've got to go down to the coffee shop before his caffeine high dips again." She takes a deep breath and continues her power walk over to the staircase.

A ping rings across my cubicle. Another email from Adam.

Jennifer,

Scrap the dog.

—Adam

It's probably for the best anyway. I wasn't going to win any awards for my peeking Pekingese pun.

"Aww." Lucy stands behind me, staring at my screen.

"Yes?" I ask, turning around halfway.

She gently places a printed copy of a story on my desk. "Since you have nothing else to do, you can copyedit for me, right? Page two."

"Yeah," I reply.

"I need it in an hour . . . can you *do* that?"

"Yeah."

"Great, thanks." She vanishes as quickly as she appeared.

One of the more senior editors shuffles past my cubicle and stops a few feet away, staring at my blank screen instead of me. "Are you working?" she asks.

I lift the story on my desk. "Copyediting. Do you need a story checked?"

"No," she replies, before walking away.

I look down at the story on my desk. Page two, tentatively titled "The Tragedy on MLK Boulevard." The story is about a Black family of five who have opened their two-bedroom home as a halfway house for teens detoxing from drugs. I cross out about twenty-five synonyms for "sad" before I'm even 200 words in.

Regina drops Adam's coffee on his desk, and he waves her away while he takes a phone call. She swings back over to my desk. She rolls her eyes at the pen marks across the page. *Lucy?* she mouths.

"How'd you guess?"

"The pity," she replies.

"*Always.*"

"Switch one adjective in the story and it'd be framed as an inspiration to the masses," Regina replies.

"Yep."

The phone on Regina's desk rings. "I'll text you," she says, jogging over to her desk to grab the phone.

I cross out another lamentation, circle three typos, and scribble a note in the margin about the tense switches in the second paragraph.

A stack of papers drops on top of the story, almost hitting my hand. The senior editor is standing over me again. "You don't look too busy. Can you fact-check these sources." It's not framed as a question. She stares down at me. "I need it by tomorrow."

"Sure." I pick up the stack of papers she dropped and move them to the side of my desk.

I try not to think about the fact that I'm just a workhorse for a group of white people who never fully acknowledge my humanity. But I do think about it. Frequently. To some degree, I keep the editorial team running. But it's never my name on the byline. I don't think I'd even make an acknowledgments page.

But hey, we had a Black president, so everything's fine. I just don't try hard enough. Or I'm not fun to be around. My writing is not as impressive as that of my coworkers. I deserve it. Right? That's what every career advancement blog I've read has told me. It's what our former Features editor told me when I asked him about more reporting opportunities. I have to put myself out there more and try to be more relatable. Otherwise, how can I make sources comfortable? Lucy, Clara, and Heather, they just have that personal touch. Except with anyone who isn't white, cis, Christian, and heterosexual. But the *Tribune* has their audience. And the editor-in-chief decides what stories we should tell. Whose stories matter to subscribers. And those? Those I can't write, apparently.

When the most recent letter of recommendation you can score is from an editor who quit three years ago, and your only story post-college is about ice cream, it's pretty impossible to make even a lateral move. This small group's lack of faith in me has translated across city lines. I don't know where else to go. And I don't know how to find the energy to put myself out there again, just to be rejected.

Once I finish Lucy's edits, I go to her desk and try to hand the paper to her. She doesn't acknowledge that I'm there, so I set it next to her. Heather smiles at me from her cubicle and I force myself to smile back.

Back at my desk I take the first of Evelyn's six stories and begin calling sources to verify their statements. I get through five out of the six stories and twenty of the twenty-two sources after four hours and a fifteen-minute lunch break.

As I start to dial the twenty-first number, an email from Evelyn pops up on my computer screen.

Article's scrapped. Don't need your verification.

I drop all of the papers in the recycling bin, fighting the urge to make direct eye contact with her while I do it.

CHAPTER THREE

After work I pull into the only empty parking space of Tía Rosa, Sykeswood's newest and only Mexican restaurant, cutting off an Escalade for the spot with my Mini Cooper. In my defense, the driver of the Escalade was being a bit optimistic about her chances of fitting into a spot where both neighboring cars were over the line. She honks at me as I step out of my car, and I jog inside to avoid any sort of confrontation.

I step into the restaurant's vestibule and pull up my email on my phone. Three copyedits to do in the morning, and no story assignments. I reported on Black Lives Matter protests in college for this same paper. I thought I'd come back and build myself up into the kind of reporter who could get a job at a top publication without rich connections. So much so that I refused to allow Jude or his family to help me with my internship search in college. I was determined to do everything myself, so that I never had to be in debt to the Landons for anything. I was not on the pulse with that one.

"Phone away. *Now*." My best friend, Mickey, holds her hand out.

"Fine," I reply, tucking the phone into my pocket. "You can put the hand away; I'm not one of your fifth graders."

"True. You're also late."

"By like two minutes."

"Four minutes. Four," Mickey replies. "You have delayed our Thirsty Thursday margarita consumption by four minutes."

Mickey flags down the nearest waiter, a Black guy with a fade that could adorn art museums. He's been our waiter the past few times we've been here, and I always find myself staring at him just a second too long.

"We're going to need a pitcher of pomegranate margs, frozen, sugar on the glass rims, please." She bats her eyes, and he nods.

"He's totally going to ask for your phone number later," I say.

"Well, he certainly meets the cuteness requirements I've set for you, so I'll give him yours instead. And I'm getting you a shot of tequila. Because your face is set to perma-glare and I need it to stop."

It's not that I'm completely opposed to dating. I've been on dates, even kept a relationship going for a few months here and there, if the guy's lucky. But work comes first, and no one has really understood the late nights and lack of progress in my career.

The pitcher appears about two minutes later, along with a basket of chips and salsa. The waiter hovers for a few moments. We always order within thirty seconds of arriving, so we can spend our real brainpower on figuring out dessert.

Mickey kicks me under the table and lifts her eyebrows. I check my menu, as though I don't order the same thing every time we come here. It probably wouldn't kill me to make an effort.

"So, what's your favorite thing on the menu?" I ask. "Could always diversify my order."

"She's unattached, by the way," Mickey says.

My head bolts up from the menu and I try to kick her back, but she's moved her legs.

"Oh?" he replies. "Good to know."

This guy is absolutely, terrifyingly handsome. He's making the slightly puffed sleeve yellow shirt work for him. He looks like the guy in college who was president of the Black Student Caucus but also the captain of the lacrosse team. The one who never actually dates Black women, despite calling them "queens" on social media at least once a week.

Ever since Jude, I've always found a guy's fatal flaw before that flaw can get down on one knee. Maybe this is the waiter's. Even if it isn't, it has severely diminished my interest in ever going on a date with him. Any anyway, I've *had* the guy who looks at me like I'm sunshine personified. But it rains. It always fucking rains. I don't know what's sadder, the state of my love life or the state of my career.

"I mean, I know it looks like we're a couple, but we're not," Mickey continues. "I play for the ladies' team, but she *totally* plays for yours. Isn't that right, Gen? Her name's Gen, by the way."

The waiter—his name tag says "Tom"—is now staring at me. He's definitely my type: at least six feet tall and gainfully employed. God, I need higher standards.

"I'm really career-focused right now," I say.

"So am I," he replies.

"That's awesome!" Mickey says. "You have so much in common already."

I try not to glare at her. I'm sure this guy is great, but if I don't focus on my job, I'm never going to get a story. Hotties with unlimited access to enchiladas and mezcal are a distraction I literally cannot afford.

"This is my night job. Parents own the place," Tom adds. "In daylight I work IT."

"I wasn't judging your job," I say.

"Yeah, tell that to your Resting Bitch Face," Mickey says. "Gen works for the *Tribune*. Very accomplished reporter."

She's being a little too generous in that job description. If he knew what I actually did on a daily basis I doubt he'd be impressed given he's working two jobs when he could almost certainly survive in this town with just one of them.

Tom raises his eyebrows, and then nods.

"Don't worry, I'm not reviewing the restaurant secretly or anything. Just a fan," I reply.

"It'd be cool, though, you reviewing the restaurant. Black reporter, Black and Mexican-owned establishment," Tom says. "Or do you not cover food?"

"Um . . . I've done a little food work. I can put in a word, but I might be a bit of a biased source. Being a fan and all. Of the food."

"And the waitstaff," Mickey adds. "Killer service."

I'm more than a little rusty, but I definitely don't need this kind of scaffolding. I can't date the waiter at our favorite restaurant. If I mess this up, we can't come back. Nowhere else within a twenty-mile radius has good salsa.

I clear my throat. "Where do you work IT?" I ask.

"A local startup. Connecting businesses with investors. Mostly helping people who make three times my salary update their computer software, so probably not the most exciting."

"Well, I'm sure it's more exciting than a lot of my days," I reply. "I mean, it sounds great. I wish I were good with computers."

Tom twirls his pen around his fingers. "Yeah, it's handy."

Someone at the table behind us waves him over and he turns back to me with a smile before he leaves.

"That was horrible," I say. "*I wish I were good with computers.* Kill me. Please kill me."

"I sense a connection!" Mickey replies.

"I hate you."

"You haven't dated anyone seriously since Named-After-A-Beatles-Song."

That's because no one has appealed to me seriously since Jude. No one has quizzed me on journalistic ethics and paid for my subscriptions to seven national publications as a continuous birthday present. No one has proofread my articles over late night cronuts and coffee.

"I've dated plenty," I reply.

"Name a guy who lasted more than three months."

"Brandon lasted four."

"Until you dumped him because . . . 'Brandon' was a smidge too close to 'Landon'? Really selling this successful dating thing."

"No," I say. "That was just a drawback. I dumped him because he hated sweet potato pie and his texts were riddled with typos."

I take a long sip of my margarita while trying to ignore the email notifications vibrating in my pants pocket. My heart still leaps like it could be an article assignment, when I know it's just something else to copyedit or sensitivity check.

"So what's wrong with this one then?" Mickey asks. "He's cute, he's taller than you, he has a job, two in fact, and he helps support his family."

"I barely know anything about him."

"He works IT! You're amazing at internet stalking! It's a love story waiting to happen," she says. "Don't pretend you had any more in common with J—Mr. Beatles."

"We had many common interests. He just wanted to party a little more than I did and had family money to fall back on when his grades slipped. I mean, we were practically perfect until the end, which was entirely his fault."

Mickey sucks the middle of her lime. She used to go out with us freshman year of college, until she realized that Jude could function on two hours of sleep and a fair amount of uppers. I thought it was just something rich college kids did sometimes. It took me another two years to find out that he was pulling all-nighters and doing cocaine more days than not. It's a miracle he's pulled it together enough to actually run a company. Though there weren't really other options to keep it in the family. Joanna never wanted it and spent what would have been her college years at various wellness retreats across Asia.

"It was mostly his fault, yes, but he's still holding you back—even though you haven't spoken to him in years."

She's not wrong. But it's hard to move on, even years later, when you never got the littlest bit of closure. He ghosted me after the funeral, full-on disappeared for months, never responding to a single text or call. After four months of waiting for him to respond to my messages, I gave up on him just like he gave up on me. Then he moved to New York and has barely been back since. Closure was apparently a luxury I didn't deserve.

Now he's back, and I've had to give up all my old haunts, since they were his too. It's been two weeks of success so far; I've only had one near heart attack when I saw a redhead in the grocery store. Apparently the redhead population in Sykeswood has expanded in the last five years, which I have to keep in mind every time I think I see him.

"What about you?" I ask Mickey pointedly. "You've been single for a while too."

"I'm playing the field. Anyway, don't try to change the subject."

"I can't be playing the field too?"

"You're offsides."

She refills my barely touched glass so it's nearly overflowing with margarita, before doing the same for herself. She licks the salt off a chip and chugs half of her drink. At my raised eyebrows, she holds up her phone, revealing that tomorrow is Spirit Day at her elementary school. The kids get to dress up and spend most of the day doing activities in the gym. Minimal effort needed from the teachers.

I sip my margarita and nibble at the edge of a chip. "Maybe I'm in the wrong profession."

"I'll tell you a story about the kid who's so sheltered that he thought lesbian was a nationality, and the parents who complained that their children heard the word lesbian in class. I promise you'll reconsider that statement."

"That would be page four material with a retweet from *Cosmo*."

She sticks her tongue out at me and grabs another chip. "What about your Black women in the workplace idea with Regina?"

Regina and I have been revising that article for the last six months, but it never goes anywhere. She tried to pitch it fifteen years ago when she was a staff writer, before she was forced down the ladder by her own Fate, Evelyn. How Regina can stand to still see Evelyn's face every day is a mystery to me. The assistant role pays better than staff writer, which helped her support her family, so she accepted it. Plus, she has more of an in with corporate than she ever did as a writer, meaning she—and by extension I—get all the best intel. Not that it's helped either of us.

"They'd never publish it."

"So pitch the story at the meeting tomorrow. For you and for Regina," Mickey replies. "What do you have to lose?"

"My dignity." The chip I'm trying to dip into the guacamole breaks off halfway down.

"Well, you lost that a while ago, babe."

Every time I've pitched an article it's been shut down within sixty seconds, without fail. For the first year I thought it was my ideas, until a week after my pitch on the racial dynamics of the College Admissions scandal, Lucy pitched the same article and got approved before she even finished talking.

When I tried to cover Breonna Taylor's murder, Adam told me that we had to have unbiased reporting, and my background made me seem biased.

"Maybe I can find it if Adam stops calling me Jennifer."

"You could try wearing a name tag to the pitch. Just write 'not the other one,'" Mickey says.

"He laughs it off every time Regina points it out. I don't want to be the bitch who calls him out."

"Burn it down, fuck your tone," she replies.

Tom appears at the side of our table. "Are you guys ready to order?" he asks.

"Shrimp tacos," Mickey says. "Extra shrimp. Same amount of taco."

"Noted, and you, Gen?"

I don't know what kind of special sauce he's putting on the pronunciation of my name, but it's working. I haven't quite figured out my angle, though. I've been firmly single for the last eight months, and my just-hooking-up phase ended with an orgasm success rate lower than my article pitches.

"The seafood medley ceviche, please," I say.

"Good choice," Tom replies, looking only at me. "I'll make sure the chef makes his absolute best effort. What made you want to try something new?"

I shrug. "Feeling adventurous tonight."

"In terms of food?" he asks.

Mickey kicks me under the table again and I smile at Tom, who smiles back. Even rusty, I can still pull it together.

"We'll see, I guess."

He smiles and nods to himself as he heads back toward the kitchen.

Mickey slams her hand on the table three times, causing people at neighboring tables to stare at us. "Date him," she says.

"He gives me big Greg Jackson from college vibes."

She pulls out her phone and starts typing. While she scrolls, I keep eating our chips. She clicks something, sighs, and then starts typing again. She lays her phone on the table with Tom's Instagram open.

"Why are you showing me a private Instagram? You don't follow him; we can't see anything," I ask.

"I'm showing you that we don't *know* he doesn't date Black women," she says.

"We also didn't *know* Greg Jackson didn't date Black women, except when he didn't date Black women."

"He hooked up with—"

"Hooked up with" being the operative phrase there. I have a radar for these things. The perils of trying to date in a relatively small, overwhelmingly white area as a Black woman. Show me a guy's picture and I can tell you whether he's willing to actually date a Black woman with an accuracy that can only be described as eternally on the money.

"A lot of people 'hook up with' Black women and then deny them basic human rights and decency. See the editor of my paper." Adam's latest girlfriend was featured in the *Sports Illustrated* swimsuit edition three years ago and has been on the long list for the *Real Housewives of New York City* for the past several months. His last fling was with a pretty well-renowned documentary filmmaker who dumped him to report on conditions in Sudan. The slant of the paper tends to make slight shifts depending on the sociopolitical leanings of his current Black girlfriend, but it's always lip service.

Mickey almost chokes on her water. "Bloop. Pitch that story tomorrow. Your first of many *Black* stories, and the universe will align. Hot Waiter will transform from Greg Jackson 2.0 into the King of Wakanda. No Black woman will ever look at Adam again."

I lean back against the booth. "I'll try. *Maybe.* If I can get a draft done tonight."

"You may draft on your phone until the food comes. *If* I get to swipe on your defunct Bumble later."

Mickey takes a small bow into the table and takes another long swig of her margarita. She'll be my benevolent queen until she swipes right on a venture capitalist who used to play Division 1 lacrosse. I shudder at the thought.

CHAPTER FOUR

My ballet flat almost slips off as I sprint through the rows of cubicles with my extra-large coffee. The line at the downstairs bodega took fifteen minutes longer than usual, and I'm getting to the office with barely a minute to spare before the pitch meeting.

My phone keeps buzzing with texts from my parents; they discovered GIFs last weekend, and they keep sending me GIFs of Michelle Obama and Viola Davis to tell me good luck. I usually don't tell them about my pitches, since they never amount to anything, but this one felt important. They don't need to know all the sordid details; they'd just worry more than they already do.

The Fates are already in the conference room with their matching coffee tumblers, whispering over their respective binders of ideas.

I slide into the first open seat I find, in the back of the room. So much for making myself more visible. I run the back of my hand over my forehead to try to vanquish the sweat beads that appeared the instant I crossed the conference room threshold. I open my bag and pull out my copies of the article draft I finished at four AM.

Adam nods at me as I sit down, and then stands. "Happy Friday, everyone," he says. "Let's begin. Does anyone have anything they want to pitch?"

I take three gulps of my coffee and slump a bit in my seat.

Regina glances at me and the stack of papers on my lap and cocks her head toward Adam. She's been trying to get me to pitch this for the last two months.

A junior editor stands up and pitches an exposé on the rumored favoring of higher-income students at the local university. Adam approves it on the spot.

A senior writer stands next. "I was doing some research on the politically correct . . ."

"George," Adam says. "You've written some of the best articles in recent memory for this paper. Do *not* pitch me another article about how millennials feel entitled to trigger warnings, written by a middle-aged white man."

George sits down and slides his papers back into his folder.

"Anyone else?" Adam asks.

Regina clears her throat and cocks her head at me.

I stand, holding my papers up against my chest.

"Yes?" Adam says. "This must be your first pitch since you started here."

"Um, sure."

Never mind that I pitched a story about a new general store run by a Black woman last week and was rejected sometime in between the words Black and woman. Evelyn, our other senior editor, had me pitch it while Adam was in the bathroom, and then told me it wasn't an appropriate story right now. I didn't follow up.

"Are you going to share? Or shall we engage in group telepathy?" he asks.

The Fates giggle. They giggled their way through my last pitch too.

"Yes. Sorry. I have an idea," I say.

"I figured," Adam replies.

"It's about women in the workplace." I shuffle my papers. "I wrote a draft." I take a sip of my coffee. "So. As is ironically clear right now, there are many women, especially Black women, who are afraid to speak up in the workplace. Whether it's to ask for a promotion, or correct the pronunciation of their name, Black women in the workplace often try to be seen but not heard. Society, through pop culture and social norms, treats Black women who are loud and opinionated as a sort of 'other,' and frequently demonizes them—"

"So, what's your pitch?" Adam asks.

"Please don't interrupt me."

Lucy gasps and I feel myself internally turning several different shades of red. "Sorry."

"Don't apologize, *Genevieve*," Regina says.

"That's my pitch. An article about the social dynamics Black women face in the workplace. I've interviewed a few of my local peers who work in white male–dominated industries, and cross-referenced their statements with interviews the *Tribune* has conducted as far back as the seventies and eighties, to demonstrate how little has changed societally in Sykeswood."

Regina gives me a thumbs up. The Fates just stare at me, their jaws slacking a bit.

"I'll take the draft and consider it," Adam says. "Next?"

I spend the rest of the meeting in a daze, after my first moderately successful pitch. A couple of people mouth *good job*, and I nod, but barely register who they are. I swallow the rest of the now-lukewarm coffee down, hoping it will help resurrect me from the undead-like state I'm in.

Once we're dismissed, I head to my desk to see if I can come up with anything to bolster my draft just in case it is conditionally approved. I text my parents a thumbs up with one hand and set my coffee down with the other. No sooner than my cup brushes against the desk, the Fates all appear at my side.

"Great pitch!" Clara says.

"Thanks," I reply.

"What made you think of it?" Lucy asks.

I bite my tongue. What could *possibly* make me think about how Black women are treated in the workplace? Truly, how could I come up with such an innovative topic?

"Just stories I've heard."

"That's definitely something we've talked about," Clara says. "But good for you."

I exhale. "You've talked about Black women in the workplace?"

"Of course," Lucy replies.

"From the perspective of white women?"

All three of them exchange a look. It's taking everything in them to not call me a bitch to my face. Not that I haven't overheard them doing it behind my back. The most recent time was two weeks ago when Lucy asked one of the interns, a Korean-American woman, where she was from in China for what must have been the fifth time in two weeks. She laughed it off, like she always does, while this sweet twenty-one-year-old intern tried to patiently explain her heritage. I stepped in, reminding Lucy that repeatedly assuming the intern was Chinese, and not an American citizen, was a microaggression at best. Lucy was absolutely floored at the idea that assuming the intern was Chinese was offensive. As soon as she thought I was out of earshot I heard her tell Heather, "She's such a fucking bitch, humiliating me in front of the intern again." I cleared my throat so they knew I could hear them. They just moved a few feet farther away and stared at me while they whispered.

"We should totally get you like a cupcake or something," Heather says.

"You don't have to do that," I reply.

"Oh, it's nothing. We have to celebrate all of our successes," Heather replies. "Anyway, we should get back to work."

They all go back to their respective cubicles, whispering along the way.

CHAPTER FIVE

When I enter my apartment after work, I'm immediately hit with the smell of something burning. I take a couple of steps and almost slip on something dusting the floor of the entryway.

Is that flour? What the hell?

Eva, one of my roommates, stands in front of the oven, which has smoke creeping out of the corner. She's covered in flour and is crying in place, making no moves to address whatever is burning. Eva's Filipina mother jokes that Eva gets her tan complexion and thick dark hair from her, and her lack of cooking skills from her white father. But even if Eva's father can't cook, as a volunteer firefighter, he'd never let smoke fill the apartment. Oliver, our third roommate and Eva's boyfriend—and a professional chef—is nowhere to be found. This would never have happened if he were home.

"Turn it *off*!" I exclaim. "You're going to set off the alarm!" I crack the oven door open a bit. A plume of smoke comes out, and I run to open the two nearest windows.

"I . . . I don't know what happened!" she says. "I was trying to bake a cake . . ."

"Eva, you don't cook."

"This is true. But it was an apology cake for working late and missing the debut of Oliver's new side dish at the restaurant. I thought a homemade cake would soften the blow."

It was a really big deal, given that Oliver has trained with some of the most world-renowned chefs, but hasn't, before now, been permitted to invent a dish of his own for the restaurant he's worked at for the last two years. But Eva's portion of the rent is the reason we could afford this apartment, so he wasn't too broken up about it. That, and the fact that they've been in an extraordinarily affectionate relationship for almost our entire post-college tenure. She's my favorite of Oliver's girlfriends, by far, even if she is a bit on the enthusiastic side.

"You work in finance, *buy* a cake," I reply. "You remember that Oliver is literally a professional chef, right?"

"Well, it's the thought that counts. Probably. I was supposed to flour the pan before baking? But I did it during because I forgot. And then the doorbell rang, and I dropped the bag of flour."

I peek into the oven. "Yeah, that thing's burnt through. Maybe put a lot of icing on it? Once it cools."

No amount of icing could save that thing, but now doesn't seem like the time to tell her that. At least it could look pretty. I'll signal to Oliver not to eat it.

"Yeah. But it might be poisonous," she says.

"I doubt it's poisonous. Did you follow a recipe?"

"Yeah. Mostly. I wanted it to cook faster, so I added some yeast and put it in at like 500."

"*Degrees?*"

"Yes. Is that a lot?"

Oh God. She's definitely not supposed to use yeast. Or set our thirty-year-old oven that high for anything.

The fire alarm begins beeping and chanting, "Fire. Fire. Fire."

I pull a chair over, grab our nearest piece of mail, and start waving it around the fire alarm. When that doesn't work, I stand on my toes on the chair and press the mute button. The alarm stops.

"Thank good—" Eva says.

It begins beeping again, this time chanting, "Carbon monoxide warning."

"Oh my God," Eva says.

I hit the mute button again and hold it down until the alarm stops. I continue waving the envelope around to dissipate the smoke.

"Babe?" we hear from a distance. The alarm was so loud we hadn't heard Oliver open the front door. "What the hell?" he asks.

"Eva tried to bake," I reply.

"You've never turned on an oven."

"Well, I did today. It was supposed to be a gift," Eva mumbles.

"It's appreciated. Now let's get whatever that is out of the oven before it's reborn in the fire," he replies.

This is not the first time I've heard him patiently teach someone how to properly clean an oven. Our freshman year of college flashes in my head, and the many evenings we spent in the communal kitchen with Jude. Later, by junior year, Jude and I were supposed to do low-key activities together, per our couples therapist—but it helped to have Oliver there as a buffer. When Oliver was there, we didn't fight. Or rather, I didn't fight. I swallow hard and blink back whatever threatens to come out.

I should actually blame Oliver for my entire life right now. We grew up next to each other, the only two Black kids in the neighborhood, and spent elementary school as a unit. When we were in eighth grade, he joined a travel soccer team with boys from all over the county. One day he invited me over to his house and there was his favorite teammate, the forward he wouldn't shut up about: Jude.

It took us about a year to acknowledge that we liked each other. Our first kiss was behind the bleachers at the homecoming game, when our school's team played Jude's team. His driver would take us out to Applebee's every Saturday night, until Jude could take us himself. We'd split spinach and artichoke dip and see who could scarf down a plate of wings the fastest. We'd see a movie, or walk around the local craft fair, and Jude would always buy me some little tchotchke. I think I own every decorative dog figurine created in the state of New York in the early 2010s.

The first time I met his parents, we brought Oliver along too. Oliver had met the Landons, but never been invited for dinner. Jackie Landon kept inquiring about the nature of Oliver's and my relationship. Why weren't we dating instead? Wouldn't we be a better fit? Joanna laughed when she said that. She told Jackie to be less racist before turning to me and declaring that Jude and I would have the cutest mocha babies.

Julian barely spoke three words to me that night. He focused all of his attention on Oliver, wanting to know about his ambitions, why he and Jude connected. It was almost like Jude's parents each thought that one of us was the worse influence, the gold-digger looking to take advantage, but they couldn't agree on which one of us it was. Jude started bringing us around more often after that. He wanted his parents to know that the three of us were a forever pairing.

He and I apparently had different definitions of forever.

Mickey helped me pick up the pieces after Jude and I broke up; Oliver was the one who helped Jude, before getting dumped too. Apparently, trying to hold a grown man accountable for driving under the influence gets you tossed aside.

If I hadn't met Jude, maybe I'd have chosen to take an internship at a different paper, instead of staying in town sophomore year of college to join his family on their boat and cover BLM protests at the *Tribune*. That was the summer his family really starting accepting me, at least a little bit. I spent two weeks with them on a yacht, lying out on the deck with Joanna, sharing the newspapers with Julian, and running an informal book club with Jackie and the boat's captain. I loved that summer, and I loved that internship. But it all gave me false hope. Hope for me and Jude and hope for me and the *Tribune*. I couldn't have been more wrong about both of them.

Once I'm sure the alarm isn't going to go off again, I step down from the chair and grab my bag, which has begun vibrating with a call. I pull my phone out and slide the answer bar over with my finger.

"Hello?"

"Jennifer?" Adam says.

"My name is Genevieve, not Jennifer," I reply with a sigh.

"Oh." Adam almost sounds disappointed.

"Is everything okay?" I ask.

"Not really. Lucy, Clara, and Heather all came down with food poisoning from some place they ordered lunch from," he replies.

A mean part of me feels a degree of satisfaction. As long as it's just the kind of food poisoning that makes you miserable for a few hours, and not the hospital kind.

"Oh."

"We need someone to cover the Pancreatic Cancer Prevention gala tonight. Not the whole gala, one of the senior reporters is in charge of that, but just a profile on the chef. He's been flown in from a Michelin-starred restaurant in France; his name is Jacques Potts."

I wonder if he called every single other employee before getting to me. This is a huge opportunity for me to remind everyone what I'm actually capable of. But, of course, I only got it because every other reporter at my level is glued to the bathroom floor. Still, I guess I've got to make the most of it. It's something. "Okay."

"There will be a press pass waiting for you at the door, just tell them your name. I assume you have something to wear. Just please, not your prom dress or something," he says. "And no sequins. You know how to dress yourself, right?"

I can certainly dress myself better than any of the Fates could. It wouldn't be my first gala, after all.

"I'll figure something out," I reply.

"Seven PM at the Renaissance Hotel. I'll see you there," he says.

Adam hangs up and I glance at the clock. It's five thirty, my hair is half-frizzed from the five minutes I spent chatting with Regina in the parking lot after work, and the most formal dress in my closet is five years and three sizes too old.

Oliver sits at the counter, poking at the charred remains of Eva's cake with a knife. He cringes. "So?"

"I have to cover a gala tonight."

Eva raises her eyebrows. "Oh. Um. Hmm," she says. "Do you own a formal gown?"

If my hips can still fit in the seams.

"Bet you wish you were still with J," Oliver says. "He'd have you in a Vivian Wang in no time."

"I don't. And it's Vera Wang."

"Agree to disagree," Oliver replies.

Eva sighs and gives me a once-over. I can tell that she's physically pained thinking of the limited offerings of my closet.

"I have a royal purple, one shoulder chiffon gown that hasn't fit me in three years. I don't want to talk about why . . . *Oliver*. And please let me handle the updo. And maybe the makeup. Definitely the makeup," she says.

"Do you not think I can put myself together for a fancy event?" I ask.

"No, I just think you're a person who has, according to Ollie, avoided fancy events on principle post Ju . . . you-know-who," she replies. "I don't think I've ever even seen you in heels."

"That and any top ten newspapers," Oliver says, winking at me.

Eva tries to elbow him, and he dodges her by jumping back and knocking into the counter. The cake collapses into a pile of chocolate dust and chunks.

Oliver starts to laugh, and Eva lets out a screech.

"I think I'll write a story about *that*. A how not to impress your boyfriend? Or how not to use yeast?" I say.

"Maybe think about how to match your complexion in the purple chiffon," Eva replies.

An hour later I'm zipped into a dress that would cost me three months' salary, with my hair wrangled into a complicated updo I would never attempt alone, a full face of makeup, and fifteen pages of research on the illustrious Jacques Potts saved to my phone.

Eva hands me one of her clutches and slips a lipstick inside.

I thrust my phone and wallet into the clutch and take a deep breath. I have a feeling it's going to be one of those nights, even if I don't know why.

Oliver rubs my shoulder. "You're going to be great," he says. "Bring the fire Eva brought to that cake earlier."

Eva rolls her eyes. "I put your keys in already, and you've checked for your wallet three times. *Go.*"

I close the clutch and try not to wobble in my heels on the way to the door. It's going to be a long night in these shoes.

CHAPTER SIX

I pull up to the venue five minutes after the gala starts, and the line to get in is already wrapped around the corner. There are two separate security checkpoints, not counting the suspicion with which the valet, whose blonde buzzcut and single earring are already giving me bad vibes, is eyeing my car. He gives me a once-over when I hand him my keys.

"Can I see your license?" he asks.

I hate to stereotype, but yep, my initial impression was clearly correct. Bad vibes central. "You need my license to park my car?" I ask.

"It's protocol."

"It wasn't with the four people who pulled in before me," I reply. "I'm press for the event. Newsroom reporter with a little extra story time this week." I make direct eye contact.

"Go ahead," he says, his lips curling together as he spits the words out.

"Thank you." Well, we're already off to a banner start to the night. I was already expecting some degree of racial awkwardness given that this is a gala in an eighty-five percent white town. I just assumed it would start once I actually made it inside. I take a deep breath; I have to keep moving, get my article, and finally make some forward movement in my stalled career. I have to.

I jog as best I can in stilettos that were designed for aesthetics and not functionality to the press line that stretches outside the venue. At least four men in the line are wearing the same suit and tie combination, and most of the women are wearing short dresses. I feel acutely aware of the fact that the hem of my borrowed dress drags slightly on the floor (a consistent reminder that Eva is three inches taller than me) and was apparently too dressy for a Pancreatic Cancer Prevention benefit. "Gown" usually means long, at least in the circles I've run in. But in this case, I'm guessing it's more Adam's ignorance about dress codes than intentional sabotage.

A woman wearing a plain black dress sits alone at the check-in table, her eyes already half closed. I hope there's coffee nearby, for her and for me.

"Purple is your color," she says.

"Thank you," I say.

"Name?"

"Genevieve Francis. With the *Sykeswood Tribune*. I was just added like an hour ago."

She flips through her box of passes. "Ah. Yes. Your handsome editor dropped off your pass on his way in." She pulls a pass out of a pile behind the box. She hands me the pass. "Enjoy."

"Thank you." Of course, the pass says Jennifer. I pause for a moment. "Do you have a Sharpie, by any chance?"

She raises her eyebrows and her eyes flick between me and the pass.

I show the pass to her, trying to find the words as heat creeps up my neck.

"Pretty big typo; didn't you say your name was Genevieve?"

"Yep."

She pulls out a Sharpie and crosses out Jennifer. She writes GENEVIEVE above the crossed-out name and hands the pass back to me.

"Thank you," I say. I slip my pass around my neck and try not to trip over the hem of my dress. Eva's generosity runs out the moment a seam rips.

The gala, which is being held in a ballroom at least three times larger than any other venue in town, is packed. The lights around the room are dim enough to make everyone's jewelry brighter, like a beacon of the richest of the rich. Judging by the sheer number of diamond statement necklaces gleaming into my eyes, there should be a substantial number of donations to pancreatic cancer research tonight.

However, nothing shines quite as brightly as the stage off to the side of the room, which is adorned with a crystal podium and a red velvet carpet leading up to it. Recycled greenery drapes the walls, making it look like we're trapped in a garden, waiting to bloom. The metaphor for my own life isn't lost on me.

A waiter walks by holding a tray of champagne and I grab a glass. Maybe just the act of holding Dom Perignon will make me feel fancy enough to be here. It always worked at Landon family events, and those featured more Harry Winston than I've clocked at this gala so far.

I move toward the back of the venue, where the kitchen usually resides, taking care to scan the room for any familiar faces. I wipe a stray strand of hair out of my eyes and almost trip into a man practically shouting about his new Lamborghini. I raise my hand in apology and he scans me up and down before deciding I'm not worth pursuing.

When I'm sure I don't see anyone I recognize, I knock back the champagne and leave the empty glass on the nearest table.

The kitchen is one of those partially open ones, with a large horizontal window that allows you to see inside. There are at least thirty people inside, all men except for one waifish blonde woman who is confined to the dishwashing station. I watch as one man minces nine cloves of garlic in under a minute. A large flame shoots up into the air from the stove, then settles down again.

I approach the window and lean over the edge. An olive-toned hand swipes at me and I jump back.

"No guests allowed in the kitchen," a sous-chef tells me, his slight Italian accent adding an adding extra emphasis on the second syllable of kitchen.

"I'm not . . . I'm looking for Chef Jacques Potts," I say.

"He's busy." Somehow his tone is even more clipped than before. He won't even look at me.

"I'm from the *Tribune*. We have an interview scheduled. I'm sure if you just let him know . . ."

"Five feet from the window."

"Sir."

"Five. Feet."

I take a few steps back. "Happy?"

The sous-chef goes back to sautéing peppers, his nostrils flared as though they're providing the cooking fire.

My stomach growls as the aromas from the kitchen waft over me. A waiter with a platter of bruschetta stops in front of me and I grab a piece, biting off half. A tomato falls onto my exposed toe. I kick it off and promise myself I'll pick it up with the napkin when I finish eating. The sous-chef rolls his eyes and turns his back to me.

"I hear he's quite the playboy," I hear a woman behind me say. "He's been seen with that heiress. The one with that hotel, or television show? Probably both."

"Well, he's only twenty-five. Lord knows his father was doing worse at his age," another woman replies.

The first woman laughs. "Perhaps he'll debut a new socialite during his speech. Shall we place bets?"

"I'll give you my Tiffany chalice if she's a redhead," the second woman replies. "Imagine the dynasty he'd create with a redhead."

I bend down and pick up the fallen tomato. I crush it into my napkin and barely deny my deeply rooted desire to toss it into the sous-chef's pan. Instead, I grab a glass of sparkling water from a table surrounded by several marble water fountains and sip it as I watch the well-oiled machine of the kitchen, typing quick notes into my phone.

After about fifteen minutes, I approach the kitchen again and tap my hastily painted fingers on the wall outside.

The sous-chef glares at me and pours one of his pans of peppers onto a plate that he passes to another sous-chef.

"If you, or literally anyone, could just ask Chef Potts to come to the window . . . ," I begin.

"Does your ape brain have trouble comprehending that he's busy?" the sous-chef asks.

Before I can curse this man out, the lone woman in the kitchen drops a dish in the sink. It clatters but doesn't break and I'm grateful for the distraction.

Making direct eye contact with me, and not even glancing at the sous-chef, she says, "I'll grab Mr. Potts. You're with the *Tribune*, is that correct?"

"Yes. Thank you."

The sous-chef grabs her arm. "Don't you *dare*. He wouldn't want to be bothered with *this*." He gestures to me as he says "this."

"He'll be bothered when an article about one of his chefs being racist is front page," she replies. "You make him look bad. You'll be fired."

The sous-chef drops the woman's arm like it's burning. He looks over to his peppers, which are on fire, and pulls the pan off the stove.

"Harrison!" a voice yells from across the kitchen.

The sous-chef—Harrison—flings his oven mitt at me.

The woman taps him on the shoulder. "By the way, women tend to have larger brains than men. Though, in your case, a worm has a larger brain." She smiles at me. "Chef Potts should be on his way over. Once he stops yelling, I'm sure he'd *love* to talk to you."

Just then Chef Potts, who scarcely looks like he's out of his teenage years, comes billowing over in a golden apron.

"You burned my peppers," he says to Harrison in accented English.

Harrison points at me. "*She* distracted me."

Chef Potts scans me, his eyes settling on the top half of my dress. He cocks his head to the side and raises his eyebrows. "*She* isn't better-looking than my hand-picked shishitos," he says. "No offense."

"She was in the kitchen, leaning over the window. Totally unprofessional."

"*She* was trying to find Chef Potts for a prescheduled interview," I reply. "And *you* attempted to sabotage an important exposure opportunity for your boss."

Chef Potts glares at Harrison. "You're fired. Miss, come back in half an hour, please, when the food has been put out."

I catch the eye of the bartender a few feet away, who had a front row seat to the kitchen soap opera. He pours something from a tumbler into a small glass and nods at me. It looks stronger than champagne, which might be just what I need. I hold my dress up with one hand and teeter over to the bar.

"Manhattan," he says as I approach. "You look like a whiskey girl, and like you're having a hard liquor kind of night."

"Thank you. I'm working, though."

"About that."

"Yeah?"

"That guy is headed over here," he replies.

I turn around and see Harrison approaching, nostrils still flared and apron flapping. I take a large gulp of the drink. It's just sweet enough for me to pretend it's not whiskey, but with enough of a kick that I feel like I could swing this clutch like a baseball bat in self-defense.

Harrison stops about an inch away from my face. "Listen here, you n—"

"I'm going to let you back the hell away from me before you finish that sentence," I reply. "Just so you can maybe take a second to figure out if this is how you want to lose your job and your reputation."

A hand nearly the size of Harrison's shoulder pulls him away from me. A man, at least six foot three with dusty red hair and wearing a heather-gray suit, inserts himself between us, his back to me. "You're causing a scene," he says.

My heart stops. That voice. I'd know that voice anywhere. It's slightly deeper than I remember, definitely more authoritative, but some variation of it has been stored in my mind for the last four years.

"She . . . ," Harrison begins.

"You're causing a scene at *my* event," the voice replies, his tone warning, bordering on hostile.

Harrison's mouth, which has barely stopped moving all night, snaps closed for a moment. "I'm so sorry, Mr. Landon."

I turn back to the bar. Shit. I am a literal journalist, how did I not do more research on which company was throwing this event? What does clean energy have to do with pancreatic cancer, anyway? Oh. Jude's dad. Of course the first public event he's held since returning to town is a tribute to his dad. There's a pang in my chest, a mix of sympathy and butterflies. Some small part of me hopes I'm imagining this. This isn't the moment I needed a literal white knight. What if Adam sees? I'll never get another story. Why trust me to handle local or national events when I can't handle a single irate sous-chef?

"Get out," Jude says. "And if I ever hear the word you were about to say, about anyone, from you again, I'll have you blacklisted from the entire industry."

Well, that's not the Jude I used to know. His tone has slipped into distinctly Julian territory, and I am not interested in anyone like Julian Landon. I respected him for a long time, all the hard work he did, the lip service he gave to environmental racism in public. But when push came to shove, he turned out to be like every other rich patriarch: willing to cover up the increasingly terrible behavior of his offspring so they never have to experience a single consequence. If that's the Jude who's behind me, then I don't want to talk to him, even if every part of me has been screaming out for closure since Julian's funeral. I wanted closure from *my* Jude, not this Julian clone.

"Genevieve Francis," the voice behind me says. "Aren't you going to say hello?"

I turn around and there he is, the CEO whose gala I'm attending on a last-minute press pass. The CEO whose proposal I turned down four years ago. I wish I had a thousand more whiskeys or some well-placed amnesia to drown out this moment.

Before he took over his father's company at the ripe age of twenty-one, after doubling up on coursework for a semester to finish early, he never grew out his facial hair. The late Mr. Landon believed that a clean-shaven face was a powerful face. It was more honest and less cluttered, in his esteem, so he and Jude used to get fresh shaves at a local barbershop at least once a week.

Jude now sports a well-trimmed beard, just a shade or two darker than the hair on his head. He's put on at least twenty-five pounds of muscle since I last saw him, and his suit is just tight enough to accentuate the definition he barely had when we were dating. He wears a platinum watch with emerald accents, the same one his father wore every day, with J.L. inscribed on the side. I catch a glimpse of his father's brushed-platinum wedding band on his right ring finger.

"Jude. Hey." I grab my glass and knock back the rest of the drink. "I'm perfectly capable of saving myself, thank you. You just drew more attention to it."

He takes the empty glass from me and sets it down on the bar. "I was just trying to stand up—"

"Congrats, you clearly read *How to Be an Antiracist* and absolutely missed the systemic discussions. I don't need a white savior, especially not when I'm at a work event, and you should probably vet your staff. But *so* glad you learned how to speak up. Anyway, hey. Long time. I assume you lost my number?"

He blinks several times, like he's trying to process what's just happened. "Can we hug, if that's okay with you?" he says, his voice moving up slightly to the tone I remember.

My heart flutters a bit and I try to shove it back down. This isn't the Jude I knew. Just like I'm not the Gen he remembers. She was optimistic. This one's a cynic. He was a sweetheart. Now he's a lower-key version of his father.

"Your takeaway from this whole thing is a hug? Is this supposed to be a happy reunion?" I ask.

"Well, I wish it had gone a bit better, but I *am* happy to see you." His arms are slightly extended, still waiting for that hug.

I sigh. "Fine. If you're going to be weird about it."

He pulls me in and absorbs me into a hug tighter than any I've had in recent memory. I almost reflexively lean my head into his chest, the way I have so many times before. He pulls back and puts his hands on my shoulders, looking me up and down. "How have you been? You look . . . purple has always been your color.

Well, to be fair, everything was your color. It was a little unfair, actually."

"You . . . you . . ." I stare down at my shoes, hoping they'll turn into ruby slippers that can send me home.

He looks perfect. He looks better than I ever imagined him, and I . . . I may look good on the outside right now, but I'm not where he is. I never will be, especially not at the *Tribune*. Or, at this rate, anywhere else.

"I always loved seeing you with your hair up," he adds. "I mean I loved seeing it down too. Should I not have hugged you? You didn't enthusiastically consent before I went in . . . Please don't write about that . . . But I also don't want to censor you, that would be wrong . . . You look so . . . Wow. You look wow."

I feel the bruschetta and champagne churning in my stomach. Why did I not check whose gala this was before I agreed to take the story? There aren't *that* many businesses in this town. And now here we are, and I have never been more unsure of how to feel.

When I imagined running into him before, it was a meeting of equals. I was walking into some powerful board meeting with a press pass that displayed my name proudly and *correctly*. There wasn't a single moment where I felt flustered. He was stammering, like he is now, but he pulled it together and told me about the work he was doing to improve global poverty. The board members echoed his responses and talked about how he'd promoted local Black and Indigenous women to senior positions in his company. He was donating vast swaths of his fortune to grassroots organizations that supported the causes I wrote about, because he still kept up with my incredible career. Seeing him for the first time was always a fantasy, where we were both at the height of our respective industries, finally ready to actually change the world together.

This moment is the opposite of everything I could have ever wanted.

"Thanks. Nice suit."

Jude flinches, and I know he hears how clipped my tone is. He shouldn't be surprised, though, given how he left things. Springing a proposal on your girlfriend at your father's funeral and then ghosting her afterward is a pretty definitive statement of your extreme lack of care. Considering that his father dumped his longtime girlfriend for Jude's mother over a particularly eventful weekend, then married her not long after, it was just a reminder that the sins of the father are the legacy of the son.

"I guess it was bold of me to assume we could just move past it," he says.

I fake gasp. "Acting like the last several years never happened? That's your MO, isn't it? Leave the girl you just proposed to in a graveyard, have your driver drop off her stuff outside the dorm a week later, and never speak to her again. Until, of course, you're in public." I gesture to the room around us. "Or should I pretend not to know you, for your image? What would your mother think?"

Jude swallows. "That's fair. I did take Mom's opinion into account instead of yours after the . . . you know, and that wasn't right. What I did wasn't right, but I've changed—"

"Please spare me the *I've changed* when you're basically Julian lite right now. Do you have an NDA for me to sign?"

Jude laughs bitterly, like this moment was supposed to be lemonade but the reality is a really rotten lemon.

"Julian lite, that's a good one. That's essentially what the board calls me behind my back, actually. CEO Jude is completely Julian lite. Looks like him, tries to act like him, but falls totally short. Real Jude, who is still very much here by the way, is having a complete panic attack. Neither one of them listens to Jackie anymore. Both of them are willing to hear you out, if you're willing to stay after my speech to talk."

I don't know if my body wants me to cry, vomit, run away, or slap him. I was never worried when I imagined this moment. But now I feel like a nervous system come to chaotic life. Fight or flight is the only question flooding my body right now. He looks better than I ever dreamed and only one of us is actually meant to be at this gala. I'm particularly reminded of that as I catch Adam beelining over to the two of us.

"Real Jude can join the club then because I'm freaking out too. But I can't have a panic attack given that my boss is headed this way," I reply.

He laughs; I can hear the undercurrent of anxiety peppering the staccato of it, but it's real. It's the way he laughed before trying to pivot a conversation with his mother that was trending a little too close to a microaggression. It's the laugh he had when he was first interviewed on TV, right after kicking the game-winning goal at the state soccer championships. It's the laugh that came after I made a joke when he was trying to say "I love you" for the first time. It's Jude. It's my old Jude.

Seeing parts of my Jude is almost worse. Loving a fantasy was kind of fun, more fun than loving the real one was sometimes. But loving the person he used to be, that's just pathetic. And if he still loves some part of who I used to be, he's about to be disappointed.

She's buried in the broken bottom drawer of my desk, withering away.

Adam appears next to Jude, and after a few seconds of staring, like he's struggling to place me, smiles. "I'm glad my staff is so charming," he says to Jude.

"We go *way* back," Jude says. "Just a natural comfort level, I suppose." His voice has slipped back into CEO Jude, even though that acknowledgment was fully real Jude.

I'm a little impressed. I know he's clocked Adam's whole deal already. I wonder if they've already met and try to push back another fantasy—one where Jude uses his considerable resources to leak an anonymous story about how corrupt Adam's newsroom is.

Adam clears his throat. "Well, my apologies, I'm just going to have to steal Jennifer for a second. Story business."

Jude furrows his eyebrows. "You mean Genevieve," he says. He glances down at my crossed-out name tag and a flicker of understanding comes across his face.

I really regret all those discussions we had about systemic racism right now. Once he learned he could be an ally, he decided to be as loud an ally as possible. In college it was charming. When I could lose my job over it, less so.

"Huh? Oh, yes," Adam replies. "I was just talking to a woman named Jennifer, natural slip."

"Were you thinking of Jennifer Warren, the reporter who covered business for the *Tribune* a few years ago? Gen's mentor?" Jude asks.

"I must have been, you know, subconsciously," Adam replies, the confidence in his voice faltering.

"The only other Black female reporter that the *Tribune* has had in recent memory. Besides Regina Brown, before she was demoted to your assistant," Jude replies. "Interesting."

Jesus Christ. He's losing tact by the second. I shoot him a look. This isn't his fight, and there's no way he's making it better. Now I'll just be the girl who knows Jude Landon, even less worthy of being taken seriously.

Adam clears his throat. "I'm going to grab *Genevieve* to talk about her story."

"Of course, Allen, excuse me, *Adam*," Jude says. "Are we still meeting for dinner next week?"

Adam's eyes narrow, and whatever smile he had has completely faded. He nods before taking my arm.

I don't miss the way Jude's nostrils flare when he sees how tightly Adam is gripping me. But I can handle Adam without Jude; I've been doing it for years.

Adam leads me over to the nearest empty corner, which is near one of the three exits I've clocked since I realized Jude was here.

"*You* know *him*?" Adam asks.

I feel myself wobbling, either from the heels or the panic. Or the whiskey. I probably shouldn't have had the whiskey.

I have a few different plays here. The truth is decidedly not an option, since that would become the entire story, and I'm almost certain Adam would print it, unauthorized. It's almost tempting, though, given his surprise that someone like me could know the likes of Jude Landon, let alone intimately. Completely omitting that we've met before tonight won't work now that Jude's let the cat out of the bag. So I need a middle ground. A half-truth, if you will.

"Yeah. I guess. Not super well."

Adam sighs. "I know his reputation, don't tell me you two . . . was it just one time? We can spin one time."

"And what exactly are we spinning? Whose business is it?"

"Twice?"

One more HR violation to add to the list. I'm running up quite the tab. Wonder when I'll get to reimburse them for something fun.

"It's nothing. We went to high school and college together. Ran in a similar crowd. We had some mutual friends, he wrote H.A.G.S. in my yearbook," I reply.

Adam takes a deep breath. "Good. That's . . . better."

Better for whom? Would knowing Jude change anything for me at the paper? Is all that's been holding me back a powerful connection to a white person that Adam actually respects?

Maybe Jude and I can go another four years without seeing each other. By then he'll have a wife and kids and a few more million dollars in his bank account. I'll probably have made page ten with a story about one of my high school classmates' local businesses. Each of the Fates will probably have a Pulitzer.

I shake my head when a waiter approaches me with a tray of champagne. I don't need anything else clouding my judgment.

CHAPTER SEVEN

Jacques Potts knows the names of every single person in his kitchen, down to the ballroom worker tasked with sweeping food scraps off the floor. I almost find it admirable until he mentions that he only does it so he can hold them accountable when they make mistakes. He has diagrams of their immediate family networks, so he can tell Daddy that little Michael or Michaela should be ashamed of his unevenly chopped onions. It's the kind of ridiculously specific anecdote that can spice up a profile, but also the kind that gets people labeled psychopathic.

The first meal Jacques ever made was a beef soufflé at the age of seven, under his mother's tutelage. By seventeen, he was working at the top restaurant in France as a sous-chef for his idol, Guillaume Cadet, and by twenty he had his first Michelin-starred bistro. He has an extensive network of chefs around the world, who personally recommend students for him to mentor. I feel guilty for burning a bag of microwavable popcorn last week. He probably has a special machine just to pop the world's finest kernels while he watches four-hour silent arthouse films.

He leads me through the kitchen, which, though a well-run ship, is still chaotic. I avoid three different dishes coming out of the oven. We sit down on a couple of upside-down water coolers.

I slide closer to him and hold the tape recorder between us, trying to keep my hand steady enough near him to catch his voice over the sounds of the kitchen.

"You were telling me about how you hand-pick all of your produce?" I ask.

"Yes. I send scouts to different areas around the world to find the highest-quality products throughout the year."

"That's incredible. So, what brought you to this particular event? Do you have strong feelings about clean energy or pancreatic cancer?"

"Well, of course I have feelings about clean air and organic produce, both of which help fight against cancer, in my opinion. And the money doesn't hurt." He laughs. "Growing up in a small village, everyone grew their own products. Everything was fresh, and the food tasted better. I wanted to bring that worldwide."

While his father was focused more on tools for the rich, Jude's tenure has been notable for a focus on increasing access to clean food and water for underserved communities. Not that I've been reading about him or anything.

"And how does Landon Energy help you do that?" I ask.

"Mr. Landon's projects increase the accessibility of high-quality food by improving the local environments and offering greater subsidies to local farmers and producers. Perhaps one of those men will be the next member of my staff," he says.

"I did want to ask more about your staff. I noticed that there only seemed to be one woman on staff and she wasn't even handling the food. It's been found that there is a significant gender disparity in higher-caliber restaurants. How do you address that in your kitchens?"

Jacques Potts stops smiling at me. "I don't believe this is relevant to the profile . . ."

Alright, I've got to rein it in a little bit. A puff piece isn't the best time to start grilling someone on sexism. "I didn't mean to offend; it was just something that's been brought to our attention since one part of helping access to high-quality food is increasing access for women in the professional realm."

He runs his tongue over his teeth, trying to calculate his next statement.

"There is a woman right there," he says. "With the peppers. Grace. And I am not in control of who is hired at my day-to-day restaurants."

Grace, the woman from earlier, has apparently been promoted to Harrison's position.

"Earlier tonight she was washing dishes. Quite a promotion."

He shrugs. "She owned her own restaurant, top ten in Spain, but very small."

"She owned a top ten restaurant and was washing dishes here?"

"Next question," he says, then adds, "I'll think about the women. Happy?"

The rest of the interview passes without incident. I have enough facts to write a stimulating profile, and the beginnings of an exposé into sexism in the local culinary world. I even grab Grace's email, in case the piece gets the green light.

As I'm leaving the kitchen, I hear the tap-tap-tap of a finger against a microphone. "Everyone, can we have quiet, please?" a voice says. "Mr. Landon would like to say a few words."

I stand in a corner, close enough to see the stage, but far enough away to be out of his view. He waves at the crowd, his veneers shimmering in the spotlight.

"Thank you all for coming," he says into the microphone. "We're here tonight to raise money for a worthy cause: pancreatic cancer. As you all know, it's a personal mission of mine to find a cure, so pony up those wallets, please."

How can he look so calm? As if we didn't just see each other for the first time in four years. As if I truly was an old friend from high school that he ran into at the reunion, said hi to, and then forgot about. Does he still have the ring?

I shake my head. He was nervous too. I heard it in his voice. But now he's CEO Jude. He can be cool when I can't. He can overlook something life-changing, a DUI, an unexpected reunion, when I won't.

"Before she even graduated from college three years ago, she singlehandedly designed a way to get clean water to three rural areas of the United States, areas where, due to a lack of clean air and water, cancer diagnoses have skyrocketed. Now, in the last year, with the help of Landon Energy, Kaitlyn Franklin has been traveling around the country to other nutrient-poor areas, to implement her system."

I clap along with the rest of the room as Kaitlyn Franklin, a redhead who's nearly Jude's height in heels, struts onto the stage in an evergreen body-con dress. It looks like the woman I overheard earlier placing bets on whether Jude's newest lady would have red hair will be giving away her chalice. A twinge of jealousy ricochets across my chest.

I recognize Kaitlyn Franklin from our gossip section; she's the daughter of a prominent investment banker and an oil heiress, who's known for her activities as a socialite. How she's kept her engineering prowess so far under wraps is something I'm dying to find out. I wonder who from the *Tribune* gets to interview her; she'd be a great person to talk to. Though talking to her might make me want to die if she and Jude are together.

Kaitlyn approaches the microphone and turns to smile back at Jude. "Jude Landon, everyone! Youngest CEO of a Fortune 500 company."

The way she's looking at him is warm, but not sexual. And his smile is firmly friendly, like the one he gives his sister. I'm pretty certain there's nothing there, and completely uncertain why I suddenly care so much.

While everyone else claps, I start inching toward the nearest exit. I got my interview; I have a potential future article, and I have to get out of here before Jude finds me again. I glance at the stage and see Jude scanning the crowd. He locks eyes with me and nods. *Stay*, he mouths, shrugging.

The moment his eyes travel to another area of the room, I slip out the nearest door and into the hallway. A couple of people meander near the other bar across from the elevators. I rustle through my clutch until I feel my phone, then hit Mickey's contact.

She answers on the third ring. "Gen, date, remember?" she answers. She mutters something inaudible to her date.

"Jude. He's here. And I—"

I hear her glass hit what I assume is a bar, and she excuses herself from her date. "*What?* I thought you were interviewing a chef. Where are you?"

"Apparently, Landon Energy's latest charity gala. I already interviewed the chef."

The tears start to prick the corners of my eyes. It wasn't supposed to be like this. Despite years of being treated like shit at the *Tribune*, somehow this is the most humiliated I've ever felt. Not only did I look like a damsel in distress to my ex-boyfriend, but I also looked like some potentially helpless, discarded one night stand to my boss. In another world my name would be linked with Jude's, and I'd command a certain amount of grudging respect as the other Mrs. Landon. In this world, I'm just the girl who peaked in high school, professionally and personally.

"Well, he hasn't seen you, right?" she asks. "Just go."

"Wrong. I was getting harassed by this sous-chef, and he just appeared. And muscles. His muscles appeared. He told me I look wow."

"That's not a sentence, Gen. Just go home. You've done your job," she says. "I'll be there in twenty for a group debrief. We need Oliver in on this."

Oliver, the other person Jude dumped. The other person who got to see Jude at his absolute worst. But I can't face Oliver right now—he's always seen through me, and this time I'm afraid he'll see something I'm petrified of, even if I don't know what that is yet.

CHAPTER EIGHT

When I pull into my apartment's parking lot, Mickey is leaning against her car holding a bottle of wine and two pints of ice cream. I pull into my usual space, off to the side, and take a deep breath before I pull the key out of the ignition.

I open the car door, holding my heels and the clutch.

"He was barely even rattled. Like nothing ever happened," I say.

"He was always good at putting up a front. Well, except the one time," Mickey says, taking my purse.

"The one time it would have fucking helped, huh?" I wipe a rogue tear from the top of my cheek.

All of Jude's and my couldn'ts and wouldn'ts were on painful display in what remains the worst moment of my life. What happened at his father's funeral is seared in my mind whenever I see his stupid perfect face in print or otherwise.

"There's lo mein for you in the car. And a bottle of tequila. In case this is something wine can't solve. Actually, I'm certain this is something wine can't solve, and those fancy galas never have real food," Mickey says.

She reaches out her arms and wraps me in a hug almost as tight as Jude's earlier tonight and I feel the tears welling up again. She pulls back and squeezes my shoulders. She nods at me and I nod back.

"Thanks, Mick," I say.

"And by the way, despite the look of panic perma-frozen on your face right now, you look amazing. I might even say you look wow."

"Too soon."

I lead the way up the outdoor stairs to the entrance. When the door closes behind us, the dog in the nearest apartment starts yipping and scratching at the wall.

When we reach the third floor, my apartment door is already open. Eva stands in the doorway and squeals when she sees me. "How was it?" Her smile falls when she sees Mickey. "What happened?"

Mickeys starts humming "Hey Jude," and I glare at her.

Eva's jaw drops. "No. No. Absolutely not. He's back in town? Does Oliver know?"

"It was his event," I reply.

"Whose event?" Oliver asks, coming to the door. He smiles when he sees the heels still in my hand and I drop them to the floor.

Eva pulls him in by his shirt collar and whispers in his ear.

His eyes widen, making the scar over the right one more prominent. A reminder I didn't need. "Fuck. Did you know?"

"Wouldn't have gone if I did."

"Well, are you okay?" Oliver asks.

"I will be," I say. I turn to Eva. "Thank you for the dress, by the way."

Eva gives me a once-over and I watch her scan the hem of the dress for any damage. She smiles to herself when she realizes that nothing in her immediate line of sight is amiss.

"He told her she looks wow," Mickey says.

"Well, you do, of course," Eva says.

Oliver grabs four glasses out of the cabinet. "I assume Mickey brought alcohol," he says. "And I smell lo mein. But I'm making grilled cheeses anyway."

"You're a saint, Oliver," Mickey replies.

"He's avoiding talking about his feelings about J . . . *him*," Eva says. "Every time he sees him on TV he makes waffle batter."

Oliver shakes his head and grabs a stick of butter. "Not every time."

Most of the time. But I can't blame him. I'm also never mad to get emotional support waffles. Oliver brought me and Jude together, and unfortunately, got torn apart right along with us in a different kind of heartbreak.

"I'm going to go change," I say. "I'll be right back."

"Hang that dress up!" Eva calls after me. "She wrinkles."

I close the door to my bedroom behind me and resist the urge to just collapse onto my bed. I've only eaten bruschetta tonight and my stomach keeps growling. I unzip the dress and slide it off onto the floor.

Mickey slips into the room wordlessly, and whisks the dress off the floor and onto the nearest empty hanger. She tosses me a pair of pajama pants and a T-shirt, then kneels in front of me with a makeup remover wipe.

"Don't cry until I pull the fake lashes off," she orders.

"Okay."

She pulls the lashes off my left eye and I feel the tears welling up. She puts her hands on my shoulders. "You've both grown up and are totally different people. He just wants to hear what you've been up to. But since you left, he'll probably let it go. It's not like he's been trying to get in contact all these years."

"True. I've had the same phone number since seventh grade."

"Exactly. It's a one and done. You came, you saw, you conquered, and you even got an article out of it. Which they will publish because you've been to war, and then I'll tweet about it, make it viral, and boom. Career boost."

The smell of Oliver's grilled cheese wafts into the room. He always sprinkles extra parmesan and hot honey over the top. It's divine.

Eva and Oliver stop whispering the second I sit down. Eva gives me a small smile.

"Care to share?" Mickey asks, staring directly at her.

Eva sighs, and Oliver's gaze shifts back to the grilled cheese. "We—" she begins.

Oliver coughs and flips another of the grilled cheeses. "Let's kibosh the we." He puts the first one on a plate and slides it over to me.

Eva glares at him. "Fine, *I* think you should call him."

I take a bite of the grilled cheese and almost burn the roof of my mouth. It silences my initial response, which I'm grateful for. I shouldn't have to be the one to call. I called every day for months. I showed up at the Landon Estate. I wrote letters, emails, Instagram DMs, private tweets. I could publish a book of the essays I wrote trying to get him to open up to me. One moment at one gala means nothing. I won't let it. Not after how badly he wrecked me last time. Why should I let him destroy what's left on the off chance that there's something still there?

"Hold up, no," Mickey says. "He's had *years* to reach out . . ."

"Maybe it was fate!" Eva replies. "The last time you saw him he was in a horribly vulnerable place, and he felt like you rejected him. Now he's in a better place."

"I don't know what kind of place he's in," I reply.

Who knows how much he's really changed. He agreed to bury it the last time he was in a bad place, maybe he would again. The cover-up may not have been Jude's idea, but he went along with what Jackie wanted without ever asking me for my opinion. It never mattered what I thought about that decision. If it did, we'd have a different relationship. He had an opportunity to take that awful moment, where thankfully no one got seriously hurt, or worse, and turn it into growth. Instead, he pretended it never happened and kept doing the exact same things until his father died. And the Landons enabled him. They never sent him to rehab, they just covered it up to the public until Jude got his act together.

"Never underestimate what the Landons can cover up," Oliver replies. He turns off the stove and slides the other three grilled cheeses onto plates, which he leaves on the counter for everyone to take.

"Well, maybe he'd just lie about it again. I'd never have to know," I say.

That lie is the one who ended our relationship, though it took a few months for the poison to really sink in, when I fully got to see just how thoroughly corrupted all of the Landons were. When his father set us up with the top couples' therapist in the county, thinking that it would repair what Jude's lie had broken, and subsequently keep me quiet. When Jude told me he was going "California sober" and cutting out every substance except for weed. When the next weekend, Jude nearly overdosed on cocaine that was laced with fentanyl, and his family bought a supply of Narcan for me to carry around instead of sending him to get help. I can't blame Jude for his addiction, but I also can't look past everything that happened in the throes of it, everything he was willing to give up, including me, in service of it.

"Technically, he omitted, not lied," Oliver says. "To give him the smallest bit of credit."

"Who told me the truth, then?"

It's a low blow, I know. Oliver was the one who told me, setting off the chain of events that led us from therapy to Jude's father's funeral. I never blamed Oliver, though—he did what was right. Jude and the Landons were the ones who refused to take accountability, spelling out the end of anything between us.

"He wanted to," Oliver says. "I forgave him for it, and I was the one actually hurt."

"Well, he didn't. And you haven't forgiven him for ending your friendship, so let's not go too far on the forgiveness train."

Eva steps in between us. "Okay, one thing I'm not going to let you do is talk to my boyfriend like that."

The look in her eyes—anger, love for Oliver—it's the same one I saw in Jude's eyes earlier after he confronted the sous-chef. And after he told Adam off. But I have to be wrong. Because he can't feel that way about me. Not after what he did.

Oliver holds his hand out at Eva. "Eva, I appreciate what you're trying to do. But Gen is my oldest friend, and we've both said worse to each other over the years."

"I'm sorry, Oliver," I reply. "I'm not my best right now and that was a shitty shot to take."

"I'm sorry too," he says. "You were hurt by that night too. You just as easily could have been the one in that car. And no, I haven't forgiven him for how he ended our friendship. But he hasn't given me a chance to. You have a chance if you want it. We both still love him, albeit in different ways. He's apologized to me for the accident, but he's never given you your due for its aftermath."

Oliver is right. Jude personally paid for his hospital bills from his trust fund. They got joint season passes for both the men's and women's national and local soccer teams. They spent more time together in the three months after the accident than they had in the three years before it. Oliver was embraced by the entire Landon family, to reward him for his silence and for being willing to keep the peace, while I was slowly iced out for pushing Jude to speak out.

Then Oliver agreed with me that Jude should use his platform to address substance abuse. He told the Landons that Jude should admit publicly what he'd done, and use the family's influence for the greater good. He even offered to be by Jude's side at the press conference, demonstrating his forgiveness. Julian told him to leave, and Jude never spoke to him again.

At the time, it all felt painfully simple. We didn't fall into what the Landons wanted, so we were pushed out.

But could there be more to the story? And why do I want there to be?

CHAPTER NINE

"It's *definitely* been twenty minutes, right?" Mickey asks, leaning her head back against the bench we're waiting on. She glares at the light-up sign screaming BRUNCH! outside of our local diner. She's deemed this meal my cheer-up brunch, even though it's doubling as a not-so-secret mission to run into her teacher-crush who mentioned coming here every Saturday at eleven.

"It's been five, and you're the one who chose the most popular restaurant in town at eleven AM on a Saturday for boozy brunch just to see your crush," I reply, sending a text to my parents to say the gala was fine and I'd call them later.

"And the hostess that looks like Shane from *The L Word*," Mickey replies. "I'm cool with whatever happens."

"Uh huh."

"What about that dude? He looks employed," Mickey says, pointing at an off-brand Bruce Wayne standing off by the parking lot.

"Suits remind me of Jude. And why is he wearing a suit to a diner brunch?"

Mickey swings her head back, almost knocking it against the bench. "That's the fourth dude you've refused to even talk to."

"He's not my type."

I barely have a type. But right now, no one looks good when they're stacked up against . . .

"Well, babes, you've got to do something besides ruminate on a certain redheaded mill-y-naire," she replies.

"Mill-y-naire?"

"To represent that millionaire just doesn't capture the moment. The scope."

"Yeah, okay," I reply.

There's a mental picture of him in that suit lodged in my frontal lobe, guiding all my potential dating-related decision making. I can invent an instant problem in any guy Mickey points out right now. Because I don't want any of them.

My phone buzzes with a text from Mom. She's texted back a GIF of a woman twirling in a dress and asks, *Did you secure the bag?*

I text back three question marks.

Dad responds, *The bag. You know. What the millennials say.*

Did you charm any rich ppl who want you to tell their stories??? Mom texts back.

I hope! I send back.

"You're going to tell me I'm lucky the wait isn't longer, aren't you? For both the restaurant and for you to pick a potential lover," Mickey asks, scrolling through Instagram.

"Look at that; you're psychic."

Mickey's head snaps up and she fluffs her hair. I open my mouth to say something, but she kicks me and nods in the direction of a group of friends. A short curvy white woman, who I assume is Helena, the teacher crush, emerges from the center of the pack and locks eyes with Mickey.

Mickey stands up, a little too quickly, and I can see the panic seize her body as she almost tries to sit back down. I give her a tiny push before she gets halfway down, and she takes a few steps toward Helena.

"Hey, Helena," Mickey says.

"Hey, Michelle," Helena replies.

I almost flinch. I've never heard anyone call Mickey "Michelle" besides her mother, and that's usually only when she's in trouble.

"Brunch, huh?" Mickey says.

"Yup. You?"

"Yep. Gotta love it." Mickey smiles at her and the two of them stand in silence.

I stand up. "Hi! I'm Gen," I say to Helena, a little too cheerfully and probably with accidental territorial undertones.

Helena scans me up and down and swallows. She forces a smile. "Hi, nice to meet you. I should probably . . ." She looks back to her friends.

"I'm Mickey's best friend. She wants me to date every man here. Make sure to try the western omelet!" I reply.

Mickey turns to either glare at me or laugh at me. Either way, she's a lot more relaxed looking than she was before my word vomit sandwich, and Helena is still standing next to her.

"She's right, about the men and the omelet," Mickey says.

Helena pauses for a moment. "Not your type?"

"They generally have a few additional parts I could do without, but some can be objectively, like a statue in a museum, attractive," Mickey replies.

"Ah. Yes. Certain parts can be unnecessary," Helena says. "Something we could maybe talk about . . . outside the classroom?"

"It'd be a *pleasure*," Mickey replies.

One of Helena's friends taps her on the shoulder and shows her their blinking restaurant pager. Mickey winks at her before she goes, and Helena blushes.

Once Helena vanishes into the restaurant, I give Mickey a thumbs-up from the bench. "That was incredible."

I really should take notes. When Mickey's on, she's on. And if I could flirt like that, I probably wouldn't be single.

"No, your word slushie was incredible," she replies, sitting down next to me.

I feel a buzzing in my lap. "Our table . . ."

"Yes!" Mickey stands up. "What?"

"It's not the buzzer."

I never changed the contact photo in my phone, but I was sure the number would be different. A picture of Jude and me at prom has taken over my screen. He wore a light blue tux to match my light blue strapless silk gown. Julian even pulled some strings so I could borrow a seven-carat Tiffany diamond pendant necklace for the night.

I stare at the picture for a few seconds too long and Mickey taps me on the shoulder. I shake my head.

"Well, the fact that he hasn't changed his number since becoming a rich-ass CEO is questionable," Mickey says.

"He definitely has more than one phone; I'm sure this isn't the same one he uses for business," I reply.

The phone stops buzzing and flashes one missed call. I take a deep breath and then a voice mail pops up.

Mickey snatches the phone from me and pulls up my voice mail. She's putting it on speaker before I can get a word out.

"Hey, Gen. It was great seeing you last night. Sorry we didn't find each other before the night ended. I'd still love to catch up if you're interested. I hope you are. You can call me or text me. Beep me if you want to reach me? God, that was terrible. Just reach out if you want. You looked beautiful," Jude's voice says.

"He sounds the exact same. What was all that about a *deep voice*?" Mickey asks.

"This is his regular voice. He whips out CEO Jude for business functions, it seems. Deeper, more Julian-like."

The less polished he sounds, the more I'm reminded of the Jude I used to know. And the cheesy jokes? They're the cherry on top of a sundae I shouldn't even want.

The phone begins buzzing again and Mickey squeals before seeing that it's Adam. She snorts and drops her voice down three octaves. "Jennifer, you can't write your Black women at work piece; it's divisive. But please authenticity check this article written by two white women about an *urban* drug dealer who's turned his life around."

I wave my hand at her to be quiet. "Hello?" I say into the phone.

"It's Adam," Adam says. "I have to talk to you."

"You hated the article that much?"

"Not at all. It was a surprisingly good profile, you must have been up all night. And I enjoyed your pitch about the gender gap in the kitchen, but that's not why I'm calling," he replies.

I try not to take offense at "surprisingly good." I've written dozens of profiles. The only person who's surprised is him, because he can't see past his own biases even with all the evidence right in front of his face. And yes, I pulled an all-nighter because I didn't want this article to somehow get snatched away from me in the light of day. I'm sure the Fates have recovered by now.

"Okay, are we going to run the gender gap article? I can have a draft to you by the end of the weekend."

"Maybe someday, but not right now."

"Oh."

"But you're definitely in the running for more articles. Maybe even some cowrites with other staff members while you find your footing," he asks.

"My footing?"

"As a writer," he says. "Since you're still pretty new to writing articles. It gets easier after the first two."

I've written more than 200 articles, just not for his paper. He's shot down every idea I've ever had and assigned articles to everyone except me. I'm such a team player that I'm of better use propping up everyone else.

I bite the inside of my lip and Mickey stares me down, trying to mouth messages to me.

"Um . . . Thanks. What kind of articles were you thinking for me, moving forward, then?" I ask.

"Of course the ones you've pitched. Down the line when you're ready. You can start with some of the lower-stakes ones. Telling some of the other ethnic stories and practicing objectivity. Helping your colleagues by adding a few sentences to get more credit than just a sensitivity read. You're on your way up."

How long exactly can one be "on the way up"? At this point, I feel like I've been stuck on the basement floor for almost half of my twenties.

"I see."

"But, again, none of that is why I'm calling," he says.

"Oh?"

"I wanted to apologize for mispronouncing your name for all this time. It's been brought to my attention just how . . . wrong . . . that is," he says.

Mispronouncing is a way to put it. I hate that I know exactly who brought that to his attention. I can't bring myself to respond to his "apology." "Will the profile be published?"

"We'll see. Lucy can help you with it on Monday; she's done this kind of thing before." He hangs up before I can say that I've done this kind of thing before too.

I lean back against the bench and lay the phone back on my lap.

"Did he get your name right this time?" Mickey asks.

"Yes, to tell me that my piece was *surprisingly good*, articles get easier after the first two, and that Lucy gets to rewrite my piece, essentially."

"Ugh, seriously? Like you've only written two articles ever? And surprisingly good? What makes Lucy so great?"

"She's Adam's favorite and is untouchable. She had next to no experience coming in, just a year on the staff of her college paper, no editorial experience, yet apparently she's the journalistic voice we've all been waiting for," I reply.

Lucy is a good writer. Minus her clear racial biases, there's nothing wrong with the quality of her writing. But she's a dime a dozen. I worked with fifteen Lucys at my high school and college papers. All of them are doing ten times better than I am, even though I know I have just as much skill, if not more.

"Isn't she the one who made one of the high school interns cry on their first day? She told that kid that she jeopardized the entire paper by making nine copies instead of ten?"

"Yep. One intern on day one and the other two interns by the end of the first week. One of them told me she berates them until they cry, or until someone is walking by. Then it's all smiles. And he only got my name right because it was *brought to his attention* that it might be . . . *wrong*."

Mickey stares at my phone, as if willing it to light up again. "He botched your name in front of Jude? At Jude's fundraiser? Which both of you were there to write articles about? How fucking embarrassing."

"Jude swooped right in with that correction and then purposefully messed up Adam's name to his face."

"Love to see it." The buzzer in Mickey's hand begins to vibrate. "Are we going in?"

"Yeah. Come on. Pivot pivot. New topic."

I spin my spoon around and around on the table, ignoring the menu in front of me. I can hear Mickey chatting to a waiter, but I can't hear anything she's saying. All I can hear is the whooshing sound in my ears. I'm about to at least get one article, maybe more, doubling my publication record with the *Tribune*. And I'm certainly not going to spend the next forty-eight hours listening to Jude's voicemail over and over again until I've committed it to memory.

Mickey taps her glass against the table. "Pivot pivot, I have a had-to-bite-my-tongue parent moment for you."

I lean forward. "Yes please. Hit me with it."

When Mickey was finishing her full takeover of a classroom, we used to play a drinking game at the bar across from our dorm. Once a week, one shot for every time someone older than both of us said something utterly insane while she was student teaching at her elementary school placement. We had to stop when one night we both ended up on the bathroom floor with the spins and couldn't stop texting our respective recent exes. At least her ex responded; I never heard back from Jude. Plus, now that she's actually the full-time teacher, she usually has too many experiences to count. Especially given that she's publicly out and keeps a pride flag on her door.

"So, remember how I told you about that kid who keeps throwing erasers at my back when I'm writing on the board?"

"Yes. How could I forget?"

"So, I called his parents. Mom and Dad come in, and straight up tell me that maybe it's not such a bad thing."

"Logic being?" I ask.

"With the recent budget cuts in education, I could probably use some additional classroom supplies. I had to *smile* at them."

"Well, are you keeping the erasers?" I ask.

"Of course. It's the middle of the year; I'm fucking low on classroom supplies."

I try to repress the cackle-laugh that threatens to emerge from me as I spot Helena coming our way. I kick Mickey under the table and cock my head.

Presumably on her way to the bathroom, Helena takes a lingering look at Mickey, who stares back so intently that I catch Helena looking flushed.

"Smooth," I say, when Helena has passed us. "Do you need to just take your omelet to go? She looks pretty hot and bothered."

"Smoother than you."

"Low bar. Low blow."

Mickey, of the two of us, has always been the better flirt by far. She can communicate entire pickup lines with her eyes. It always floors me when she's single because I have no idea how anyone resists her.

She shrugs and picks at one of the sugar packets in the corner container. She stares off in the direction of the bathroom, and pulls the sugar packet out of the container, then stuffs it back in, over and over.

I thought she'd be happier. She's definitely got Helena interested, but something's up.

I reach out for her hand and she pulls it back, leaving the sugar packet lying on top of the rest of the sugars. "Mickey, what's going on? Now *you're* off."

Mickey sighs. "I'm really into her."

"And? Is that a bad thing?" I ask.

"I figured out that she likes women at the beginning of the year with a thorough Twitter stalk session. But I don't know if she's into Black women. And I'm too afraid to ask."

"She's been flirting, it seems like. She gets all flushed when you look at her."

"Yeah. So do a lot of girls I end up going on dates with. And then what happens? Never goes anywhere. I think we're having a good time, but there's always just *something missing* for them. Usually when it comes time to maybe meet each other's friends, or better yet each other's families. I've been in four different exclusive relationships in the last two years and I've never met someone's family."

I thought her last couple of girlfriends were just closeted. But then, boom, a couple months later there's a social media pic of them with their new white girlfriend and their entire extended family.

"I'm sorry. It sucks."

"I know. And you know. But this isn't the biggest town. Imperfect and complicated as Jude is, I bet he'd take you back in a heartbeat. I've exhausted at least four different dating apps and all of the gay and bi women in a twenty-mile radius." She drops her head to the table again.

"You're right. You know I'm good with an online search. Do you need me to do a little vet before you get more invested in the flirtation?"

I know I have it hard in the dating world, but Mickey, sitting at another intersection of marginalized identities, definitely has it bad too. We're two employed mid-twenties Black women with sparkling wits and a pretty solid education. Why won't anyone take us seriously?

Mickey shakes her head. "I think I'll just do a more thorough social media stalk and see if she maybe knows any other Black people that aren't connected to the local school system."

"I'll stay on standby," I reply. "I'm feeling spicy, maybe."

Mickey pulls her plate back toward her and begins cutting into her omelet. "Stay spicy and direct it at Jude. Settle *that* action item."

"Fine. I'll consider calling him. But don't you want to know? With Helena. Before you get hurt?"

"I don't," she replies. "The fantasy bubble will burst at some point. But I'm kind of having fun with it right now. It's exciting and new and I have no idea what could happen. I like the excitement. You can too, if you'd stop being scared of it."

I cut a piece of omelet and stuff it in my mouth before I have to respond. I'm not scared of Jude the person; I'm scared of Jude the public entity. I'm scared of being on the front page of the newspaper as the subject instead of in the byline. It may not be the best reason, but it's mine. It's my protection, against a system I know will treat me badly both on the inside and outside, in the front-page picture and in the back cubicle.

Twenty minutes later, there is a line out the door, and we're both leaning back into the booth, debating whether or not to unbutton our top pants buttons now or when we get to the car, and whether or not we should stop in some of the boutiques before going back to my apartment.

Mickey picks up the check and waves my hand away when I try to offer my credit card. "Walk off the omelet and take a moment for yourself outside; I'll meet you at Chic," she says.

"So you have another date this weekend," I reply. "You only shop at Chic for a date. An impressive date."

"She's an OB resident," Mickey replies, "4c curls, impeccably maintained, president of the LGBTQIA social club two towns over, and all of her app pictures were professionally taken because her ex was a photographer, and she was her muse. I need to be immaculate."

"You *are* immaculate and just as impressive as she is. I'll see you there. Thank you for brunch!"

I swing my purse over my shoulder, grab my phone off the table, and smile at the hostess on my way out to the parking lot. I notice that there do seem to be a lot more women in the waiting area than on previous Saturdays, and many of them do seem to be staring at the hostess. I wonder if *she* dates Black women; maybe I need to do a little Mickey-esque meddling.

The parking lot is now completely packed, as are the surrounding side streets. Main Street is as busy as ever, with families walking to the local park and teens swinging in and out of every little shop.

I shake my head and make a mental note to pick up oven cleaner from the Black-owned supply shop next to Chic. Our basic kitchen cleaning supplies were no match for the remnants of Eva's cake, and neither were Oliver's household-item hacks.

My phone buzzes in my hand, and I glance down at it. A headline flashes across the screen: *Pulitzer Prize Winner Resigns After Newspaper Misprints Name.* I roll my eyes and stick the phone in my pocket. A gross understatement, per usual. A staff writer for a prominent Midwest newspaper quit after the newspaper she worked for, the newspaper she earned a Pulitzer for, published a photo of a completely different Black woman in their congratulations to her, *and* spelled her name incorrectly. Even a Pulitzer can't protect Black women from being "misidentified" by the papers they've worked at for decades. What hope is there for me?

I barely make it to the curb at the edge of the parking lot before I feel a hand on my shoulder. "That was fast, Mick. You won't believe this headline," I say, before turning around to find that Mickey isn't standing behind me, Jude is. "Oh. Hey."

How many times can this happen in twenty-four hours? It hasn't happened for four years even though I pass Landon Energy on the way to the *Tribune*. Was I recently implanted with a GPS?

He stands far enough away so we're not touching, but close enough that I can smell his cologne, the same cologne his dad used to wear. He looks just as good as he did last night, but there are bags under his eyes. Like he couldn't sleep either.

"I have to meet Mickey at Chic," I say.

If he didn't sleep for the same reason I didn't, I can't stay here. I lay in bed, every facial expression he made at the gala, from our conversation to his speech, replaying in my mind. I turned each one over and over until they heated up my entire body with embarrassment, anger, sadness, maybe even wonderment. He was always charming, at least to me, but he hated public speaking. He had the stutter, and he never thought he was good enough to be a Landon in the way his father wanted him to be. But there he was, with the eyes of an entire room on him, and he fit like a glove. And if he fits into that world now, then where does that leave me? Was I always a different pair of gloves, destined to someday be tossed aside?

"May I walk with you?" Jude asks. "To Chic. I have a . . . a question . . . about your article."

Of course, the only thing he'd want to talk about would be the article. Please. It's been a while, but he's still easy to read.

"The Potts profile will be perfect, and I'm sure the paper will rave about your gala. No need to worry."

"That's not . . . Jesus, this is awkward."

"Yep."

I stare straight ahead as we walk, trying to avoid glancing at Jude, or noticing the way his shoes click-clack as they hit the sidewalk.

"I hope I've caught you in a particularly forgiving mood," Jude says, trying to force out a laugh.

"Well, I hate to dash your hopes."

I could be nicer. Actually, I probably should be, even if I don't want to. How long can I hold a college-aged grudge against him? As bad as it was for me, it couldn't have been a walk in the park for him either.

"I was headed to the farmers market and saw you out here on your phone. Did you see the *Times*? Isn't it fun knowing you're treated the same as a Pulitzer winner?"

"Fun," I reply. "You think racism is fun?"

His jaw drops, and he waves his hands in front of his face. "Fuck! No. Of course not. Come on, we used to joke. We were always friends."

"Well, not always."

For three blocks, neither of us makes any more physical or verbal moves, just one foot in front of the other, past the local ice cream shop and a DryBar.

"I was happy to see you last night. And I thought maybe you'd want to talk. Especially after Adam."

He must have amnesia. Or this is a body double. We're not casual friends who've run into each other a few years post-graduation. I can't imagine a deeper well of feelings than the one bubbling up between the two of us.

"What do we have to talk about, Jude?"

"Our entire lives for the last four years? Jobs, friends, other things? Like, how's Oliver? And Mickey, going to Chic, that means she has a date, right? Is Adam as much of an asshole as he seems? The way he acted like there's no way I could know you."

"Speaking of, nice cover last night," I say. "Pretending we're just old friends."

"Well technically, we are—were."

"And more. We were."

If he'd had his way we'd be married right now. Well, probably divorced. I'd have gotten a nice settlement, though. I could have started my own paper. Maybe I *was* wrong.

"I wasn't sure if you wanted our past out there," he says.

"I don't. Neither do you, since you had all of our photos scrubbed from the internet."

"That wasn't my idea."

"It never is," I reply.

He fiddles with his father's ring, and I catch flashes of light as the sun radiates against his watch. One block away from Chic he stops and turns to me.

"Were you ever going to answer the phone?" he asks.

"Were you ever going to answer mine? After the funeral?"

His voice softens, and his eyes suddenly look sad. "I should have."

How different would things have been if he had answered even one of my calls? If both of us could have completely moved on from everything that happened in those last few months.

"I understand," he says. "I do. I have a lot of regrets from that time." He stares down at his loafers, which are slightly scuffed from the dirt we're standing in.

"Good," I reply after a few seconds of standing in silence. "I don't know why you want to talk to me anyway. Didn't I break your heart? That's what you said while you were dumping me."

A couple of women stare at us for a few seconds too long as they pass by, trying to place Jude and figure out why I'm with him. Jude makes eye contact with one of them and they put it together, chattering to each other about how they're certain it's *the* Jude Landon.

"Didn't I break yours?" he asks.

"You did," I reply, forcing my voice to stay level, even though I feel the tears starting to brim in my eyes. "Into a million pieces."

"And you broke mine. In pieces I'm still picking up."

I'd pay to see what he has to pick up. I never wanted him to be perfect, I just wanted him to be the best version of himself. I wanted to be the best version of myself too, personally and professionally. Everything I did in that graveyard was out of the ultimate love for him.

"So, what are we doing here?" I ask. "If all we do is break each other."

"Well, we've never given each other the chance to do anything else. Being older and wiser now . . ."

I snort. We're not that much older, and I don't know how wise I think I am. As hurt as I still am, something is keeping me here, next to him. Maybe we have some of the same pieces left broken.

"What about being older and more pessimistic?"

Jude smiles. "I did mean it, about catching up. If you ever want. On or off the record. If that's more appealing."

I raise my eyebrows. An interview with the elusive Jude Landon. He's never been formally interviewed.

"There are other reporters."

"Never found a reporter I liked," he replies, smiling at me. "Well, I did but then I gave her an ultimatum during a proposal at a funeral."

Despite myself, I crack a smile back. "Rookie mistake."

Whoever gets that exclusive will probably have all the career opportunities in the world. Like writing about more than ice cream. Like being the one writing the stories about Black people instead of just being the diversity reader. It probably couldn't be me, though, given the ethical dimensions. Heather was allowed to write a glowing review of her now-fiancé's new seafood shack, without ever disclosing their relationship. I doubt I'd be given the same grace.

Mickey has just appeared in view, up the street.

"See you around, I hope," Jude says.

He's gone before Mickey can spot him.

CHAPTER TEN

The next morning, I wake up to the smell of pancakes wafting into my bedroom. I roll out of bed, cap intact, and pull my T-shirt down. I almost trip over the slippers by the side of my bed as I stumble to the door.

Oliver's standing by the stove, flipping pancakes.

"Where's Eva?" I ask.

"An engagement party breakfast for a friend from work," he replies.

"So, this is a 'we have to talk' breakfast," I say, pulling off my cap and laying it on the table near the bathroom.

We had one of these when Oliver told me about the accident. He made French toast in our dorm kitchen and showed me a photo of Jude's mugshot. By the end, we were both crying, and neither of us was particularly hungry. Whenever Oliver tells the story now, he pretends that I had to force it out of him, or that I figured it out entirely on my own.

The truth is, I knew that Jude wasn't telling me everything, but I never wanted to believe that he'd actually risk anyone's life by driving drunk. The light above us started flickering and I was certain it was a sign that Oliver was lying, that this was all some cruel joke. But the mugshot was impossible to deny. To this day, I've never asked Oliver how he got a copy, considering it was never released to the public.

Oliver stands across from me with his plate of pancakes. "I know you, and I knew him too," he says, drizzling syrup across his pancakes. "It's been a long time since he and I had anything to do with each other, but I remember the two of you together and, in my opinion, you never fully moved on."

"I see." I take a bite of the pancakes and chew for as long as I can until Oliver fills the silence.

"That doesn't mean that I'm hoping you two get back together. Eva thinks it's a rom-com or something, but I was there. That proposal was horrifying. But I think you still love some part of him, despite everything. And based on what you told us about the event, I wouldn't be surprised if he felt the same way."

"He could have killed you. How can I love someone who'd do something like that, Ollie?"

"Because he's more than his worst moments," Oliver says. "We all are."

Oliver tried to blame himself, saying that he knew Jude shouldn't drive, but he was drunk too. That he convinced Jude that because they were only going a mile up the street, it'd be fine. But, in the end, Oliver and I both knew that Jude's drinking was out of hand long before they hit that tree.

I sigh. "I ran into him again yesterday. Outside of the restaurant before Mickey came out. He said I broke his heart; he still wants to catch up and he's willing to make it on the record."

"What would that open up?" he asks.

"A lot of shit, but maybe also opportunities. Especially since I told Adam that we only ran in the same group in high school," I reply. "I don't know, but it's compelling."

He picks up his fork. "Just be careful." He takes a bite of his pancakes. "And if you do this, you have to tell Adam."

"Do I?" I ask. "I could just pretend."

"Yeah, I'm sure the internet and your coworkers would be kind about you downplaying a long-term relationship with a multimillionaire to get a scoop."

I groan.

We eat the rest of our pancakes across from each other in silence. A few times Oliver looks like he wants to say something, but he refrains. The moment after I take my last bite, he whisks the plate away into the sink. When all of the dishes are loaded in the dishwasher, he turns back around to face me as I nurse my coffee.

"What are the odds Adam assigns you the Pulitzer article, now that he knows your name?"

"What are the odds we even cover it?" I reply. "And even if we do it'll have to go to a white woman who will frame it as the Black unemployment rate rising."

I can see the headline now: "Black Woman Gives Up Job for No Reason at All." And I'll get an email asking if devaluing hard work is cultural. Maybe I *should* have just been Jude's trophy wife. Falling out of love with a job seems worse than falling out of love with him.

"Touché. Maybe you could get a job at Landon Energy. They could definitely use a sensitivity reader on some of those press releases."

"You're not funny," I reply.

"Au contraire," he says. "But I figured you could use the joke. We literally went through puberty together, Gen. I saw every part of that relationship, from how it started to how it ended. And your face the entire time we've been talking about him . . . there's something there for you. It's complicated, it's not all sunshine and roses, but it's there."

Oliver's right. I don't know where I want Jude to end up, but I do have a nagging feeling that I want to see him again—just from a distance, where I don't have to risk anything yet.

CHAPTER ELEVEN

Everyone at the *Tribune* office Monday morning is staring at me. I smooth my shirt down, wondering if I have a stain on my pants or something. I reach up reflexively to touch my hair. If a strand or two is out of place, I hear whispers about how disheveled I seem, usually from Evelyn. I notice every eye that's trained on me as I place my bag down on my desk.

Regina stands and makes a point of looking around the room, trying to make eye contact with as many people as possible. She claps three times and whistles. "I see a lot of looking and not a lot of working," she says.

Heads duck back into their desks, but I still feel myself growing hot. I can hear some pretty furious typing in what I assume is Slack, not a Word document.

Regina makes eye contact with me across the room. She slides a stack of documents on the edge of her desk over toward the middle, leaving a space for me to lean.

"What's going on?" I ask.

"Your profile of Jacques Potts from the Landon gala. Adam copyedited it himself and ran the piece pretty much as written."

"Seriously? I have a *published* story?" I ask. "That wasn't torn apart with edits?"

"Yep, top of the culture section. *Congratulations.*" Regina leans in. "Adam plans to give you more stories; he floated it by Evelyn this morning, who was none too pleased. After this weekend's story over at the *Times*, there's a lot of scrutiny. A former intern posted on Twitter, and now Adam's dedicated to proving he's not racist."

"Which involves me getting published?"

"You getting published with minimal oversight. Essentially, copyedit your own pieces, because he's willing to run them pretty much as is, and you can take the fall or the success."

I blink at her, trying to put the pieces together. Usually, we have college interns copyedit, or, for the Fates, me. Adam only ever does line edits for the biggest stories, which tend to only involve senior staff writers. For someone who keeps his big break on his office wall, he gave up actually writing stories notoriously quickly.

"So to be not racist he's going to not do something for me that's done for everyone else?" I ask.

"Pretty much."

"That makes very little sense."

"A course correction that veers so far left it's actually a mistake. Send your pieces to me for a second look if you want."

"Thanks, girl. Is that it?"

She sighs. Great. My one good career moment in the last four years is taking another turn.

"No. Someone—I don't know who—told Evelyn who told Adam that you're a story thief."

All three of the Fates are gathered at Lucy's desk, their heads ducked together beneath the cubicle dividers. It was a bold move to report me for an article that Adam personally assigned to me while they were all home with food poisoning. What was I supposed to do, say no? Write their name on the byline instead of mine?

"Do we know who?"

"Whoever it was said something that Adam felt that he shouldn't repeat about your *tone* when you talked about the story yesterday," Regina says.

"My *tone* in what? I called Lucy to ask if she felt up to copyediting the story once Adam approved it yesterday, since it was hers originally, and when she said no, Adam apparently did it personally."

"Apparently, that was quite offensive," Regina replies. "Your *tone* made it sound like you were reveling in her being sick. And copyediting is not something she does, as a staff writer."

I roll my eyes. Hello, also a staff writer here, and they don't have a problem with me copyediting *their* pieces.

"So essentially tread lightly . . . in doing my job," I reply.

"Yep. Watch your tone around the white folks."

The moment I get a story, only because no one else was available, I get tone policed. That's just perfect. I'm even getting positive emails from local culinary people on the profile, thanks to Oliver, who I'm sure told every single person he knows about this article between Friday night and this morning.

"I'm really fucking sick of this. I really thought I'd get to do something here."

Evelyn stares at both of us as she passes. She lingers a few feet away until Regina makes eye contact with her, and I hear her whisper something under her breath as she heads into her office.

"I'm really freaking sick of *her*," Regina says. "She's been like this for two decades."

I roll my eyes. "So, the Fates never change, they just get promoted."

"Yep. And get the best stories at the most conveniently early times."

"Speaking of, any word on who the mysterious CEO profile is on?" I ask.

Regina glances around surreptitiously and slides over a business card. My breath stops. *That's* why Jude mentioned catching up professionally.

I run my finger over his name.

Regina leans in more, her eyes lighting up. "Wait a minute, do you know him?"

I nod. "We dated."

"Good for you," she whispers, tapping me on the arm. "Get it, girl."

"For six years in high school and college."

"*Six years?* So you *know* him know him. And he's not your secret husband? Shouldn't you be working at like *Vogue* or *Newsweek*?"

"We broke up at Julian Landon's funeral; people had to sign NDAs, it was a whole thing," I reply. "I didn't want anything to do with them after that so I came here instead of the places that were reaching out because of my connection to the Landons."

Regina's eyes widen. "He broke up with you the second he was anointed? Just *like* a man." She takes a sip of her water. "You could have taken those opportunities, though."

"Um, actually . . . I technically broke up with him? I refused his casket-side marriage proposal."

Regina starts choking on her water and coughs so loudly that everyone in the cubicle area stares at us. It takes her several seconds to catch her breath. She waves at all of the onlookers to indicate that she's fine and slowly heads start turning back to their desks.

I shake my head. "I ran into him at the gala and again yesterday. He mentioned potentially having a conversation on the record, but I didn't think much of it."

"You'd have to disclose to standards and practices. This kind of thing is heavily frowned upon."

"I know, that's why I would want to avoid it," I reply. "We ran into Adam at the gala, and I told him that we went to high school together and had some of the same friends. That's it."

Regina sighs. "I can't say for sure, but he's been on with the ethics board for the last hour. And he had dinner with Jude Landon last night."

"Fuck."

"You've *got* to make sure the other person is in on your lie. Just a friend from high school? You were basically married," she says. "Have those three taught you nothing?"

Lucy and Heather covered for Clara last week when she was two hours late for work. They both claimed they personally witnessed a near-fatal car accident near her apartment that jammed traffic. She lives four blocks from the office and hasn't had a car in the last two months.

I nearly throw my phone into Regina's trash can as Adam spots me across the newsroom. I wait for him to reach us before following him into his office.

The stack of papers he drops on his desk are almost as loud as the breath he takes before sitting down. I'm supposed to take the seat across from him, I assume, but he hasn't said anything yet.

"*Genevieve*," he says.

"Yes."

Regina slips into the room and hands Adam a coffee. He nods at her, and she gives him a small smile.

"Do you prefer Gen?" Adam asks me.

"Either is fine."

"You know, Gen is often a nickname for Jennifer, so that's why I thought that was your name. It wasn't like the *Times*. And, of course, you haven't been here half as long. Or won a *Pulitzer*."

Regina, standing in the doorway, makes eye contact with me. I bite my tongue, wondering if I should tweet that my boss just mansplained my own name to me. I could create a real viral moment for the paper.

"I see," I reply.

Regina slips out the door, but she leaves it open a crack to listen from her desk.

"You lied to me about the nature of your relationship with Jude Landon," Adam says. "You could have been Mrs. Landon."

I take a gulp of air. So Jude *did* tell him the full nature of our former relationship. "Theoretically."

"Why did you lie to me about that?"

"Because I didn't think it would matter."

Because I knew it would look bad, somehow.

"It's an important conflict of interest."

"I don't write about business."

I don't write about anything anyone actually cares to read.

"Not with that attitude," Adam says. He leans back in his chair and pushes the sleeves of his shirt up to his elbows. He leans forward and places his elbows on the desk. "And you know that's not the conflict of interest I'm talking about. You've been specifically requested to write the profile of Jude Landon for the *Tribune*, Genevieve." He sighs. "Mr. Landon has made it clear that if you're not the writer, we won't get the story. No one will. Not even the *Times*. I've got to be honest, Genevieve. This is the kind of piece that makes careers."

The way Adam says it confirms my suspicions. He would never voluntarily give me this article over one of the Fates. Jude must have pushed really hard behind the scenes. But why? Does he think I'm going to go easy on him?

"What about ethics?" I ask.

"It's a profile, not a strictly business article, and there's a precedent of profiles being written by people who have known their subjects personally—some would argue it makes for a more honest piece. Additionally, per Mr. Landon's admission, your . . . personal relationship hasn't been active in four years. And you would need to disclose that relationship either before the profile or within it. Preferably more directly than you disclosed it to me."

He isn't wrong. Our past does give me a unique prism into how Jude became the man he is today, and how he filled his father's shoes. We have rapport, so I can probably get him to open up. If I do it right, it could be groundbreaking, for both of us. Plus, it would give me the chance to see who Jude is now, compared to who he was.

Of course, it could also only benefit Jude and the *Tribune*. Jude gets a good dose of local publicity, and the *Tribune* gets to benefit over the bigger New York papers with an exclusive story. Per usual, Adam, who thinks the only interesting part of this situation is that I gave up the opportunity to be Mrs. Landon, is going to benefit from my hard work, while my career remains in limbo. If I do this profile, will it allow me to write the stories I want to write going forward or will it be the end of a barely started career? Will it give me some degree of positive attention for my work, or will I just be the tragic almost–Mrs. Landon?

"Noted."

He whistles. "I'd love a piece on why you said no."

And I'd love a job at a different publication that would give me stories I'm actually interested in, professionally. I can find out how Jude overcame grief over coffee or maybe a glass of wine more expensive than my monthly rent. I can't change this paper from the inside out with a fake feminist take about turning down the marriage proposal of my fucking ex-boyfriend, no matter how impressive he is. If that's the only article I get to write after this profile, I'm going to burn the building down and laugh at the flames.

"I'm going to say no to that one," I reply.

"But the profile?"

I raise an eyebrow. "Do I really have a choice?"

"There's always a choice," he replies. "Maybe you can write your Black piece when this is done. Once we've established that you can do more than just Black issues."

He quite literally hasn't even given me the opportunity to write Black issues, yet that's all I can do? The *maybe* rings around in my head too. He can't even guarantee anything when backing me into an ethical dilemma. So I can't really say no because this doesn't sound like an optional assignment, and it's all I'm guaranteed to get for the rest of time. Right now my prize is just a "good job!" sticker from two white dudes.

I stand up. "I'm already getting backlash for the Potts profile in the newsroom," I say. "What are you going to do with this one, given the personal component?"

Adam shrugs. "You can handle it. Feminism, right? Girl power. Black Girls Rock. Love that special."

I close my eyes for a moment, hoping Regina is still listening and will burst in with a monologue that perfectly captures every problematic aspect of this moment in biting fashion. Adam would never fire her, and I live on the chopping block.

If the Fates are this mad that I got a profile due to extenuating circumstances, then they'd be livid if they knew I got the coveted Jude Landon profile based on a personal connection. After they overcame the shock that Jude Landon could be interested in the likes of me, they'd start actively trying to ruin my life instead of just making the process a slow IV drip of workplace politics.

"Fine," I say. I'm a coward. I should stand up for myself.

Adam smiles. "Look forward to seeing a draft on my desk in the next two weeks. And in the meantime I need five hundred words on that incident downtown. With the Asian woman. Track her down, get a quote from her family, even if it's broken. Something emotional. Don't take no for an answer. And find some statistics."

A Chinese woman was assaulted at the bus station by the mall yesterday afternoon, in broad daylight. News crews have been banging down her door trying to get an interview for the past eighteen hours. My ethical bind with Jude sounds infinitely more appealing than berating someone who doesn't want their face in the media to cry for me so I can describe it with a twenty-word simile.

I think I nod, but I can't be sure. I want to push back. I want to say no, tell him it's racist to assume that this woman or her family can't speak English. But better me than one of the Fates, right? Even if I let these comments go.

I push myself out of the chair, trying to blink back my tears. I compel myself to smile back at Adam, but it comes out as more of a grimace, gritted teeth and all.

I'm a hypocrite. Imploding my relationship with Jude after his DUI because he wouldn't publicly own up to it and use his platform to raise awareness. Begging for him back even after he dumped me in front of hundreds of people. Here I am with a growing platform, an actual important article assignment, ignoring everything I've learned for my own gain. How am I supposed to stand up for myself if I can't even tell my editor that it's racist to assume an Asian woman speaks broken English solely on the basis of her Asian-ness? I can write a better story than any of the Fates, I can give her her humanity back in print . . . so why can't I do it for myself in the newsroom?

I take a moment to breathe once I close Adam's door behind me, even though I know people are looking.

I shuffle through a couple of papers on my desk. Most of them are old copyedits or research verification on someone else's article that I could drop in the shredding bin, especially now that I have my own assignment.

My desk phone rings.

"Genevieve Francis?"

"Yes," I reply.

"This is Lauren, Jude Landon's assistant. I wanted to schedule your first meeting with Mr. Landon about the profile."

She must have the office bugged; how could my acceptance have gotten around this quickly?

"Oh . . . great."

"Are you available tomorrow at nine AM?" she asks.

"Sure."

"Wonderful!" Lauren says. "We're very excited over here. We loved your Jacques Potts profile and are thrilled you'll be writing a piece about our esteemed leader."

"Thank you, Lauren," I reply.

An email pings in my inbox with a map to the parking garage and Lauren's direct line listed. She works fast.

"Thank *you*! We'll see you tomorrow. Bye."

I hang up. If only we could all be as excited about this profile as Lauren. Though, if I were, it'd probably be to my detriment, given every way Jude has disappointed me thus far.

I just have to treat this like any other assignment. Jude is my subject, a person I'm getting to know. He's not the Jude of my past. He's not the Jude of my anything. He's an article coming to life, a story I'm trying to tell. And right now, I have other stories too. Stories I actually care about. Even if I have to get them all the way to print myself, I'll do it. This is my shot to turn the hellscape of my career around. Plus, I've put off dealing with whatever feelings linger about past Jude for this long. I can handle two weeks.

I hope.

CHAPTER TWELVE

I'm making page four tomorrow, with the quote Adam wanted, and I couldn't feel worse about it.

"I can't eat; I can't sleep. If I close my eyes, I know he'll come back. If I take a moment to breathe, he'll be there."

Since press has been camped outside of the woman's daughter's house, she's afraid he knows where she lives. She called us vultures. Adam won't let me run *that* quote.

This isn't why I got into journalism. These are important stories to tell, but not the way Adam wants me to tell them. I don't want to write trauma porn to keep white suburban moms up at night, worried about something that won't happen to them. Mrs. Li is a person, a full human being with a rich life that I was told to cut. Five hundred words, Adam told me. Five hundred words that are only allowed to reflect the worst moment of Mrs. Li's life.

He really wanted a picture to run alongside the article. Close-ups of the bruises. I told him the camera on my phone is broken. It was the least I could do. Not that it worked, of course. He said I could use Mrs. Li's phone. While looking at her fresh iPhone, sitting between us, I texted back that she doesn't have one. *Of course*, he replied. *She doesn't speak English.*

Mrs. Li has lived in Sykeswood for thirty years and speaks three languages fluently. All three of which she used when she was responding to texts from her friends and family on her phone. Also, since when do non–English speakers not use cell phones?

She does, I responded. *Her phone was just lost in the assault.*

Adam texted back a shrug emoji.

I've been playing it over and over in my head for the last three hours, trying not to let it distract me from copyediting my own article.

It wasn't that Adam doesn't care about who Mrs. Li really is. But what he told me is that it doesn't matter how we *feel*, because this is bigger than the two of us. Most people, you see, aren't like us. They don't have that empathy for those different than them, so we have to describe her attack in PSTD-by-proxy level of detail. That's what will make the readers really care.

What really gets me is that he genuinely believes that. He believes that our readers can only empathize with an Asian woman who was brutally attacked if we highlight the violence, instead of who she is beyond that. To me, it's a gross underestimation of the quality of our readership and an indictment of whose stories Adam thinks are worthy of telling. Jude gets a full write-up for existing. Mrs. Li immigrated to America, runs her own business, and raised a thriving family who have gone on to their own successes too. But her write-up is her pain. The pain of an entire community. Prioritized over everything else.

My plans to frustrate-eat the hunk of brie in the fridge are interrupted by Eva and Oliver. They're staring at an elaborate, entirely purple floral basket that rests between them, completely stunned silent.

I've never seen so many varieties of flowers in one arrangement. They stick out all over the sides, making the basket look more like an abstract art sculpture than a floral arrangement.

"There are six different kinds of purple flowers in this arrangement," Eva says. "And it's half the size of our table."

"Do you not like it?" I ask. "Who sent it to you?"

Eva snorts. "To me? You think someone got this for *me*?"

They're being weirder than usual. I reach into the arrangement for the card. I pull it out, shake off a bit of dirt, and read:

Gen,

I hope you finally make the front page. No one deserves it more.

Respectfully yours,
Jude Alexander Landon

I sigh.

"He has decided to be the subject of a profile," I explain. "He's never participated in one before, and he is willing to let the *Tribune* break his story. It'd be a massive win for the paper and whoever gets to write it," I say. "I'm the whoever."

"Well, congratulations then!" Eva says. "That's a huge win for you."

Is it? I only got this profile because a rich white guy decided I was worthy. The same way I've missed out on probably hundreds of articles over my career because a different rich white guy decided I wasn't up to the task. I don't feel great about this. Of course, part of it is the knowledge that once our past relationship gets out, there will be people, even fellow journalists, who think I only got the profile because I used to date him. It's a potential kiss of death as a woman, particularly a Black one, if the general public thinks I'm getting "special perks" when I don't deserve them. But it'll give me the cachet to get a better job, if the strings don't take me out first. That's what I have to keep telling myself, otherwise I'd give up this article in a heartbeat.

"Is it? Like you've blown him off already. *Twice.* This seems like a bit of a manipulative thing to do to resume contact," Oliver replies. "Like I said before."

"Oh, come on!" Eva says. "It's *romantic.* He wants her to have it all, the thriving career, true love. It's like a movie."

"A stalker movie," Oliver mutters.

"Well, what are *you* after, Gen?" Eva asks. "Besides pissing off the triad."

I shake my head and continue standing. But I do high-five her. Pissing off the Fates might be the best thing that happens in all of this. I'm not particularly enthused to spend more time with Jude. Hell, if today is how all of my new "diverse" articles are going to feel, then I'm not even happy to get more assignments. At least when Adam was ignoring me, I wasn't actively contributing to the harm of people I wanted to highlight.

Oliver scoots his chair back from the table and leans away from the floral arrangement. "When are you seeing him again?" he asks.

"Tomorrow morning. His perky assistant Lauren called me earlier," I reply.

"He wastes no time," Oliver replies. He rolls his eyes and moves further away from the table.

Eva watches him, her eyes searching his face up and down, but he doesn't show anything.

"He's always been efficient," I say.

"Hence the proposal. Get the funeral and an engagement out of the way as soon as possible," Oliver says.

"That's a bit harsh, Ollie," Eva says, reaching out for his hand.

"I don't have fuzzy feelings toward the guy who threw away our relationships because of his own bad decisions," he replies, pulling his arm back.

"Are you referring to Gen's relationship with him, or yours?" Eva asks.

"All of the above," he replies. "The grand gestures, the flowers, the dazzling wealth, it all means nothing if you're not there when it counts."

I wonder if Jude will be there after the profile, when my career is either ascending or imploding. Would he want to be beside me if the public thinks he gave me the profile as a favor to a jilted ex, instead of on journalistic merit? Will he stick around once he's gotten what he wants from me this time?

I shake my head at them and leave for my room. When I close the door, I hear their voices drop and I know they must be talking about Jude, and probably me too.

I sit down at my desk and open my laptop. My cursor hovers above the search bar on my open Chrome tab. I could still refuse. Tell Adam to let one of the Fates attempt to charm the notoriously private multimillionaire. I would honestly watch a reality show of them trying to get him to open up.

I type "Jude Landon" into the search bar and let it sit. It's not like I've never googled him before. This time shouldn't be any harder; it's professional, not personal. It's just a preliminary search; I'm not even looking for anything that could hurt. Plus, the worst things he's ever done won't come up in an internet search, or even a background check.

I press enter and the first link that comes up is a news story from this morning. The picture is of Jude and Kaitlyn Franklin at the gala, his hand on her arm and both of them grinning twin veneered smiles at each other. The headline reads: *Jude Landon spending his "energy" on fiery socialite Kaitlyn's "project."*

I roll my eyes and click the article anyway. It's absolute tabloid trash and probably completely false anyway.

Another article: *Jude Landon, the twenty-five-year-old playboy CEO, is investing his funds in buxom beauty Kaitlyn Franklin's thirst project.*

Jesus Christ. The photo they used of the two of them shows them leaning into each other over dinner on Kaitlyn's family yacht. They really would be beautiful together. And I am so annoyed that I'm a little upset at the thought. But I'm a reporter, one who absolutely is not allowed to have deeply unresolved romantic feelings welling up for her subject.

I close the tab before it occurs to me that it's from the *Tribune*'s gossip page. Jude's romantic life, or lack thereof, takes up at least a column or two of space in at least seventy-five percent of the issues we put out. None of the speculation has ever been proven true, and Kaitlyn Franklin is just the news cycle flavor of the month. I'm sure one of the Fates will float the idea that he's been messaging *Bachelor* contestants to the gossip editor. Only the blondest, thinnest twenty-two-year-old whose job title is Content Creator.

I actually wouldn't be surprised if Jude was dating Kaitlyn Franklin. She's age-appropriate, from a similarly prominent family, and, of course, stunning. But even if they are dating, their personal relationship doesn't make her project any less valid, considering that Landon Energy is almost exclusively known for providing solar panels and wind turbines to the already rich. They'd be a match made in Jackie Landon's personal heaven, the exact opposite of the ring of hell she thought she was in when Jude first brought me home.

I didn't look like the wife Jackie envisioned for Jude. It was a running theme at every family event I attended, where Jackie alternated between ignoring me and making "jokes" about how Jude was trying to rebel, or be "woke" by bringing me home. Kaitlyn fits the part. I shouldn't be jealous. It's better this way.

There's a knock on my bedroom door before I can run another search. I technically didn't stay for Kaitlyn Franklin's speech, so I don't have a full grasp of what her professional partnership with Landon Energy is, regardless of the personal.

"Come in," I say, closing my laptop.

I hear the door open and close behind me. I swivel my chair around and swing my legs up onto the side of it.

Oliver is standing against the door, looking how I felt when Regina told me about the profile.

He sits down in the middle on my unmade bed. "I didn't mean to project my feelings onto you," he says. "We don't have to feel the same way about him, or about this."

"I know. It's just . . . it feels like he thinks it was easy. I never wanted to break up. I would have married him if he'd just waited a few years. And if we were in a better place," I say. "I was put between two hard places, and I didn't really get to choose which path we took."

Oliver shrugs and stares off at the wall where I hung up the "Bitches get stuff done" poster right out of college. I'd just been hired at the *Tribune* and had a binder full of pitches about everything from the newest African market a town over to the Black teacher from Sykeswood High who was in a bid to run for Congress. Her campaign never got off the ground, and neither did my stories.

I turn my phone over in my hands.

"Why'd you sign the NDA, Oliver?" I ask.

He sighs. "He was my best friend. We talked it out, and as far as I know he hasn't done anything like that again. I walked away from the deal with a concussion and a college fund."

"It's that simple? Just talk it out? Get some money?"

I regret saying it as soon as it's out of my mouth. That money helped Oliver follow his dreams of being a chef. Even if I disagree with the Landons' motives, at least some good came from it for Oliver.

"Don't do that," Oliver says. "Don't lash out at me when you're mad at him. Maybe this is the start of him using his platform for good, like we both wanted."

"Maybe. Or it's a ploy to cover up some other scandal that's popped up in the interim."

"Is that really who you think he is?" he asks. "Even I don't think that, and I'm the one with the visible battle scar."

I shake my head. No, I don't. It wasn't his idea to use family money to cover up the DUI, but it was his choice to go along with it. Maybe he's changed into something worse, but hopefully he's someone better.

"He put you in danger and he didn't even have the balls to tell me."

"Well, if we're litigating, you've rightfully made it clear how you feel about drinking and driving. And only the car was permanently damaged in the accident."

"Well, don't forget the relationship," I reply.

"He offered to go to therapy, and you did. Who knows what would have happened if his father didn't die and you'd have kept going."

I bite my lip, but it doesn't stop me from pushing back. We wouldn't have needed therapy if Jude hadn't done what he did to Oliver in the first place.

"Really sounds like you're defending him."

"I'm playing contrarian. Take the opportunity. May you never have to caption another dog picture."

"Would you forgive him? For ending your relationship?" I ask.

"I haven't. But if he's changed, I'd consider it, maybe. And if he offered me the opportunity of a lifetime, I'd do it. When you're in the trenches, fighting a system that's rigged against you, you do what you have to."

There's a nagging feeling spreading out in my chest. I was already accused of misconduct for writing the chef profile, by default. What is going to happen when the newsroom finds out I've gotten the most sought-after story at the paper?

CHAPTER THIRTEEN

It's Tuesday morning, the day of my first official interview with Jude, and I have nothing to wear. Well, nothing that looks professional, like I'm a serious journalist but also just a girl trying to make her ex feel like he's not the one doing her a favor. Everything I own feels either too regular, like my normal work outfits, or too visibly try-hard. I don't know which one would be worse in this situation.

I settle on a purple blouse with a ruffle in the front tucked into a pair of black jeans, with silver flat shoes. I guess purple is now the color of our rekindled conversations; I don't remember purple ever being a theme in our actual romantic relationship. I braid my hair as best I can to keep it out of my face and try to shade in my brows.

I use silver eyeliner on my waterline and brush foundation all over my face. I swipe some highlighter down the bridge of my nose and try not to hold my mouth open while I put on mascara. I haven't worn more than some concealer and a bit of eyeliner to work in about a year. Somewhere in there I felt so beaten down it didn't seem to matter whether I was wearing a full face of makeup or barely any, so I went for whatever let me lie in bed the longest.

When I step into the kitchen, fully ready with my work tote bag, Eva, who is sitting at the table, whistles. "Yes, girl," she says. "Love this look."

"Thanks," I reply. "Where's Oliver?"

"Gone already. They've got a huge party at the restaurant later and he has to help prep," she says.

"Ah."

"If you need help with any of the financial stuff about Landon Energy, let me know. Those private energy companies tend to have some weird loopholes in their structures," she says. "And I'm the only one who hasn't met him."

"Thanks, but you're not missing much. I should get going."

She smiles at me and waves as I grab my keys out of the dish on the counter.

I hurry out of the apartment and out to the parking lot. I've left myself just enough time so that I get to Jude's office right at nine. I don't want to seem too eager by arriving before then, even though I try to be fifteen minutes early to everything. Plus, the less time I have to sit around waiting, the less time I have to think about what's about to happen.

The Landon Energy building is in the heart of the city, a few blocks from the newsroom, and if company reports are to be believed, it's run entirely on solar energy. It stands taller than any of the other buildings in its immediate vicinity. As I stare up at all of the windows covering the building, I wonder if Jude is sitting in any of them, waiting for me. I shake my head. Here, now, he is not Jude Landon, my high school sweetheart, he's Jude Landon, my subject.

My watch reads 8:57. Perfect timing. I'm sure there are high-tech elevators that can shoot me up to his office in three minutes.

A green light flashes and the security gates open. When I get to the third elevator it has another scanner, which I have to press my visitor pass against before I can get on. Security was definitely not this high-tech when Julian was alive. I wonder who Jude's trying to keep out. I'm shocked I wasn't on the blocked entry list, given that he'd blocked me everywhere else.

On the elevator there's a man sitting in a chair in a vibrant dark green suit. "Floor?" he asks.

"Twenty-seven," I reply.

He nods and swipes a badge before pressing the button.

The elevator shoots up and I almost lose my balance. Great start. Completely thrown off both physically and emotionally. That's exactly how I want to walk into this interview, like a tornado of instability. I reach out for the nearest railing and readjust my bag on my shoulder, trying to catch a glimpse of my reflection to see if my hair is still intact. Can't show up looking disheveled. Especially not when he looks like . . .

Ugh. I can't go there. I'm keeping it completely professional. It's times like these that I really wish I weren't so aggressively single. If I had a boyfriend, Jude and I could both pretend that I wasn't secretly admiring his chest muscles and penchant for tailored suits.

I step outside into a seemingly endless wooden hallway and the elevator doors close behind me. It smells familiar, somehow. I catch a glimpse of a small plaque on the wall across from the elevator. It reads *All Wood Recycled from Landon Family Farm est. 1878.*

"All of the wood in this hallway was repurposed from the farm when it was torn down after the late Mr. Landon's death," a voice says behind me.

Jude tore down our dream wedding venue. God, why am I almost tearing up? It's not a big deal, and we're not getting married. I need to pull it all the way together, fast. My heart thuds and I turn around to see a long-haired, long-limbed blonde woman standing behind me in a navy blue and white striped skirt-suit. "Thanks," I say.

Jesus Christ. Does every woman here wear a skirt-suit? Is there a dress code they don't tell guests about?

"I'm Lauren, Mr. Landon's assistant. I heard your shoes," she says. "Follow me, please."

While my shoes continue to make noises that echo throughout the entire hallway, Lauren's heels don't make a sound. I wonder if she's floating slightly and I just can't see it.

Lauren stops in front of what, to the naked eye, looks like a normal panel of wood and presses her hand up against it. There's a beep and then the wood slides back to reveal a door. She opens the door to reveal an office waiting area.

I follow her inside and she takes a seat at the desk that's pressed up against the wall. "I'll check with Mr. Landon to see if he's ready for you," she says, taking her phone from the receiver. "Yes, she's here. Okay. I'll send her back." She puts the phone back on the receiver. "You can head back. It's to the right at the end of the hallway."

"Thank you," I reply. I can feel the dread rising from my stomach to my chest. Maybe I should have at least had some toast this morning; it feels like my entire esophagus is burning.

Lauren is still smiling at me as I turn the corner by her desk. I clutch the strap of my bag so that it's digging into my palm. Maybe the floor could open up and suck me in whole.

Jude's office is behind a relatively nondescript wooden door with a gold plaque that reads *Jude Landon, CEO*. I stand at the door for what feels like several minutes, trying to remember how to breathe.

The door swings open and I jump back. It takes me a moment to adjust to the light, and I find myself trying to look anywhere else than at the figure that's rapidly coming into shape in front of me.

Jude, in a radiant dark navy blue suit, faces me. His beard is somehow even more impeccably trimmed than at the gala, and it looks like he's gotten a fresh haircut. He's holding a tablet with the front page of this morning's *Tribune* in one hand and smiling at me. He extends the other hand toward mine, and it looks as though he tries to say "Welcome," but I don't hear him over the ringing in my ears.

It'd be great if my eyes would go blurry too, so I could avoid seeing that he looks even hotter than he did two days ago. I don't know what's worse, the tug at my heart or the pang between my legs.

There's no way I'm going to find a boyfriend in the next two weeks, but I at least need a friend with benefits. One skilled enough to wipe my mind of the way Jude's button-down is straining against his pecs.

I step past him into the office. Jude's office is about half the size of my two-bedroom apartment and, with the exception of the wall that Jude's desk is against, is covered in floor-to-ceiling windows. I stare out of the one in front of me and I can see the entire north side of the city. It makes me feel like I could fly away in a moment, carried by the wind out of this place.

"Page four," he says, waving the tablet in the air. "Congratulations."

"Thanks."

"Really insightful piece too. You didn't turn it into trauma porn."

"I did my best." *Despite Adam's best efforts.*

"Exactly why you're perfect for this piece," he says. "No one can do it better."

"Yeah," I reply, staring at the windows. Is he comparing his story to Mrs. Li's? Who exactly is denying *Jude Landon's* humanity? Big oil? However will he and his solar panels persist? What even are the specs of the solar panels running this office right now? Would he know, or is that someone else's job?

He even moves like his father now. Visible confidence, straight posture, an ease that betrays nothing of how he actually feels. Julian all the way.

My brain has to be as mean as possible to him because my mouth can't. When he was the one whose dad died, the one who was hurting, I wasn't allowed to be bitter. I had to shove down the judgment over his drinking, the hurt over his lying, all of it, to be the supportive girlfriend while he pushed me away. While he humiliated me at his father's fucking funeral.

"I feel like I should explain," he says.

If I let my guard down, who knows what could happen. I barely understand how I'm feeling; if he moves any closer or, God forbid, touches me again, I might slap him—or worse, kiss him. I want to hate him, but right now my rational brain is fighting with the fact that I haven't been this physically attracted to someone in years.

"I don't need to hear a reason. I'm . . . grateful," I say. I swallow the acid that is rising up into my throat again.

I'm not grateful, actually, but I'm trying to fit into some artifice of professionalism. As if pretending my hardest that this is an average interview will somehow manifest normalcy. He's just a guy. I've written articles about powerful figures before, I just have to act like he's one of them.

"I think you deserve one. I know how this could look. Like manipulation at best, coercion at worst—"

He sounds like Oliver. Even post-friendship they're somehow on the same wavelength. I'm almost jealous. I'd love to be inside Jude's head, but I'm also afraid of what I'll find there.

"I'm grateful for the opportunity," I say robotically.

He studies me. "If you want to back out . . . I get that this isn't ideal," he says. "I can put in a good word and get you a different story. Not that you need my help. And you don't have to be grateful. You earned this; I can't expect gratitude for what you deserve."

I turn so that we're fully face to face, and he's already turning red. Finally, a show of actual emotion. He's turning back into the Jude I knew. Before he fully grew into a Landon. But if he's the Jude I know, then I might still love him a little. And I can't allow that.

I straighten up. "Where would you like to conduct the interview, Mr. Landon?"

"Gen . . ."

"Your desk would work. I could put the recorder between us, as long as you make sure to speak up. It's a very spacious area," I say.

"Okay." He nods. "I see how it will be."

I sit in the chair across from him and pull the audio recorder from my bag, placing it between us on the desk.

I press record. "This is your first full official interview, ever, in your four years as CEO. You've been famously guarded—what is your reasoning for opening up now?" I ask.

"I felt it was time." He fiddles with his father's ring.

"And what makes now the right time?" I ask.

His cell phone, which is on the desk beside him, buzzes. He turns it over so the screen is pressed against the desk. I wonder who he's hiding. A one-night stand? Secret girlfriend? His mother?

He hasn't been seen out with anyone besides Kaitlyn in recent memory. All reports of him being a playboy hinge on an occasional paparazzi photo, and "unnamed sources" that I'm certain are his mother using aliases to make him seem more desirable. He could never actually *be* a playboy, in case anyone wanted to talk to the press. But if he *looks* like a playboy without any of the bad behavior, then he's just a young guy doing what he's supposed to. And if Jackie is the one putting it out there, maybe that means he hasn't seriously dated anyone long-term since me.

Not that that's relevant to the profile, of course.

"I felt like I finally had some credible ground to stand on, as a CEO. I earned an MBA through an accredited private program last year, and the company has been expanding quite a bit in the last six months, taking on new projects that have pleased the board."

"Do you have an upcoming project that you're most excited about?"

"Yes, Kaitlyn Franklin's water system."

I feel my heart drop and try to shake it off. It's better if he is dating her. No one would object to that pairing, and I'm not here to figure out his dating life. *Keep it professional. Ask the questions, write the profile, never speak to Jude again, and write your article about Black women in the workplace.* Plus, I could sense at the gala that the vibe between them was mostly platonic. There's no reason to overthink it. *Smoke and mirrors, smoke and mirrors.*

"And why is that?" I ask.

"It's the cutting edge of innovation, like I said on Friday in my speech at the event. And the lack of access to clean water in this, one of the most highly developed parts of the world, is profoundly disturbing, don't you think?"

"Definitely." I swallow. "Since you've mentioned Ms. Franklin and the event, I overheard . . ."

"I can't comment on any of the gossip pieces about her, if that's what you're getting at. I know the *Tribune* has a vested interest in which club she's seen at on Friday nights," he says.

He says it as if I'm the one writing the stories. As if their relationship matters to me personally.

"Would you be willing to issue a definitive comment on the pieces that have insinuated that the only reason you're funding her project is because of a personal relation—"

"I'm single," he interrupts.

My heart leaps up in my chest. He wasn't saying that for the record professionally; he was saying that for me, personally. Goddammit, why did he have to say it like that?

"Single people can still have personal relationships, right?" *But not us. Anyone else.*

Jude takes a deep breath and adjusts his tie. "I just meant that . . . no, that's not the reason I'm funding her project, and for anyone to insinuate otherwise is insulting to her hard work and deeply sexist. Ever since I took on this position there has been speculation about the state of my personal life, and for it to come at the professional expense of someone else is just unconscionable to me."

I feel compelled to roll my eyes. He's allowing his professional expansion to come at *my* personal expense by asking me to do this profile. My eyes make it halfway up before I just blink instead, staring at my lap for a moment to gather myself. *This is just a stepping stone. An inconvenient stepping stone.* My mantra until the profile is in Adam's inbox.

"How have you coped with the speculation around your every action?" I ask.

"By, frankly, not having a personal life. I can quell the speculation around the company by presiding over something successful. I can't stop speculation on my personal life without inviting people into some part of it," he says.

"I see. One area where the personal seems to bleed into the professional is through your family. Landon Energy is family-owned and controlled. How has your family influenced the way that you run the company?"

"They mostly let me run operations without interference," he replies. "They were never particularly involved, even when Dad, um, my father, Julian, was head of the company."

"Mostly?" I ask.

"They sometimes offer suggestions. For example, my mother introduced me to Ms. Franklin, since she runs in the same circles as Mr. and Mrs. Franklin. That's how I discovered the work Kaitlyn's been doing here and in Boston, at her alma mater."

I try not to cringe at the mention of Boston as if he doesn't know she attended Harvard. But I'm not surprised Jackie had something to do with Jude and Kaitlyn's meeting. Jackie Landon has been trying to force girls on Jude since junior prom. She literally brought in an alternative date for him who showed up at the Landon pre-prom party. Oliver, who was dateless, ended up taking her instead and they dated for six months. Jackie was furious, but it didn't stop her from bringing up all of her friends' eligible daughters over dinner conversations in front of me. She never wanted me to belong, and always made sure I'd never feel like I did.

"Ah, so is your mother as dedicated to the clean water crisis as you are?" I ask, knowing the answer.

He snorts and finally makes eye contact with me again. "No. She's interested in the crisis of me approaching my late twenties without a wife."

"She wasn't happy to see you in *People Magazine*'s Most Eligible Bachelor issue last year? Most eligible executive, I believe."

"The picture they used wasn't flattering enough, in her esteem," he replies. "Also, *People* isn't exactly her favorite publication."

For once, I agree with Jackie. He looked too stiff, like his arms were stuck in front of him, too tightly crossed to adequately reveal the width of his newly buff chest.

"Did inclusion on that list, and others like it, help or hurt your credibility with the employees at the company?"

"Well, I'm a good deal younger than most employees here. I've tried to hire some bright young innovators, but I'm still always the youngest and the least experienced person in a room."

"So, what do you do to combat that?"

"I try to prove that I'm not just a rich kid who inherited a company. Even if that is technically what I am."

There's a framed photograph of Julian that hangs on the wall behind him. In it, Julian is wearing a navy blue suit, similar to the one Jude is wearing now, with a clean-shaven face and a severe expression. It was the expression I saw him give Jude most often, when Jude used to skip nine AM marketing classes to sleep in after a night out or grab breakfast in the dining hall with me.

"And how's that going for you?" I ask.

"Better today."

He reaches over toward the recorder and I pull it away from him.

"Why is it better today?" I ask, my hand still on the recorder.

He holds my gaze. "I finally feel comfortable enough, secure enough to start to share some of my story."

"Some of?"

"Some things should be off the record between you and me. For privacy's sake, please." His tone is curt, but his eyes are pleading.

My mouth suddenly feels completely dried out and I find myself unable to get words out. I sit, silent, while the recorder ticks on and on.

Jude's office phone begins to ring, and he stares at the phone for a few seconds before answering. He gestures toward the recorder and mouths *stop*.

I stop recording and try to avoid making mental notes of everything he says on the call.

He nods at me. "Hello? Can we postpone?" he says into the phone. "Okay. Okay. Yes, I'll be there." He hangs up. "Sorry about that."

"Do you need to go?" I ask, picking up my bag. I tuck the recorder into my pocket, since I'm hopeful he does. Whatever he wants to be off the record between us will have to wait until after the profile, when I've had time to mentally prepare.

He holds out his hand. "Not before we talk, for just a minute, please. Off the record. Please don't go."

Please don't go. It's what I said to him in the graveyard before he was swallowed into the crowd. Somehow, mine sounded less desperate than his right now. There's a break in his voice that turns my insides even more mushy for him. God damn. All it takes is a little vocal crack to get me. As if I wasn't privy to his voice cracking for the tail end of middle school. I'm twenty-five, I cannot let myself be swayed by the same tics Jude had when we were thirteen.

So I put my bag back on the floor and nod. My gaze goes to every part of the room except him, from the portrait of Julian to the mantel which is covered in family photos and everything unrelated to Jude's role as CEO. I spot a signed baseball, but I can't make out who the signature belongs to.

"Gen, I am so sorry," he says. "I am so sorry for everything I did to you. It was completely unfair of me. You were right to say no. And you were right about what happened with Oliver. It was wrong of me to lie to you about the DUI, and it was wrong of me to expect him to do the same."

He's never apologized for it before, not genuinely. I believe him, and that almost hurts more than the fake remorse when it happened. It means that he's grown since then, but he still never thought to reach out before now. And he still hasn't publicly used his platform to address the mistakes of his past.

"Do you regret the NDA?"

"I don't regret that it gave Oliver what he needed to follow his goals, since his parents couldn't have paid for culinary school. But yes, I do regret how it was handled."

The businessman's answer. So diplomatic. Whatever feeling he let slip earlier when he asked me to stay is fading fast. He asked his closest friend of nearly a decade to sign an NDA because his family didn't trust Oliver to keep his mouth shut. Meanwhile, Oliver's held onto hard evidence of the DUI ever since, and never would have said a word. Jude should have known that.

"You think I'm supposed to forgive you when you can't even definitively say you regret using your resources to silence our best friend?"

The words come tumbling out before I can find the willpower to censor them. I've probably ruined the professional as well as the personal at this point.

"You're not *supposed* to do anything," he replies. "And I regret it every day. I ruined my relationship with you when I did that, regardless of what happened at the graveyard, and I put Oliver in a terrible position in both situations."

"Better answer."

"You know, you're not the only one feeling weird about this," he says. "I've turned this profile over and over in my head. But the only person I trusted to tell my story in its ugly, privileged, weird entirety was the person who first asked me to use my platform for something other than wealth porn. Seeing you is like having knives poking me in the heart, but I don't want it to end for some reason."

My heart skips a beat. Something in my heart doesn't want it to end either, even though my head is screaming.

"I shouldn't have—"

"You had . . . you *have* every right to feel that way," he replies.

I shake my head. "It was unprofessional of me."

"This was off the record. It wasn't about the professional. Professionally, I think we are on the same page."

But personally . . . lingers between us.

His eyes travel over to the mantel above the fireplace, a literal shrine to the people he's lost.

I realize that he's not looking at the baseball. He's also not looking at Julian Landon's framed ID badge, leaning against the wall. He's looking to what's next to it. A small black box. A jewelry box.

His mother's, maybe? That seven-carat diamond and platinum bauble that was the centerpiece of every outfit. She was always chic, but her outfits were simple, so that your eye was naturally drawn to the flashiest thing she was wearing. It was her ten-year anniversary present, an upgrade to replace her already beautiful original two-carat ruby engagement ring that Jude's sister Joanna now wears as an heirloom. Maybe it hurt too much to see it every day, after Julian died.

"No," he replies, following my gaze, and I realize that I said my last thought out loud. "Not hers, she still wears it."

I feel my breath catch for a second.

"You'd better get to that meeting," I say, feeling the tears prick my eyes. "I'll call Lauren to set up our next . . . you know."

I could text Adam my letter of resignation, and this would be over. But who's going to hire me with three articles to my name in a four-year tenure at a local newspaper? I burst into tears.

Jude reaches out to comfort me, and I pull away.

Jude and I might actually still feel the same way about each other, and I don't know if there's anything more terrible.

CHAPTER FOURTEEN

There's no way out of the office except to pass Lauren's desk, and I can't do that with my tears streaking my makeup. I stop a few feet into the hall outside of Jude's office and pull the pack of tissues out of my bag to wipe my eyes. There's a mirror on the wall, revealing just how red my face looks. I dab more foundation under my eyes and try to blend it in with my fingers. It's rough, but it'll do if I duck my head until I get to the parking garage.

I'm putting my compact away when I hear the click-clack of heels. I pretend to be digging through my bag as a whiff of lavender perfume wafts past me.

"Excuse me," the woman says, as her bag swings into my shoulder.

Her voice is a little huskier from a steady diet of cigarettes for the past decade, but I'd recognize it anywhere.

"Sorry," I reply.

She grabs my arm. "Oh my," she says, giving me a once-over. "Please tell me you didn't see my brother with your foundation streaked like *that*."

Joanna Landon's face should show concern, but she's rather obviously fresh off a round of Botox. Her mouth muscles look like they're pulled more tightly than the cerulean blue satin dress clinging to every arch of her body.

"A mistake in reapplication," I reply.

"Genevieve, darling, did I teach you nothing?" She whips a wipe out of her snakeskin purse. "What are you even doing here?"

I hold my hand out as she starts to wipe my cheeks.

"I'm here on assignment. A profile of the CEO."

A laugh comes out of her mouth, but her expression remains the same. "Baby Brother only agrees to an interview when it's being done by the one who got away. Anyway, how have you been, babe?" she asks.

Further evidence that Jude hasn't moved on either. No, not either. I'm in the process of moving on. I'm unpacking our past, recompartmentalizing the difficult parts, and putting everything back, permanently sealed.

"Been fine. Working, living. You know. Still at the *Tribune*."

She swats me with the brand-new foundation brush she's pulled out of her bag. She holds her hand out and I hand her the foundation bottle I brought with me. She squirts a bit on her hand, dips the brush in, and starts applying the foundation across my face.

"You deserve the world. We always liked you. Well . . . most of us," she says, pulling highlighter out of her bag. She pulls out another brush and swipes the highlighter across my cheekbones.

"How *is* Jackie?" I ask, silently hoping she's not making me look too glammed up. I still have to face the office.

"As lovely as ever. She'll be devastated to hear you're back. I can't wait to deliver the news."

"It'd be amazing if you didn't," I reply.

"Yes, amazing, and unlikely. You know how Mother and I love to one-up each other," Joanna replies. She bops me on the nose with the makeup brush, which she wraps in a handkerchief and drops back in her purse.

"Yes, I think I remember," I reply.

"The rest of us always loved you," she says. She looks up at the plaque on Jude's office door. "And some of us still do."

"Ah, there goes the pot-stirring."

I think she's trying to smile at me, but her face remains in place. She closes her purse.

"Genevieve, love, he'd marry you tomorrow," Joanna says.

"He doesn't know me anymore. Whoever he claims to love is a relic."

"Write your profile," she says, sliding her sunglasses off of her head and into her purse. "Earn your accolades. But don't play with him. He just had to wake up."

I wonder what he needed to wake up to; he's had four years to say something. I watched my phone for six months, jumping anytime a text or call popped up, and it was never him. He sent his chauffeur to pick up the sweatshirts and toothbrush he'd left in my dorm room. Someone dropped off all of the things I'd left with him in a box outside my room in the middle of the night. He dropped out of school to take over the company, and was out of my life just as quickly.

"You just want me back in his life to piss off your mother," I say.

"A little. But you know why I really want you back, and why he chose you to write this profile?" she asks. "Because, of all the women in all the world, you're the only one who ever matched him. You challenged him to be better, you showed him parts of the world outside of our little bubble. You made him the man he is today."

"Well, he's doing a hell of a lot better than I am right now."

"Because he got a fluke of an opportunity. And now he's giving you the same thing. On the off chance there's still love there," she replies. "Excuse me." She pushes open the door to Jude's office behind me. "Jude-y!"

While I'd love to inherit a few hundred million and the ability to actually change the world for the better, I've never wanted it to be on someone else's terms. I didn't choose this profile, so even if it does launch my career, it has barely anything to do with me. Jude gets all the credit. He *gave* me this opportunity.

It's the exact narrative that's going to make all my coworkers really hate me. They already think I don't deserve this. And when they find out that Jude insisted I was the one to do the profile, they'll know for sure.

My face looks better; the streaks are gone. I have a *bit* more sparkle than when I came in, but it's not too much, at least in the limited light of this hallway. I stuff my phone back into my pocket.

Lauren smiles as I round the corner. "Ms. Francis, how was your meeting?"

"It was . . . productive," I reply.

It's not fully a lie. I got information for the profile and for my own closure. At this point, I'm not sure which one of those will turn out better than the other.

"We're all very excited to hear Mr. Landon is making efforts to become more open with the public," she says.

"As is the public," I reply. "Speaking as a member."

"I liked your piece about the ice cream. I don't eat ice cream, but it made me feel like I could taste it," Lauren says.

"That's the . . . most interesting compliment I've received, but thank you."

She smiles at me again and ducks her head back toward her computer monitor.

"Would tomorrow at one PM work for you? It's Mr. Landon's lunch half hour. You'll eat together in his office. The company cafeteria is completely vegan. What would you like?"

"I'll have whatever he has."

"Perfect," she replies. "It will probably have lots of veggies and some plant-based protein. You'll have lots of energy to take on the afternoon! See you then."

I'd love to know when Jude started voluntarily eating vegetables as full meals. He used to slip me his broccoli under the table at both of our family dinners and thought that tofu was an affront to his right to eat red meat for any meal he wanted.

The door in front of me slides open and I wave to her before stepping out into the hallway. This profile had better change my life for the better, because I don't think I could take it if the professional *and* the personal both blew up in my face right now.

CHAPTER FIFTEEN

Not wanting to sit alone at home poring over the immigration numbers Adam asked me to make sense of for tomorrow's issue, I drive to the office. I have to circle three times before finding a parking spot almost in the very back of the lot. I'm never late for work and never go anywhere I have to drive to for lunch for this exact reason.

I slip into the more comfortable pair of black flats that I have on the floor of my passenger seat, grab my bag, and jog into the office building. Security waves me through; I've been on a first-name basis with them since my first week, as one of ten Black people in the entire building.

No sooner do I step off of the elevator on the fourth floor, than the Fates, having spotted me through the glass windows surrounding the newsroom, collectively run over to me from their cubicles.

"Oh my God, I can't believe you got the profile!" Heather says, reaching out to hug me.

I sidestep her. "Yeah," I reply.

Lucy rolls her eyes.

I fight the urge to roll mine back at her, especially since I know she's the reason I got in trouble for my *tone* yesterday.

"You should work on your objectivity, by the way. If you're going to do the profile," Lucy says.

My mouth goes dry. No way. Adam wouldn't have told them . . .

"My objectivity in what?" I ask.

"Your piece on that woman," Lucy says. "Slanted bent, according to Adam."

"Slanted bent in what way?" I ask, genuinely confused.

"What is this, an interrogation?" Clara asks. "Like, oh my goodness. Learn to take feedback. He's your *editor*."

Imagine if any one of them could take feedback. Maybe they wouldn't make it their mission to create a working environment that's only affirming and productive for them.

"Excuse me, I'm going to my desk," I reply.

"Oh, I borrowed your charger. It was just sitting there and no one was using it," Clara says. "Hope that's okay."

I ignore them as I make my way to my desk, which is once again covered in papers that aren't mine. I pick them up and lay them on the floor before sitting down.

Lucy plops a binder down on my desk, causing a thump so loud it makes me jump in my chair. She smiles as if she's holding in a laugh she knows would look bad.

"Who'd you have to pay off to get the profile?" she asks.

I begin shuffling through the papers from my meeting with Jude, as if she's not hovering just over my shoulder. If she thinks I'd

139

have the money to pay Adam off, then I've inadvertently fixed at least one of her inaccurate stereotypes about Black people.

"The copier's broken," she says.

"Okay, thanks for letting me know."

She stands at my desk for several more seconds, tapping her finger on her arm in my peripheral view. "Why is the copier broken?" she asks, loudly enough so the entire newsroom can hear. Just your friendly office Karen, trying to get a supervisor to come over when something isn't done exactly to her personal liking.

Just because I've cleared a paper jam or two doesn't qualify me to fix the entire machine. She really is completely deluded about my role here, and I have Adam to thank for that misconception.

Adam pokes his head out of his office. "Gen, grab an intern and see if you two can fix it," he says.

"Do you want me to call IT?" I ask. "They'd have a better idea than any of the rest of us."

"Sure, if you're too busy to handle it," Adam says. "Actually, I'd like to see you in my office, Genevieve."

Adam is leaning back in his chair when Regina and I come in, staring at the wall. Once he sees me, he springs up in the chair. "Thank you, Regina," he says as she sets his coffee down. "Can you please confirm my reservation tonight? And call IT for her."

She nods and leaves the door open a crack as she goes back to her desk.

Adam gestures for me to sit in the chair across from him. This chair is starting to feel like my second home.

"Are you pro-immigration?" he asks.

"Um . . . yes? Why?"

"It showed, in your article yesterday."

"How so?" I ask. "I wrote about the assault, contextualized it with prior incidents, I got the quote you asked for—"

"Yeah, but I could just tell."

I bite my lip to keep myself from asking if he can tell because I'm Black. I'm already a hair away from being labeled difficult today. That brand is impossible to shake off. Especially if the Fates are whispering to Adam about my objectivity.

Adam looks back at the framed newspaper behind him, the story that put him on the map. A deep-dive exposé of a local restaurant chain that was mistreating its immigrant workers, where he went undercover for a day at the flagship store. It was the kind of piece that made me think a leader like him could help fix the racial issues in the newsroom. Until I actually heard him speak on racial issues.

"I'll look into it," I reply.

Adam shuffles a stack of articles for tomorrow. "So, let's talk about the piece that's going to put you on the map," he says.

"Do I deserve it, though? To be put on the map with *this* piece?" I ask. I genuinely want an answer. I want to be taken seriously, and an article on Jude does not seem to be the way to do that.

Adam raises his eyebrows. "You got this profile because after years of preparation, Jude Landon finally feels like he will be taken seriously. And he turned to the journalist he knew would take him the most seriously. So, if you're going to be self-deprecating, get out of my office. That's exactly the attitude that's keeping you down."

So I only got this assignment because Jude personally requested it. Noted. Fantastic.

"If I'm so great, then why am I the only person who does sensitivity checks? Why am I copyediting everyone else's breaking news? Why are you accusing me of lacking objectivity right now?" I ask.

I shouldn't even be asking him this. What's he going to say, *Because you're Black*? It's my attitude, of course; if I were more confident or burst into his office saying I'm a girl boss who's worth it, he'd hand me the world. That's what they all say, but it's a lie. I'd be here no matter what I did because this is exactly the position people like Adam and the Fates want me to be in.

"You're the best copyeditor. You're detail-oriented. It makes other people better. You wouldn't have the extra time to also be writing every article. See, being the best at sensitivity checks pays off."

You're better where you are. Stay there, make no noise, and elevate your coworkers at your own professional expense.

"Now, how was the meeting? Did you get anything good?" he asks.

"Yes, he told me about why he's consenting to a profile and a bit more about his collaboration with Kaitlyn Franklin, professionally."

"Are you going to be including the personal in this article?" he asks. "People will have questions. It's juicy."

This isn't a tabloid piece. I'm not about to sell out on what could actually be a thought-provoking profile of a prominent local figure to appeal to the speculation around his love life.

"He mentioned the rumors about him and Kaitlyn Franklin. He called them sexist and demeaning to her, and confirmed that he is single," I reply.

"There's a lot of history there," he says. "But there's going to be enough scrutiny once this piece comes out, especially once *your* past with Mr. Landon is dug up. Buckle up, Gen. You're going to be on the front page."

I wonder in what way. As the writer of a well-regarded piece, or as the subject of a gossip section hit job. I guess it all depends how much the Fates decide to ratchet up their extracurricular undermining activities.

Adam takes a long drink from his coffee. He sets the cup back on his desk and looks at me as if he's wondering why I'm still here.

"Adam, if—when—our past relationship does come out, what will happen here?" I ask.

"What do you mean?"

"I don't imagine that all of my colleagues will take it kindly that I got this profile. Depending on the extent of what comes out about our past relationship and breakup, it would be a potential scandal for the paper, would it not?"

"Potential. But you won't be fired. You'll be courted," Adam replies. "By bigger publications. They'll want to know the Landon family secrets. You might get a book deal. Maybe we'll just have to let you fly off to greener pastures. You'll have free rein to write whatever you want. I can't wait to see a draft. Next week."

My phone buzzes in my pocket.

"I'd better get to work then," I say.

The phone buzzes again and I stand up. It keeps buzzing as I try to grab my interview folder from Adam across the desk. Whoever's calling me better be on the verge of death; this is absurd.

I pull it out and see three missed calls from Landon Energy. The phone begins ringing again and I answer on the first ring.

"Oh, thank goodness," Lauren says. "I need to confirm with you. It's Lauren from Landon Energy."

"For tomorrow? We're already confirmed."

"No, for tonight," she says.

Adam is leaning so far forward he might collapse onto his desk.
"Tonight?"

"A six PM reservation in the private room at Fellini's. Can you
make it?" she asks.

Seriously, Jude? We're supposed to be keeping it professional
and he's trying to get me to go on a date? "I just think it's
inappropriate . . ."

"For you, Mr. Landon, Ms. Joanna Landon, and Mrs. Jacque-
line Landon."

Well, shit. There's no good reason for me to be invited to a family dinner. "Excuse me?"

This is either an intervention to stop the profile from going
forward or a mafia-style family meeting where the terms of our
professional and personal agreement are arranged for the benefit of
everyone with the last name Landon. Either way, there's no way I'm
going.

"Off the record," Lauren says. "Mrs. Landon called a few minutes ago, demanding your presence. She sounded upset. She wants
to talk to you about the profile. She doesn't seem pleased. I'm not
sure how she found out since Mr. Landon hasn't spoken to her."

"Thank you, Lauren. I'll see what I can do."

She sounds so panicked, it would be mean to tell her no. She'll
figure out Jude's and my history eventually, and everyone will be
fine. It's not like Jackie actually wants to see me.

"Also, off the record, it's black tie. Mrs. Landon is hoping you'd
show up underdressed and be turned away at the door," Lauren says.

So she wants to meet with me to control the direction of the
profile, or nix it entirely, but would prefer it with a side of embarrassment. It's not entirely surprising coming from the woman who

actively tried to break Jude and me up but who stood by while he proposed to me in front of all of their friends and family. She's all for protecting the family image until it looks like any drama could be traded off with harm to me.

"Thank you, Lauren. That's *very* helpful," I reply.

I end the call and slip the phone back into my bag. At least someone is in my corner, even if I have no idea why Lauren's so invested.

Adam raises his eyebrows. "So?"

"So, Jackie Landon wants my head at a family dinner tonight, black tie."

"If they threaten you, make sure to get it on the record," he says. "It'd be a real win for the paper. You'd *have* to write that article. Scrap whatever else you're doing; this dinner should be your whole focus."

Everything that's a win for the paper seems to be a loss for me. A woman like Jackie Landon, wealthy and white with connections all over this town and the next three counties over, could destroy my career with a single phone call. I don't know what mood I'm getting her in, but there's no way it will be triumphant for me.

"If this is an intimidation tactic, I think it would be better to not go. Can't give up the power if I'm not in the room. Plus, I was really looking forward to covering the refugees coming in."

"Oh, you're going to that dinner. This isn't about *power*. This is about a story. And I want to hear every detail of the conversation tomorrow. Preferably in print, but I can be flexible. To clarify, this is non-optional."

As if I needed the clarity. Adam's been pretty clear what his expectations are for me, and it's to play ball with whatever the Landons ask for.

Why does it feel like I have one card when everyone around me gets at least fifteen? Whether I make a mistake or write the perfect profile, my entire life could detonate, and no one involved in it seems to care. If anything, it's like Adam is rooting for me to fail. So I can't. I won't. Which means I'm going to have to grovel to either Eva or Mickey for outfit help, once again. Maybe the outfit can make the woman this time, if the actual assignment won't.

CHAPTER SIXTEEN

Mickey comes over to my apartment after school to help me figure out what to wear to dinner. When she arrives, she has two hot pink garment bags draped over her arm. She holds the two bags up in front of me in the doorway.

"As much as I appreciate the sentiment, we are not the same size," I say.

She rolls her eyes, still holding both bags up. "I swung by Chic and got these in your size."

"How much were they?" I ask.

She waves her hand. "I introduced the owner to her wife, so I got these at an incredibly reduced price. It would be practically criminal if I told you. Also, they were both on clearance."

She shuffles further inside until she hits the living room. She lays the bags on the couch and gives me a once-over.

"Yes?" I ask.

"You're going to be sucked back in," she says. "To that world. Or as Eva says: the glitz, the glam, the intrigue."

"I'm writing a piece," I reply. "The piece ends, so does that world. That world and my plans to be an active, well-respected reporter do not go together."

"You still need to be able to hold your own with them. Hence, why I vote for the less traditional option," she says, unzipping one of the garment bags. She pulls out a sleek black jumpsuit with cut-outs on the side.

I'm pretty sure black tie doesn't include cut-outs, but I keep my mouth shut.

Mickey pulls out a black wrap lined with silver, that I assume is to cover me until I sit down in whatever private room the Landons have booked. It's not like they'd kick me out if I said I was with the Landons.

"Pretty sure I'm supposed to wear a dress, but I can make it work."

"Plus, you can wear those gorgeous sapphire drop earrings that Jude got you back in the day."

For our six-year anniversary, three weeks before his dad died, Jude surprised me with a pair of sapphire and diamond drop earrings that he bought on a family vacation to France. They're my favorite thing that I own, even if they were an apology gift. I haven't looked at them since I threw them into their box after the funeral.

"Oh no . . . ," I say.

"Don't fight me on it. I also grabbed that two-carat sapphire ring my mom never wears from her room. Don't worry, she approves. I'd tell you to pretend you're engaged, but that'd be cruel, so just wear it on your right ring finger."

If Mickey told her mom, then my mom already knows too. I'm going to have to stay up half the night giving her all the details, and she'll still be mad I didn't tell her earlier. I'm shocked she hasn't called me yet.

"I half expected a call from Jude," I say. "Not his *assistant* telling me I've been summoned."

"Oh, sweetie, this is an ambush," Mickey replies. "Jackie didn't tell Jude you'd be there. She wants to ambush him and steamroll over the direction of the profile."

"Fuck. You're right. I have to call him."

Mickey unzips the other garment bag, which is a lovely deep V-neck navy blue chiffon dress.

"Jackie's going to try and scream over you and expect you to sit there and nod like you did when you were sixteen. You can't let her do that. I've met moms like her. You have to be louder, and more confident. She'll respect you. You can wear this to the next event."

"She'll never respect me."

"She already does, trust me."

She lays the ring on the coffee table and goes into my bedroom, presumably to search for the earrings.

I pull out my phone and scroll through my contacts until I get to Jude's. I take a deep breath before pressing the number. Maybe he won't answer.

He answers on the second ring. "Gen." He says my name like it's a relief.

"Hey," I say.

We sit in silence for a few seconds.

Mickey emerges from my room with the earrings, which she somehow unearthed from the absolute back of my closet, and sets

149

them next to the ring. When she sees the phone, she backs away into the bathroom and closes the door.

"I'm glad I got to see you again today. Even if it wasn't the easiest of conversations," he says. "Three days in a week, how lucky am I?"

"Jude."

"I don't regret asking you to do the profile. Maybe I should, but I don't. I know it will be great. There's no one better. Plus, we've established that we don't really know each other anymore, right?"

I blink back tears that are threatening to trickle out, even though I don't fully understand why they're even there.

"You have dinner with your family tonight?" I say.

"Yes," he replies. He pauses. "How did you know?"

"Lauren called me. Your mom has demanded my presence."

"I didn't know," he replies.

"Yeah, Mickey told me it was probably an ambush."

I don't know why I'm telling him. It's not really my business if Jackie Landon is trying to be manipulative. I don't have to try to protect him from his meddling family anymore, it's not my job, personally or professionally. It certainly doesn't fit with my get in and get out with no reason to speak to him afterwards plan.

"Of course," he replies, annoyance prickling in his voice.

"I'm sorry."

"It's not your fault my mother is meddling," he replies.

"It is, a little. But also, I'm sorry for how things went at our meeting. It may have been honest, but it wasn't necessary."

"For me, it was both," he replies. "I'll see you tonight. Thank you for warning me."

The Only Black Girl in the Room

The line clicks and in the seconds of silence that follow I realize how much I missed his voice. If my name is a relief for him, his voice is a home for me.

Mickey comes out of the bathroom holding heat protectant spray, my flat iron, and Eva's smoky eye shadow kit. She nods toward the bathroom door and I follow her inside.

CHAPTER SEVENTEEN

It seems silly to let the valet park my tiny car; there are at least four spaces within my line of vision that I could slip into in the fifteen minutes before the reservation. But in an effort to play the part expected of me tonight, I hand the keys to the valet, who can only have had a license for three years, maximum. I adjust the wrap on my shoulders and silently pray that there isn't red lipstick on my teeth. The valet holds open the door for me and I grip the railing as I go up the stairs to the hostess stand.

The hostess looks me up and down. "Reservations only."

"There's a room reserved," I say. "Landon."

Her jaw drops a bit. "Um, name?"

"Genevieve Francis," I reply.

She scoops up a drink menu, her lips pressed together. "Are you a member of the family?"

"Press," I reply. "For the *Tribune*."

"Oh. So you're the one doing the infamous interview. Follow me."

Oh fuck. The Fates eat here all the time because Clara's roommate gets them discounts during Happy Hour. I'm betting this hostess is that roommate. Meaning they're all going to know I was here by tomorrow. An impromptu dinner at the fanciest restaurant in town isn't completely out of the realm of possibility, but it strains credulity. Unfortunately, cruelty doesn't make you stupid. They're going to be on another level tomorrow.

She leads me all the way to the back of the restaurant and down a flight of stairs that leads to the wine cellar.

The table is empty, except for Jude sitting at the head. He's wearing a tuxedo and is fiddling with his cuff links. He has a small, but still noticeable, earpiece in his ear. He stands when he realizes that it's me.

"You're early," I say, trying to keep my voice steady. I have to remind myself that I *am* here for the article, and if anyone asks, the Landons were just trying to do some additional vetting and asking some basic questions about how I plan to frame the profile. Plenty of the rich people we've covered have done the same, at this very restaurant. Just because it's me this time doesn't make it somehow untoward.

"I knew you'd be," he replies. "Didn't want my mother to claw your eyes out with no witnesses."

I hate that he's still charming. It's making this so much harder. "Thanks."

He adjusts his cummerbund, which is already crooked. "I hate black tie," he says.

"I barely knew what it was," I reply. "Where should I sit?"

"Next to me," he says. "So you can kick me under the table when I say something impolite. My shin remembers."

"That happened once!" I say.

I'm taken back to the Sunday dinners his family insisted we attend weekly at the Landon estate. They were mostly business casual, with the occasional formal event. Jude, ganglier then, could never get his cummerbund to stay straight. His dress shirts were frequently wrinkled, and he only wore suits that were slightly baggy. His clothes fit better now, to my admiration and anxiety, but he still has that general air of discomfort, as if he doesn't have to dress like this most days.

When I'm standing next to him, his eyes scan my body, stopping at the cutouts that the wrap doesn't fully cover, and I feel myself heat up. Every part of me is hyperaware that we're almost touching, and I feel butterflies fly from my stomach up and down the rest of my body. We used to stand like this at Landon family events, waiting for the opportunity to run upstairs and fool around while everyone hemmed and hawed in the foyer.

"Mickey has a flair for the dramatic," I say, trying to break the moment.

"You look wonderful, Gen," he replies. "Once again. You could probably try to tone that down, for fairness."

"So do you. Whatever plant protein you're guzzling means that now you wear that cummerbund, instead of it wearing you."

He grins. "Are you saying I look good?"

"You know how you look," I reply.

"And now you know too."

He looks me directly in the eyes and I find myself reaching out for the table to keep steady. He reaches out for my hand, and I don't move. Why won't I move?

Before he can take it, the door to the room swings open and Jackie Landon strolls in. She's wearing a faux fur coat, even though it's seventy-five degrees outside, and a bateau-neck plain black dress underneath. She hands her coat to the attendant before noticing Jude and me standing together.

Jackie's eyes flick from my face to my feet and her mouth tightens. She turns back toward the attendant at the door. "Please give us a moment before anyone else comes in," she says. "Including any other members of the family."

The attendant nods and backs out of the room, closing the door behind him. I've clocked that almost every employee we've seen, with the exception of the hostess, is a man and my gender disparity in the culinary world idea comes back to the forefront of my mind. Yet another article I probably won't get to write at the *Tribune*.

"Mother," Jude says.

"Jude," she says. She's more focused on the table centerpiece than my face. "Ms. Francis."

"Mrs. Landon," I say. "Good to see you."

Mickey's words about standing up to Jackie ring around in my head. *You have to be louder, and more confident. She'll respect you.*

"Hmm," she replies. She stands behind a chair several seats away from us.

"Thank you for inviting me to dinner," I say, forcing myself to smile at her.

"Oh, I didn't say dinner," she replies.

"*Mother*," Jude says.

She shrugs. "It's family dinner. This is a meeting."

"So, on the record?" I ask.

I ignore the butterflies in my stomach as Jude snorts. Looks like I can still make him laugh. I pull out my audio recorder and wave it in the air. Why not, right?

Jackie glares at me. "Put that away. I always knew you were a gold-digger."

To be a gold-digger, wouldn't that imply that I've actually gotten some gold? That's always been Jackie's favorite line: that I was only with Jude for his money. It would have been an exceptionally long con, given that before his father died, he wouldn't have had access to his trust until age thirty-five. But I guess fourteen-year-old Gen was really on the pulse, planning out her life for two-plus decades.

"Takes one to know one," Jude says.

I kick him under the table. We're nineteen again, with him debating his father on the merits of a wealth tax. They always loved to discuss current events, even getting into impressive disputes in front of a table full of board members. The wealth tax debate was the only one where I ended up kicking Jude, accidentally hard enough that he bruised, after he told his father that billionaires were hopelessly morally corroded, and he'd never want to be the son of one.

Jackie rolls her eyes. "I was naturally a world-class bachelorette. It wasn't forced."

Jude opens his mouth to speak again, and I put my hand out in front of him.

"If I were a gold-digger, I would have taken the ring that you, I'll remind you, didn't stop him from giving me," I reply. "Jude's an adult, and he asked me to write this profile, so I'm doing it, regardless of whether or not you like it. Will it advance my career? Maybe. But it also could end it because of a violation of journalistic integrity."

"Social climbers can be calculated," Jackie replies. "Risk versus reward."

"And you think reward will win out," I say.

"With our family name versus yours, of course," Jackie replies.

Of course. The Landon family name can get you anything. We've all learned that over the years, in increasingly illegal ways.

"Gen's family name is just as esteemed as ours," Jude says. "Don't play the financial class card, Mother."

"She wants money. To sell this family out," Jackie says. "Or money from you, Jude. She wants her stake in the Landon inheritance."

"I don't have a stake, what are you talking about?" I ask.

If I had a stake, best believe I'd have cashed in by now. I'd move to a remote town, buy all of my loved ones property within a five-mile radius, and start a newspaper that isn't built on the sweat and tears of underpaid, underappreciated Black women.

"If I recall correctly, you worked at a department store when you met Dad," Jude says.

She shrugs. "Honest work."

"Of course it is. But was it before or after he'd bought a ring for someone else?" he asks.

Jackie looks like she may reach across the table and throttle him. The story of how she and Julian met is pretty well known, but she hates any reference to her past. Middle-class life isn't something she ever wants to be associated with.

For some reason, I can never repress the impulse to defend Jude, but only to his family.

"I'd love to record this for historical accuracy," I say. "In case the *Tribune* asks me to write an article on upward mobility into the highest class."

As the story goes, a freshly thirty-year-old Julian Landon walked into a local department store, looking to buy an engagement ring for his then-girlfriend of about a year. His girlfriend was a family friend; they were set up by their parents before Julian even founded Landon Energy. The clerk at the jewelry counter was Jackie Hanson, a twenty-two-year-old college graduate who was working her very first shift at the store. The intervening series of events is unclear, but it's well known that Julian never proposed to his girlfriend, and Jackie appeared on his arm at an event the very next week.

Jackie's eyes flick over me again and she nods once. "Unimportant. Sit. You're staying for dinner, Genevieve."

"I'm sure Gen has better things to do," Jude says.

"I'm sure she doesn't," Jackie replies.

I take a deep breath. Mickey was right; show a little fire, earn the slightest amount of respect. Except it wasn't me who showed any. Maybe I should start throwing erasers like one of Mickey's students. Or caviar. It's gross but costs more than any school supply. If I'm going to run in an elite circle, I guess I'll have to make any shenanigans high-class.

I've never seen Jude talk to his mother without absolute reverence. He'd barely even let me complain about her when we were dating. Now he's practically throwing her under the bus, for what? My honor? Maybe he *has* grown up. What's more adult than finally figuring out that your parents can be massive hypocrites?

"Joanna is late, per usual," Jude whispers, spinning his spoon around on the table.

Jackie lets out a sound akin to that of a wounded deer as the gold reflection from the spoon ricochets into the lighting fixture. It's almost a comfort to know that, after all this time, seeing Jude and me together still wounds her.

As if she sensed Jackie's discomfort, Joanna comes in wearing what looks like a purple version of the dress I saw her in earlier. She gives me a once-over, runs her hands down the dress, and winks at me.

Jude nods at Joanna and pulls the chair next to him out. His arm brushes against mine and the hairs on my arm shoot up in response.

Joanna sits next to Jackie instead. Both of their faces are frozen, Joanna's, perpetually neutral, to avoid lines, and Jackie's, narrowed and filled with contempt. Joanna looks from me to Jude and back several times, and I'm sure she'd be smiling if she could. For someone who seems perpetually out of touch, she's always been surprisingly perceptive about the two of us.

The waiter pours white wine in every glass but Jude's, while another dashes in the room with hors d'oeuvres. The second waiter lays a plate of tuna tartare on the table and gives Jackie a small bow.

If Jude orders a vodka cocktail instead, I might have to leave. He's been perfectly pleasant so far, and the last time I saw him under the influence of Smirnoff, it wasn't pretty.

Jackie takes a several-second gulp of wine the moment the waiter steps away from her glass. She waves the waiters out of the room and turns back to me.

"This profile could be monumental for Jude, *if* done correctly," Jackie says. "And it's a family business, so the portrayal of the family needs to be tasteful."

"In my understanding, while the family was influential in Jude's upbringing, since inheriting Landon Energy he has been working to develop his own set of skills and values to bring into the company. So, while of course you will all be mentioned and interviewed, the profile will focus on Jude's tenure as CEO," I reply, taking a sip of wine.

"And what will it say about Jude's personal life? And his . . . past?" Jackie asks.

"There isn't much to report about Jude's personal life that would be relevant except that it appears that he doesn't have one. He's focused on his work. As for his past, only the formative events that led to his tenure as CEO would be mentioned, as anything else is . . . confidential in the eyes of the court system," I reply.

"Well, Kaitlyn Franklin . . . ," Jackie begins.

I turn to Jude, who is glaring at his mother. He looks like he wants to get up and leave. And I realize that now, he actually might.

"Mother, you know there is nothing going on between me and Kaitlyn Franklin," Jude replies.

"You'd make an excellent match." Jackie takes another sip of wine. "Both families think so."

"I'm not her type," Jude replies.

Jackie rolls her eyes. "You're everyone's type."

"She's gay," Jude replies.

Well, *that* hasn't made the gossip pages. Kaitlyn Franklin has been spotted at every local hotspot, usually with a different guy every time. She's been spotted with Jude at dinner at least four times in the last couple of months, fueling the speculation about their relationship. Which, now that I think about it, was an obvious ploy to take attention away from whoever else they'd be interested in seeing.

Jackie waves her hand. "A phase, obviously."

"Not how it works," Jude replies. He leans into me. "Don't report that, please."

"Noted."

"Well, we'll find someone," Jackie says.

"Not my priority," Jude replies.

Joanna watches me and, in the silence, straightens up in her chair. She tilts her head to the side.

"Perhaps it's not a priority because Jude already has someone," Joanna says, winking at me.

Jude turns red and stares down at the tablecloth. He reaches for the tuna tartare.

Oh. Maybe I read this wrong. His playboy image isn't to hide that he's alone, it's to hide that he has a partner he'd rather keep private. But then why has he been flirting—no, not flirting. It's been something else, it has to be. Just platonic tenderness. Like he has with Kaitlyn.

"You know, it's not relevant to the profile I'm writing, but maybe bring up Jude's relationship status with *People* before they name him most eligible again," I say.

Jude squeezes my hand under the table and I feel electricity shoot through my entire body. He doesn't let go right away, but I do.

"I have a feeling he won't be eligible," Joanna says. "Just a hunch."

Jackie sighs. "Of course not; he'll be with Kaitlyn. And on that note, I think it would be prudent for Genevieve to find an alternative romantic prospect. As publicly as possible. We can set you up with someone respectable who will be willing to put up with you for a reasonable amount of time."

Could Jude have an entire relationship that Jackie doesn't know about? Or is she just willing it to go away, like she did with me? Oh my God, I need to stop thinking about this. The state of Jude's romantic life is unimportant. We can blow up the idea of romance in general. I am not allowed to think about romance until the profile is published and I have a job at a paper that doesn't make me want to scream every other hour.

"I won't be doing that. Back to the article, I would love to highlight and interview some of the innovators, like Kaitlyn Franklin, that Jude has decided to bring onto his team," I say.

"Highlighting his commitment to his own social circle," Jackie replies.

"Highlighting his commitment to young voices looking to solve chronic issues like water access," I say.

Jackie runs her tongue over her teeth before baring them in my direction. "For someone who dropped him at the first sign of conflict, you seem to have quite the favorable view."

As if she'd respect me more had I stayed. I can only imagine the absolutely monstrous prenup she'd have had me sign before the wedding. I wouldn't see a penny, and she'd drag my name through the mud the second things went south. And they would have, the way Jude was acting. We couldn't have made it work.

"It wasn't the first sign of conflict, as you know," I reply. "And I didn't initiate the breakup."

"Yeah, Mother. The first sign of conflict was when you told me I should use privilege, connections, and money to hide my alcoholism," Jude replies. "And that if I told anyone, including my long-time girlfriend, I'd end up in jail because she'd sell me out in a second for a story."

She said *what*? Seriously? I would never have sold him out. It takes me a moment to realize that he's admitted to being an alcoholic. He didn't even have a caveat about how he was a functioning alcoholic, like he'd joke in college. This is such a massive change for him. What other changes has he made? Maybe I haven't read him as well as I thought.

"Well, look what she's doing now," Jackie says.

"I'm writing a story. One where he'll probably come off pretty well, because he's done a lot in his tenure as CEO. And I don't know if it's because of our history or because of his new lifestyle, but I notice that despite the awkwardness of this meeting, Jude is the only one not drinking," I reply.

Maybe it's for my benefit, given how things ended the last time he drank before a family event with me. He's been drinking sparkling water this whole time, even though I'm sure every person at this table wants to completely obliterate their senses right now, myself included.

"I don't drink," he says, his voice cracking. "I tell the public it's because I'm practicing a radically healthy diet, but I haven't had a drop since Dad's funeral." There's regret in his voice when he mentions the funeral. I don't know whether it's about the proposal, or the vodka, or both, but it's there, and he looks like he's holding back tears.

"Oh. Oh, Jude. That's . . . that's really great."

I can't believe he actually quit. Right after. A little bit of me feels even worse. So he ghosted me once he got sober, like I wouldn't have been there for him? Or did his family keep him from me?

"Two of my worst moments happened while I was drinking. And both of them cost me the love and respect of someone I didn't think I could live without. So I stopped."

"That easy, huh?" I say, trying to make a joke I realize is ill-timed.

Jackie is still glaring at me, but Jude spares me the smallest of laughs.

"My leave of absence for a semester wasn't to recover emotionally or learn the ropes of the business. I went to rehab in Malibu and didn't get out until the start of senior year. I go to AA meetings twice a week, still. And therapy."

And none of that will make the profile. Even though it would actually be incredible to have such a public figure talk about his disease. And now I'm realizing that for six months, he wasn't ghosting me, he was literally across the country, changing his entire life. He never reached out after, but maybe it was too late. Would I have answered if he tried? Probably not.

Jude taps his earpiece.

"What?" Jackie asks.

"Training," Jude says. "Lauren has me running a new employee training tomorrow morning and I forgot to get the materials prepared at the office. Sorry, I'm going to have to head out and take care of that."

"What about dinner?" Jackie asks.

"I'll have the kitchen box me up something. The *training* is important."

I feel my heart stop. We were pretty transparent with training in our college years.

I clear my throat, and everyone turns to me. "As CEO you still run trainings yourself? And gather materials? Isn't that something that usually a more junior employee would do? I'd love to get a glimpse of that for the profile—do you mind if I tag along?" I ask.

"Of course not. Do you two mind?" he asks.

"Have fun," Joanna says, winking at me again.

She knows. And since she's teasing us about it, that must mean he's actually single. Joanna was cheated on in ninth grade and she keyed three of his family's cars and slashed the tires of his bike. The Landons had to pay off the family. Point is, she's radically against cheating, to the point of property destruction.

Remembering all of that should not be making me smile.

Jackie purses her lips. "Fine," she replies. "Manage your time more efficiently next time."

"Will do," Jude says, standing. He straightens his jacket before pulling out my chair.

I stand and watch as Jackie assesses my full outfit again. Her eyes stop at the earrings, and she flushes two different shades of scarlet. I stare at my feet and follow Jude out of the room. When the sliding door closes behind us, I lightly punch him in the arm.

"Bold move," I say.

"I'm glad you remembered."

"It was my idea!" I reply.

One of the waiters, the one who brought the tartare, hovers nearby.

"Can we get two to-go bags of the usual?" Jude asks. "We'll wait outside."

The server nods, as if there's nothing weird about this. I must not be the first woman the waitstaff have seen leave with Jude from a family dinner.

"How often do you call training?" I ask when the waiter is out of earshot.

"Not since Joanna's third twenty-fifth birthday party when we snuck off to . . ."

The shivers return, firing off from the pit of my stomach, all the way to my toes. I don't know why I agreed to this in the first place. Well, I do, and it's not because my brain is telling me to.

"I remember," I reply. I'd love to forget it. I can barely control my face, which already feels flushed.

"Vividly." His voice sounds gravelly, and he looks me directly in the eyes.

"Parlay," I whisper.

He takes a step back. "Well, if you have to call hiatus on even the thought . . ."

He isn't wrong, but the thought can spiral into something much worse. At the very least, I need a parlay on this part until the profile is over.

"The rules of parlay were established under the bleachers, tenth grade, when you wanted me to go to that soccer team party—and I stand by them today," I reply. "We have to pause."

"Well, can we at least eat pasta out of paper containers in your car, for old time's sake? My driver won't be here for another hour or two," he asks. "Please tell me you have a new car."

There are still an assortment of sauce stains in and around my passenger seat from our pasta excursions senior year of high school.

Every time I see the one on the side of the passenger seat cushion I think of Jude.

"Excuse you, Miss Minnie Cooper still runs almost perfectly, except on hills."

"I bet there's still a scuff mark on the passenger dashboard from my loafers."

"Yes, and? There are actually several," I reply.

"Come on, let's pick her up from the valet," Jude says, holding out his hand for the ticket.

I hand the ticket to him, and he strides up to the front of the restaurant. The hostess still looks stunned as we pass by her. However normal it feels for me, apparently being seen next to Jude Landon is still something extraordinary. I'm pretty sure she's texting Clara about it already.

The waiter runs outside with our food, in four large bags, just as the valet pulls my car around.

Jude slips them both what appears to be at least two hundred dollars at first glance.

I lean in toward him. "Remember when you never tipped because your mom told you that you were of European descent and it's gauche?" I whisper.

"Thank goodness someone taught me otherwise," he replies. "I looked like such an asshole."

I smile and climb into the car. Jude sits in the passenger seat, his knees up against the passenger dashboard, just like old times. We both slam our doors shut at the same time.

"Where should we go?" I ask.

"You drive; I'll navigate," he replies. "I know places."

I nod and turn the key in the ignition. Miss Minnie Cooper doesn't so much roar to life as she sputters, and I ignore Jude's concerned face as she struggles to life. I buckle my seat belt and hit the gas.

We pull out of the restaurant parking lot and onto Main Street, heading in unknown directions.

CHAPTER EIGHTEEN

We end up parked by the pond next to the local library, where we used to picnic in high school, with the sun setting behind us. Jude's legs are bent slightly to the side, wrinkling the delicate material of his tuxedo pants. My audio recorder is balanced in the cupholder between us.

We're sharing a to-go box of bruschetta, which is resting on my dashboard, and we're each holding a box of tagliatelle Bolognese, made with Impossible meat, in our laps. Two slices of tiramisu are sitting in a fourth to-go box in my back seat, one for me and one that I'm supposed to bring home to Oliver as a peace offering.

"This whole thing better end up in the profile. It makes me sound relatable," he says.

"I disagree," I reply, then ask more seriously, "Do you care about being relatable?"

"I don't know that I can be," he says. "I'm a—so far as I know— straight, cisgender, wealthy white man. I've had every advantage in this world. I had a company given to me like a consolation prize for the one hard thing I've been through."

He pops another piece of calamari in his mouth and twirls tagliatelle around his fork. The restaurant gave us real silverware because they know that Jude wouldn't use plastic cutlery. He doesn't even have to return it, and I imagine a sad drawer in his apartment filled with mismatched silverware donated by Fellini's.

"But look what you've done with that company," I say, taking a bite of my Bolognese.

"I like to surround myself with extraordinary people. Professionally and personally. I think they lift me up and show me more than I'd ever have discovered on my own."

"What do these extraordinary people show you?" I ask.

"Landon Energy, under my father, started as a company that mainly made solar panels for eight-bedroom California mansions. He expanded to funding research with hybrid cars, and some windmills for high-performing farms, but he and the company had a lot of blind spots," Jude says. "The importance of using non-potable water as energy and using sustainable measures to improve access to clean water was a big one."

Hence his interest in Kaitlyn Franklin's project, I assume. I still wonder why he chose her. Other people are doing similar projects— was it just a matter of personal trust since they're family friends?

"What were his other blind spots?" I ask.

"Methods of improving air quality and quality of life in densely populated low-income areas. Improving infrastructure in those areas to reduce toxic waste and lead paint leaching into the ecosystem. The company's focus has long been on the financial, even though it was changing parts of the world for the better."

"Driving an electric car doesn't make you a good person," I say.

"Having solar panels on your roof doesn't actually mean you care about the legacy you leave for your children," he replies.

Jude smiles for a moment, no doubt remembering how we used to recite this mantra to each other after particularly bad fights between him and his father. They were, to some degree, the best of friends, and also the fiercest of competitors in their worldviews. To me, Jude was always the better version of Julian. Julian without the drawbacks. But now I'm starting to see that he's not really like Julian at all. Sure, he's got some of that same business acumen, but he's evolved. He's a better version of the Jude I used to know, a more mature version. He's so close to being exactly who I wanted him to be when we were together.

"Do you think that by surrounding yourself with extraordinary people, you've become one yourself?" I ask.

He smiles faintly. "I hope so. I hope someday I can be just a little bit worthy of everything I've had."

"Professionally?" I ask.

He nods and makes eye contact with me. "And personally," he says.

"Can you elaborate?" I ask, trying not to want the answer.

"On the record," he says. "I was in a relationship for a very long time with someone who transformed my view of the world and my place in it with the privileges I have. Someone who asked more of me than I'd ever thought to ask of myself. Trying to build up something professionally and improve the lives of people who can't utilize their resources in the way I have changed me."

"She sounds pretty great," I reply, only half joking.

"Eh. She wanted a 'democracy dies in darkness' tattoo before Jeff Bezos took over the *Washington Post* and once went undercover in the dorm cafeteria for a month. She smelled like stale spaghetti and only wanted to talk about abuse in the workplace. Real weirdo."

Yeah . . . I got the story but lost three features editors who didn't want to be in the office with me. I found panko crumbs in my hair, even though I wore a net. And don't even get me started on how many times I was disciplined for "over-seasoning" the food. Like a few extra teaspoons of paprika were going to bankrupt a state university.

I stop the recorder and lay it completely inside the cupholder. "Yeah, but she had drive. She got shit done."

"She still can."

"Yeah, you're not in the newsroom. Be nice to me, whatever, I get it, but I'm not the same girl I was. And I'm not successful, so."

I probably shouldn't have said all of that. Or any of it. He doesn't need to know how things are going in the newsroom. This is professional, and if he knows how bad it's gotten, his white savior is for sure going to come out. I bet he'd offer to buy the paper. Which, while well-intentioned, doesn't exactly get to the core of the issue.

"I'm sorry. I didn't realize that was a sore spot."

"Why would you? We haven't kept in touch. I didn't even know you went to rehab. Like, what the fuck, Jude? You could have called me afterward. Or asked Joanna to. You should have told me."

He looks toward the ground, and I can see that he's blushing. "I didn't know how to articulate it at the time, but I have never been more ashamed than the moment I came to at the wheel, watching my best friend bleed from his head. Until I had him sign an NDA because my parents told me it was the only way I could keep my inheritance. How was I supposed to look at you after that? After I humiliated you too?"

It was mostly a surface wound, but a pretty nasty one nonetheless. Even the best detailing couldn't get the bloodstain out of Jude's dashboard. And even the best intentions, whether the Landons were operating for Jude or for themselves, couldn't erase the damage of that night.

"Maybe things would have been different," I say quietly.

Maybe I would have taken another job, and actually risen through the ranks on my talent and connections. Maybe I wouldn't have to rely on Mickey to remember to check my Bumble messages. Maybe I would never have even made a profile.

"Don't remind me. I've wondered about it almost every day. Especially when I've been reading the *Tribune* pretty religiously and I didn't see your name on anything besides that ice cream piece. I know how hard you work, and I wanted you to have this. It seems like it's already working. Three bylines in the last few days? That's great, right?"

I can't believe he's been checking the paper to see if I make it in there, and that he remembers my one article pre–Jacques Potts. It reminds me of how he read every article I wrote, from high school to college, and left little notes telling me his favorite parts. He'd star the sentences he loved the most, and leave a copy of the day's paper on my desk, covered in his dark-blue ink.

"I guess. But I have been repeatedly warned that our past will be dredged up, not just what we decide to share in the article, but the good, the bad, and the ugly. And the ugly will mostly be directed at me, for getting the article based on our past," I say.

"That is highly likely. And that is the only reason I hesitated on having you do this. Because of my past. And because I had to quiz you on ethics in college, I know this is a murky area at best.

But if you write this, beyond being the best person for the job, you get to control the aftermath and how much of the focus is on us. I hope."

He hesitated. He wasn't just thinking of what he wanted at my expense, there was actual thought behind this. If anyone else wrote it, they'd find out about me before I could give my side of the story. It'd actually be worse if it was someone else, especially one of the Fates.

"And if someone does dig it up? Will your mom be the one throwing me under the bus?" I ask.

He smiles. "She doesn't hate you."

He takes a sip from one of the sparkling water bottles the restaurant gave us and hands me the other one.

I take the bottle and our hands brush again. "Debatable," I reply, trying to ignore the butterflies fluttering lower and lower when we touch.

"There's a reason she didn't stop me in the cemetery. Wrong time, right person," he says.

He was easy to hate when he was a memory, and very hard to hate as the person in my passenger seat, eating pasta and laughing with me like we're still sixteen and in love.

"Wrong time? I *personally* can't think of a more romantic setting than your father's funeral during an eighty-five-year-old woman's speech," I say.

He grins. "Hey. Give me some credit. She was ninety and had stage fright. I was taking some of the attention. Out of *chivalry*."

"A regular knight of the Round Table, you are," I reply.

He leans his head back against the seat. "I get it if you hate me forever. But sitting in your very old, possibly unsafe car, eating fancy pasta, has been more fun, and more honest than anything I've done in a long time. Even if it's all for work. But I feel something here, something in the air. Even if you think I'm the devil."

He's right; this *has* been fun. It's like we've traveled back in time to how we were, but better. He's different than I imagined, but in a good way.

Fuck.

"I don't think you're the devil. And I feel something here too. Possibly only because of your biceps. And maybe because I feel like I've gotten through the Jude Landon veneer a bit. I see my old friend."

I probably shouldn't have admitted the thing about his biceps, but I simply can't stop staring at them. Is that what it looks like when someone eats enough vegetables and protein to no longer qualify as having an overall vitamin insufficiency?

"Does it have to be a veneer? Maybe I've matured." He makes his voice deeper, slipping back into CEO Jude. "Late-stage puberty has worked wonders for my career."

I restrain the urge to give him a laugh. "Eh, have you?"

"Yes, but part of me still wants a full journalistic description of my biceps in the profile."

"Only if you let me use a comparison shot of you in middle school and you now. I was hoping your mom would give me photos since I deleted my copies."

"Perfect. She definitely won't, but I can dig up the old albums."

After that *People* cover, I know any photos of Jude between the ages of nine and twenty-two will be locked down. The Landon family has a certain image, and Jude at sixth grade soccer camp with his spindly limbs and cheese puff–covered jersey is not it.

"And please, I'd like it if you only use your real voice with me, except at professional functions. As nice as the deep one is, it's weird."

He clears his throat and puts on a high-pitched Mickey Mouse voice. "Deal!"

It's so off-putting that he can do that, but I guess voice acting camp paid off. Rich people are huge weirdos, even if it is a good party trick.

I lean back in my seat and take a bite of focaccia bread from one of the food bags. If every dish didn't cost as much as an entire two-person meal with drinks from Tía Rosa's, I'd definitely be going back tomorrow.

Jude smiles at me over his Bolognese.

"You really don't drink? At all?" I ask.

"Haven't touched it since. Does that change anything?" He looks at me with hopeful eyes.

"Are you asking me if we can be together because you stopped drinking?" I ask.

"Not *because* of that," he says. "But does it change how you feel about me? Could we make this work in some way once the article is over?"

It was so easy for me to hate Jude when he wasn't here, right in front of me. When I could fill the gaps with everything that went wrong. When I didn't know that he thinks I changed his life. When I didn't know what he'd done to change his.

"I don't know. Maybe we could be friends. I don't know about more. Not yet."

"Do you think it would mean anything to Oliver?" he asks.

I wonder if Oliver will feel the same way. But I can't answer that right now. We both loved him so much in different ways. But letting him back in the way we did before doesn't feel possible right now, with all the hurt all of us have endured.

At least now I know what I have to do for this profile. I have to put Jude out into the world as he is and as he was, and to do that ethically I have to do the same to myself. Whatever comes with that is something I'll have to face, and there's a chance I could be facing it with Jude by my side for the first time in half a decade. The wound he left that I haphazardly stitched up four years ago is now reopened, but at least it hurts less.

CHAPTER NINETEEN

The next morning, before my next meeting with Jude, I sit in the principal's office of Sykeswood High School, next to a longtime respected English teacher and across from the longest-tenured principal in the county—my parents. They called me in, via our family text thread, after Mickey's mom called them last night.

Dad taps his fingers on the desk and stares at me, while Mom stares at the floor and wiggles her foot every couple of seconds. They've been doing this for the last ten minutes, as we all sat in complete silence after a couple of pleasantries and questions about my immigration articles.

"We have concerns," Mom says. "We're very concerned. How did this even happen? You ran into him at a gala? He just bombarded you after all this time?"

"Jude had me in mind from the beginning, but he hadn't told Adam yet. Apparently the gala was a coincidence, and once he saw my dynamic with Adam, he requested me personally the next night."

"He's a nice young man and we liked him quite a bit," Dad says. "Minus the end there."

"But this is a big step," Mom finishes. "And you didn't tell us."

I've avoided telling them too much about any aspect of my life ever since the *Tribune*. If they knew how bad things really were, they'd probably be in Adam's office, threatening to call the ACLU.

"I know. I'm sorry about that."

"Why? Why didn't you tell us?" she asks.

"I didn't know if I wanted to take it. And I figured you two would be less than thrilled. Since you were there . . . after everything."

"People can grow," Dad says. "You have, I'm sure he has too."

"I feel like I'm in the exact same place I was four years ago, but with worse job opportunities."

Maybe it's what I deserve. I chose the *Tribune* to avoid using the internship opportunities that the Landons had offered to secure for me. Worked out great, right?

"Making mistakes is how you grow," Dad says. "We all make a lot of them."

"Some more than others," Mom replies. "Jude was lovely most of the time, but some of the things he did . . ." She waves her hand at Dad and shakes her head.

They were the first people I told about the DUI, and the last before Jackie tried to shoehorn me into that NDA. I always wondered if that's part of why Jude proposed to me. Maybe he thought, as a misguided college junior, that if we were married I couldn't tell anyone.

"Four years ago. Which, in the life of a twenty-year-old, is more like a decade," Dad replies.

"True," Mom concedes. "But this profile business . . ."

"Your privacy will be destroyed. At least in this town," Dad says. "And the sanctity of the family group text."

"All we ask for is honesty. And the story will be picked up all over the country. Even in the gossip magazines. They'll find your social media, your pictures," Mom adds. "Who knows what the school board will think."

Why would the school board have anything to do with it?

"It will blow over," I say. "And I'm sorry I kept it from you both."

Dad raises his eyebrows, while Mom coughs.

"Well, I don't know if that logic adds up," Dad says, smiling at me and then Mom.

Neither Mom nor I react. He loves to make math jokes and we love to pretend they haven't happened.

"I'll do whatever I have to do to handle it," I reply.

"We wouldn't be upset if the two of you got back together at some point. Or surprised, for that matter," Dad says. "Your dating path since has been . . . limited? Is that the right word?"

"Dad!"

"We liked Jude, quite a bit. His family less so. Especially not his mother. Truly a witch," Mom replies. She shudders after mentioning Jackie. "We want you to be happy and secure financially. He offers both, in spades, from what we've seen."

"And you haven't been. Happy. Between feeling stuck at your job emotionally, plus never having received a promotion and, in our minds at least, never moving on from Jude, we haven't seen this kind of shine from you in a long time. You're finally excited about something again," Dad says. "Even if you're trying to pretend that you're not."

I really didn't expect this meeting to turn into a psychoanalytic session from my parents, but here we are. I don't know if I'm more annoyed that they're reading me, or that they're correct.

"Where am I supposed to find someone who supports me emotionally and professionally, who also can at least try to understand my reality as a Black woman? There isn't exactly an app for that."

"Set the dating apps to 'just as incredible as your father,'" Mom says.

I roll my eyes. They're disgustingly cute, and I hate that if I were ever on *The Bachelor* I'd say they're my relationship goal.

"It's about your own discernment. Trust your gut. And find someone who will give us cute grandchildren, please," Dad says.

"I can provide cute grandchildren on my own, in a minimum of five years. I was *adorable*."

I don't know that I would I ever be able to rely on Jude again, the way my parents rely on each other. There's a mutual respect between them that I'm certain I can't find when I'm maybe trending toward unemployed with minimal prospects. How am I supposed to face him if I do this profile and it ruins my life?

When I'm in the hallway, I check my phone and see that I have been added into a group text with all of the Fates.

Good luck with your meeting today! Heather texts.

Clara texts a succession of winking face emojis. *Hope you enjoyed dinner last night.*

Lol Clara hopes you get her a date, Lucy texts.

I could toss my phone into the path of the maintenance man trimming the grass outside the front of the school. Let the lawn mower eat it and give me the perfect excuse to not respond to this text chain.

Gen's too good for us. Hanging out with the Landons, can't even get a text back, Clara texts.

Sorry, I was driving, I reply. *I'll put in a good word for everyone.*

Slip him my number, Clara says.

Mine too, Lucy adds.

Invite him to my wedding, L or C, Heather replies.

Or does Gen want him all for herself? Clara says. *Since she left with him. JK. Heard his mom was a terror and you had to escape to get an interview.*

Okay, that's new. Well, not exactly new, but Jackie doesn't usually slip in public. And she definitely doesn't blow up enough to scatter witnesses.

???, I reply.

APPARENTLY, she was livid that the staff let Jude leave in your car. Had a whole thing about it being unsafe and a hazard to the health of one of the restaurant's biggest benefactors.

I close my eyes for a few seconds. My car, despite her age, is not actually unsafe. But it did break down on the highway in the middle of the night the week before Jude and I broke up. Jackie was inconsolable when we came in at three AM, and we both thought she was overreacting because of his accident. She never believed that only Jude had the problem. If he was drinking too much, it had to be due to bad influences. I was ready to fight her on it, defend myself to her for the very first time.

That was the night that Julian died.

It's weird, but there's a backstory w/the family. Can't say anything more, but I'm sure your roomie will get a lovely apology gift before the dinner rush, I reply.

Jackie can frequently be terrible. I would argue more often than not. But on this, I get it, even if it's unwarranted. I don't get to judge how she reacts to reminders of the most traumatic time in her life. In the whole family's lives.

A text from Adam pops up. *Can't wait to hear about the dinner. Sure you don't want to do the piece on why you said no? Landons sound a bit godfather-esque, no? If not, we need three sensitivity reads and 600 words on that sinkhole downtown by EOD. You rock!*

I squeeze the phone. I have to be eligible for an upgrade soon; I could totally burn it. I stick it back in my pocket and fish out my car keys instead. Can't be late.

CHAPTER TWENTY

One look through Jude's calendar gives me enough material for a follow-up article on why he loves a Wednesday lunch meeting. Without fail, every Wednesday for the past year he's had a lunch meeting in his office with someone he deems important, from other CEOs to investors to board members to new talent he wants to collaborate with. Unless he were to take a vacation, which he hasn't during his tenure as CEO, he will never have a Wednesday afternoon free.

"Wednesday used to be my least favorite day of the week," he tells me. "Hump day, you know? So I gave myself something to look forward to every Wednesday." He takes a bite of his vegetarian poke bowl.

"You look forward to meetings?" I ask.

My poke bowl is in my bag inside a climate-controlled lunch container that Jude is testing out. Apparently I get to be a fellow guinea pig and I'm supposed to text him at the end of the workday to verify whether or not it worked. I told him I wasn't hungry yet, but in reality, my stomach is in knots, thinking about our Bolognese bonding in the car.

"With interesting people, yes," he replies.

"Who is the most interesting person you've gotten the chance to meet?" I ask.

He cringes. "I'm so sorry. I hate that question. I find value in every person I meet, I can't compare them," he says. "Sorry if I offended you."

"You didn't."

I fiddle with the zipper on my jacket. It makes a barely audible click every time I push it back and forth.

"You said that too quickly," he replies. "When you're unbothered you take a couple of seconds to respond. And don't try to tell me I'm overthinking it—you haven't changed *that* much."

"This Jude Landon is more blunt. Is that just professionally?"

"It's more of the Julian Landon veneer. I try to be like him, and fail most days. So now I'm trying to figure out how to be the best version of myself. The best leader that isn't a pale imitation. Literally. I'm paler than he ever was."

I snort. "You're both pretty pale, though I concede that he could at least tan without . . . becoming the mascot for Red Lobster."

"Ouch."

I shrug. "Don't shoot the messenger."

"You're making a huge sacrifice for me," he says. "I'm grateful. And if they're terrible about it at the paper I'd hire you in a second . . ."

I turn the audio recorder off.

"I don't want another handout, Jude."

His face falls and I watch in real time as he remembers that our breakup isn't the only potentially problematic dichotomy between us. It's not like we'd never talked about being interracial, especially given the class distinction, but it just never seemed to matter when we were sharing pizza in a dorm room.

He shrinks in his chair. "I'm sorry," he says, his voice lowering. "I don't understand why we're always fighting."

God, I feel terrible. I want to be more open to him, I do, but something is blocking me. "Maybe we just need to. Because we didn't when we were supposed to."

"Well then, can we please make up?" he asks.

"The profile will be fine, no matter where we stand." And it will; I can keep this professional. I'd never ruin this opportunity for both of us just to be petty.

He pushes back his chair and stands up.

I feel hyperaware that our breathing has started to line up, and neither of us is breathing particularly normally.

Then he kneels by my chair, and my brain scatters in two distinct directions. The first is horror, the idea that he could propose again since the ring is here. The second is anticipation, that he might make a physical move. I hope the door is locked, in either case.

"Let's make it simple. What can I do to make it simple?" he asks.

"Literally nothing." This will never be simple, because our past is so complicated. I can't imagine things between us ever feeling easy, the way it did when we were kids.

"Then can we embrace complicated?" he asks. "I just . . . I've changed so much. And so have you. We can start over, brand new.

With your consent. I miss you. I miss how things were when we were happy together. Nothing and no one has compared since. Do you think we could even try?"

Before I can answer, the door opens and he jumps back away from me. Lauren leans into the room. Her eyes widen when she sees Jude on the floor. "Um, Mr. Landon, your next appointment is here."

Jude jumps up. "Of course, yes, send her in," he replies.

I can't tell which one of us is sweating more right now. I'm almost grateful that Lauren interrupted. I still don't know what to say.

"Are you sure? If you need a moment . . . Please take a moment."

"I don't, no, send her in," Jude says, jogging back behind his desk, his face flushed.

Lauren is shaking slightly. Jesus, who's coming in for the appointment, Vito Corleone?

Kaitlyn Franklin, wearing an evergreen skirt-suit straight out of *Vogue*, with stilettos to match, power-walks in without pausing. She might be worse than a mobster, given the glare she's shooting out in every direction. She's giving off major "boss bitch" vibes, like she'd embrace the title and do her best to live up to it. I'm immediately intimidated by her, her energy, her beauty, the way she looks like she wants to slit my throat.

Jude unbuttons his suit jacket and sits back in his seat; anything left of the moment between us is long gone. He smiles at Kaitlyn, and she blinks at him, looking unimpressed with whatever she has found.

"Sorry to interrupt," Kaitlyn says to no one in particular. She turns to me and offers her hand. "Kaitlyn Franklin, I'm designing a world-changing water system. You look familiar. Oh. I remember."

I shake her hand, aware that my own is clammy. "Genevieve Francis. I'm with the *Sykeswood Tribune*." I make sure to hold eye contact. I read in a business book that it makes people respect you more.

Kaitlyn raises her eyebrows and, after a few seconds, turns back to Jude. "A member of the press. That's new. Even if she's not."

Since she was a couple of years younger than us, she never made too much of a splash at Landon family events. Jude, Oliver, and I were pretty insular, even from the other young people. Jude didn't really have close friends from his family's extended social circle. I never really found out why. But I guess she remembers me too.

"Gen's writing the very first authorized profile of me," Jude says. "She's very talented."

"Ah. A real catch," she replies.

She smirks for a moment, as though she's thought of a joke that no one else in the room knows. She makes direct eye contact with me, and I see her tongue run along the inside of her mouth. For someone who can't be attracted to Jude, she's sure relishing the precariousness of our current situation.

Interviewing her is not going to be fun. Maybe I can outsource that to one of the Fates. She'd eat them alive, and I savor the idea.

Jude turns red. "Um . . ."

"For Ms. Francis. Landing this story; it's a good one," Kaitlyn says quickly. "What on *earth* did you think I meant?"

She knows what Jude thought she meant. She's Jackie Landon thirty years ago, with her ambitions pointed elsewhere. My being here is funny to her. Just like it is to everyone else. She's delighting in making Jude uncomfortable, the way Jackie does. I hate it.

"Play nice, Kait. She's going to be talking about your work too," Jude replies.

"Oh good. Something in the *Tribune* that isn't about who I'm allegedly sleeping with," Kaitlyn says.

The paper is pretty horrifying in their coverage of Kaitlyn. There aren't a lot of pieces I'd completely turn down, but I'd never write about her—the way she looks, who she might date—the way the gossip writers do. "I don't write those pieces," I say, feeling a little defensive. Even if I'm not the offending writer, I'm still a part of the institution.

"Of course you don't. You actually give nuance instead of leaning into your most salacious impulse. I *wish* you were the one covering me," she replies.

I try not to look visibly shocked, but Kaitlyn's facial expression tells me I'm failing. Women like Kaitlyn, the rich society women who feel entitled to men like Jude—their time, their resources, their affection—almost always resent me for being in his orbit. I'm sure some of it is class; I'm from outside their circles. But I also don't look like them. And that's probably worse. At least if I came from money, they could justify why Jude would find me interesting or desirable. But maybe Kaitlyn isn't like that. She's already being nicer to me than Jackie has ever been.

"I would love to cover you," I say. "Clean water engineer masquerading as a socialite? *That's* a story."

"See, that's what I'm talking about," she says. "Anyone else from your paper would want to run with the lesbian angle, take it public. You're pretending like you don't even know."

I take a beat. It makes sense that Jude would let her know that he'd told me about her sexuality at the Landon family dinner. "Well, no offense, but I don't think the lesbian angle is the most important thing here, unless you want to make that part of your platform as well. In which case, I'd make it tasteful," I reply.

"Talk to your editor. We contain multitudes, right? Let's do both. I'm in. I'm tired of everything about me being related to men. Let's come out publicly," she says.

Seriously? That wasn't just flattery? I've got myself another story on one of the *Tribune*'s favorite subjects, given to me by the person themselves? But this time, no potential ulterior motive. No guilt. Kaitlyn doesn't owe me anything. Is this how I'm going to make a name for myself? By becoming someone the powerful people in town trust to not exploit their private lives for the sake of a story?

"Me too. I'll talk with Adam today and see what we can do," I reply. "Thank you, for trusting me."

"Anytime. Now I'm going to have to ask you to go. We're talking business, and it's a little too juicy for media presence," Kaitlyn says.

She hands me a copy of her business card; a white piece of card-stock that simply reads *Kaitlyn Franklin LLC* alongside her email. Holy shit. We're actually doing this.

Jude almost looks . . . no. He can't be jealous. This is what he wanted, me getting the opportunity to write more stories. I guess he just didn't anticipate that those stories would involve anyone else in his immediate social circle. Plus, even if I do have an affinity for redheads, Kaitlyn scares me just a tad too much. Even CEO Jude would be more my speed.

It would give me the tiniest bit of satisfaction to make him jealous, even if it's over something silly. I feel the societal power imbalance so acutely in our current relationship that sometimes I still wish I didn't have to do this profile. If I built myself up a bit more, like with Kaitlyn, then my profiling Jude would make sense. Then maybe my coworkers wouldn't look at me like I'd kicked their puppies.

But then again, maybe this is just my problem. I'm feeling inadequate because I'm everything that Jude Landon and Kaitlyn Franklin are not.

The only way I know to change my inadequacy is to address it. But I really have to figure out if the *Tribune*'s newsroom is the place I can do that.

CHAPTER TWENTY-ONE

I sit at my desk in the newsroom, listening to my interviews with Jude while flipping through the documents Lauren gave me. No wonder Jude felt insecure about his performance. Company stock prices plunged when Julian died, and while they've improved, they still haven't reached the levels Julian had them at during his tenure. From a purely financial standpoint, Jude has not been beneficial for the board members' profits. Remembering all the tears from Julian's funeral, I once again wonder if everyone knew that Jude wasn't ready to take over.

Out of the corner of my eye, I can see the Fates once again gathered at their desks. A message from Clara pops up on my computer screen. *Come over!*

She motions for me to come join them. Oh good. I'm sure this will be the biggest treat and not the worst moment of my day.

I push back from my desk and try to make alarmed mental contact with Regina, who is on a call. She doesn't notice, and I grit my teeth.

"Hey," I say, approaching their collection of desks. "What's up?"

Heather pats a space on her desk. "We just wanted to chat."

"Did you see *Housewives* last night?" Clara asks.

"Wasn't it amazing?" Lucy asks. "The *table. Flip.*"

"Pretty crazy," I reply.

Truly, what are they getting at here? We haven't had a casual conversation since the last presidency.

"Even crazier, you were right. About Jackie Landon. The apology basket she sent Lisa for flipping out at Fellini's was incredible. You've totally figured the Landons out," Clara says.

Ah. Now that they think I truly understand the Landons, I have some sort of special in. I'm useful, so I matter.

"Do you want to grab lunch with us?" Heather asks. "We're grabbing hot bar from Whole Foods. We'd love to hear what it's like to eat with the Landons. Does Jackie even eat?"

"I think I'm going to stay here and have a working lunch, but thanks for thinking of me! And yes, she does," I say. I silently pray they never think of me again. They can find out about the Landons from my profile, and I don't want to give them anything else. Anything I say will somehow end up in the gossip pages or on Twitter, I just know it.

"Can we pick you up anything?" Clara asks. "What would *Jude* eat?"

Jude from college would eat literally everything the hot bar had to offer; his container was always a mélange of flavors I'd never want to put together. The Jude of today would probably stick to the salad bar, as long as it was fully organic. If we're going to ever be friends again, I hope Jude is still willing to eat pizza, grocery store or otherwise.

"I'm sure something very sustainable. I promise, this profile's not as glamorous as it seems," I say. If Jude hadn't called training, I probably wouldn't have even gotten the fancy dinner. Any glamour they think this profile brings is most likely going to be snuffed out by Jackie expeditiously.

"Well, I want the next one," Lucy replies. "So hands off. I'm stuck with Drier Park, ugh. I hate going there. It's so . . . you know."

Yeah. I know what she thinks of Drier Park. I only hear about it three times a week and have to bite my tongue before I flat-out call her racist to her face. I try to keep my expression level, and I'm literally biting my tongue.

Drier Park is the predominantly Black and Hispanic town barely six miles away from the center of Sykeswood. It's pretty firmly middle class, with a couple of parts generally acknowledged to be rougher. According to the *Tribune* it is essentially the ghetto, and the only stories reported are ones of either extreme poverty or triumph over the worst circumstances.

"There are actually some really cool things going on in Drier Park," I say. "If you can look past the stereotypes."

Lucy's face drops. "No, I didn't mean it like that. Oh my God, was that racist?"

"Not racist, just insensitive," Clara replies. "Right, Gen?"

I bite my tongue again and try to force a smile that I suspect comes out like more of a grimace. The everyday people who live in Drier Park are endlessly more interesting than most of the wealthy Sykeswoodians we cover.

"I would argue that thinking of Drier Park in an exclusively negative way is, at the very least, a product of the systemic racism that has impacted the area. Which doesn't really get covered a lot," I reply.

"I wrote about racism last week. And you had your article yesterday too," Heather says. "So we're covering it. Even if Adam isn't thrilled about it."

"What do you mean?" I ask.

"We heard Adam was . . . a little insensitive about your article yesterday," Clara says.

Insensitive is certainly a way to put it. Tepid language aside, this is the closest they've ever come to acknowledging racism in our stories. I might be hallucinating, but this is a welcome escape from the normal drone of our conversations. Or the microaggressions.

"There were some comments that I definitely found, let's say, problematic," I reply.

"Then it's a good thing you got the story, right? You got underneath the surface. Adam wouldn't have," Lucy says.

Okay, I'm definitely in a fever dream. I contracted some kind of crazy food poisoning from the day-old tiramisu and am currently weaving a fan fiction of my own life in my mind. They have literally never expressed genuine happiness for me before.

"I did my best," I reply, waiting for them to leave. Their being nice to me is honestly more disconcerting than their usual blend of hostility.

Once they're out of the newsroom, I pull up my notes document, and stick my headphones back into my ears.

The Landon Energy board has not changed in fifteen years; the same people who worked with Julian when Jude was in preschool are still there. Something tells me that they still see the four-year-old who once ate Play-Doh under a conference room table, instead of the twenty-five-year-old man who has been trying to diversify their assets. They've approved a couple of Jude's investment ideas over the last four years, but none of those investments have broken even yet. No wonder Kaitlyn's trying to swoop in with her new system. Her idea seems to be the only thing generating revenue.

I pause the recording as I get to the documents about which projects the board has rejected. There are at least twenty-five proposals in here, mostly related to addressing environmental equity in impoverished areas. The only projects of Jude's the board has approved are expansions of solar panels in high-SES neighborhoods and, most recently, Kaitlyn Franklin's water project. I flip through a few more pages until I reach a press release for Kaitlyn Franklin's project. It looks like her family put up a large amount of the capital for her project.

There's no reasoning given for any of the proposal rejections, and Lauren didn't give me the minutes from the board meetings. I pull up my email and begin drafting a message to Lauren to ask for the meeting notes.

Lauren,

Thank you for the resources! I just wanted to check and see if I would be able to get access to the board meeting minutes. I want to know more about the proposals that were rejected and accepted.

There are several proposals included that seem very similar to Kaitlyn Franklin's water system. I make a mental note to look up more general information about how water systems have worked in other parts of the US or other countries. Maybe Kaitlyn's system really is at the cutting edge of innovation.

Hannah, the intern, runs past me holding a stack of papers. She stops for a moment, and I can see her whispering to herself trying to figure out which direction to go. She looks at me panicked, and I point to the copy room on her left. She nods and mouths *thank you* before running inside. The door, which frequently jams, slams behind her and several people startle in their cubicles.

I abandon the email to Lauren and start googling the names on the rejected proposals. Most are pretty low-level researchers or engineers at the various Landon Energy plants. Several are international, and about half are women. There are only four proposals that have been funded by Landon Energy in Jude's tenure. One per year since Jude has been CEO.

My phone buzzes again. I have an interview with the owner of a bodega that's been employing low-income students after school in fifteen minutes. I lock my computer and gather all of the papers on my desk.

Adam texts me. *Can you get a quote from the security guard at the liquor store on 8th on your way to bodega? Thx. And have both articles on my desk by 3:30.—Adam.*

On it, I reply. *Can we chat later about another project?*

Heather needs a sensitivity cowrite, so read what she has so far and add on the underrepresented perspective. By 3 if you can. Feel free to copyedit as well. Plus the earlier 1s. After that, sure.

It's twelve thirty. They're definitely waiting for me to fail.

I jog to the elevator. Thank God I changed into flats.

CHAPTER TWENTY-TWO

Last month, an unarmed Black man was shot by police outside the city mall. The official story is that he stole a pair of sunglasses and fled the scene. The police claimed they saw a gun and the sunglasses, but neither was recovered at the scene. Police brutality protests have been happening in the area for the last two weeks, and I've been dodging my coworkers' bad takes on it for what feels like a month. I'm just hoping that if I'm determined enough at my computer right now, I can force flow. I can pretend I haven't gotten five requests for cowrites tomorrow, with my name on the byline, to provide, as Adam says, "the minority perspective," in addition to three assignments related to the white people protesting both for and against police brutality three blocks away. It would be a step in the right direction, if it wasn't just to cover up the fact that there aren't any other Black staff writers. According to Regina, Adam's already arranged a photo op where he's pictured holding a #BlackLivesMatter sign in the crowd, and he even asked her to sensitivity read his letter from the editor. She joked that we should go and hold #BlackStoriesMatter signs. Well, I don't know that that one was a joke. I don't know what's worse, being the only Black girl in the room and being looked over, or being the only Black girl in the room when there's the hypervisibility of a racial incident.

Evelyn is standing by Lucy's cubicle, surrounded by all the Fates. She swipes her hair back out of her face, holding out her phone.

"Every week another protest," Evelyn says. "Just blocking the downtown. So disrespectful."

"It's so scary, they were *so* close to my car," Heather replies.

"Maybe if they just said it more nicely and didn't, like, disrupt everyone's lives . . . ," Clara begins.

Hate is a strong word, but I'm starting to feel it bubbling up. Imagine keeping a straight face while telling an entire group of people to be nice when they're upset about public lynchings. They just have a complete unwillingness to see the humanity in anyone who isn't just like them.

My phone buzzes and I see a text from Regina.

Do. Not. Engage.

I begin to type back, letting out a huff of air.

No! she adds before I even send my text.

"And did you see that activist defending them in the Op-Ed section today? It's violence. Like against their own community," Lucy says.

I hit my hand against my desk, temporarily zoned solely into my frustration. Now they're all looking at me, while I'm pretending to still be focused on writing.

"Wait, is she actually mad? This time it wasn't even insensitive," Lucy says. She's turned to Heather, who's smiling up at her.

"She." Like I'm not even there. Truly, I would like to vanish from this spot. I dig my nails into my palm, because the only thing that can distract me from how angry I am is the physical sensation.

It's on the list, Regina texts.

The list? I reply.

The one I keep of every racist incident that happens here. Let me know if you want a real cowrite. No sensitivity required.

My email pings. I've become a one-woman tip line for every person on the ground at the protests who wants their story told. The closest area newspaper that covered Mrs. Li's attack never even spoke with her. Their entire framing was from the perspective of her white neighbors and how scary this attack was for *them.* Now it seems like, practically overnight, I'm starting to become the person people trust to tell their stories of racial violence. Some of them are stories I wanted to write, to avoid the clichés my coworkers lean into. But do I really want to submerge myself in other people's traumas when I haven't even dealt with my own?

One message stops me. It's from my old mentor, Jennifer Warren.

Gen,

I hope you've been well. I've been really impressed by your recent articles and pleased to see that you're finally getting your shot at the Tribune. I moved into an advocacy role, and I'm working with the National Association of Black Journalists on a more in-depth statement on the incident at the Times. We're looking for up and coming journalism stars to give input and share their experiences, if you're interested. Leaving was the best option for me, but I often think about you at the Tribune. Let me know if you want to catch up, on or off the record. We'll protect you.

Sincerely,
Jennifer Warren

God, Jennifer. I wanted to be just like her. Her pantsuits were always pastel, her sister locs were always impeccable, and she was on the front page almost every day. She was a rock star. I never understood why she left when she was on top of her game. Until I realized that, no matter how good you are, this place will spit you out. But she was as big a name as you could be as a local journalist, and she quit without really giving an explanation. Had I left every time I wanted to, I would have had to start over from the bottom somewhere else. What if every place is worse than this? If it can happen at the *Times*, if it can happen to a Pulitzer winner, who am I?

The op-eds have already started. The *Times* writer was "cold" and "unpleasant to work with." Her coworkers lived in fear of a biting retort whenever they expressed something slightly less than politically correct. All of this conveniently comes out as soon as she exposes the racism in her newsroom. Now she's tainted, regardless of her talent, of her reputation. If I speak out here, can NABJ really protect me? Or will I just be an unemployed whistleblower who stood up for herself at the expense of everything?

College Gen was on the front lines of every protest, every town hall, anything having to do with addressing injustice. She spoke at any event she could and made sure to cover it in the school paper.

She submitted articles to every newspaper in a forty-mile radius and networked like nobody's business.

I wish College Gen were still here. She had the stomach for all of this. This Gen's a coward.

Three minutes left in the workday, three minutes until I can pick up savory crepes and leave. Three minutes until I don't have to notice them all sneaking glances in my direction.

My phone buzzes again. A text from Jude. *You okay? After today?*

Do you have spies in the newsroom or something?

The three minutes are up and I'm booking it out of the newsroom and down the stairs. I try to pick up my pace; I can already see the workers folding up the chairs outside from one of the windows.

I plead the fifth. I meant with Kait. And the protests by your office. Another unarmed Black man. I'm sorry.

She's all bark, I've faced worse. And thanks. I'm holding up, best I can.

I almost run into the sign outside advertising the spicy crispy shrimp crepe special for this week.

The worker stacking chairs raises her eyebrows at me. "You must be Genevieve, the to-go?" She holds out the bag to me.

"Yes, thank you!"

Trust me, she has bite. I got an earful about conflicts of interest and distractions, Jude texts. *Wanna talk about the shooting? Are they asking you to cover it?*

I take a deep breath. *Well, count me out as a distraction; you've given me enough quotes to pull together a compelling narrative. And not right now, but thanks for asking.*

Can't wait to read it. Apologies in advance for whatever quotes you get from my mother. I'm here, anytime.

I'm sure only one to two will be fit to print.

Makes it simple, right?

Ehh. Your mother is definitely a complication.

If you had a rough day at work, does that mean you're grabbing . . . some form of shrimp?

I snort. *Who said shrimp is my comfort food?*

You, three hundred times. What form tonight?

Crepes.

Yum.

I almost crash into an unsuspecting businessman who's coming out of the *Tribune* parking garage. I raise my hand in apology before ducking my head back into my phone. I realize that I'm smiling. We're bantering and I love it.

You know what goes great with crepes? Jude's texted.

My brain flashes back to Mickey's crash course in dating advice, for my first time on the apps after Jude's and my breakup. She said that a double text means you're too interested. Triple text is basically an embarrassment.

The third text comes in, and my heart jumps. *Wine. Bottle of rosé incoming to your place. Delivery driver's ETA 20 minutes.*

And you have my address how? Stalker?

Were the flowers that forgettable?? Background check Landon Energy runs on anyone spending time in the company.

I swear I did my best to keep them alive. Should I have composted them?

Restraining the urge to send a composter to your apartment.

New headline idea: How Jude Landon Makes Eco-Friendly Sexy

Wait . . . you think I'm sexy??

Oh . . . look at the time. About to drive. See you later. Thanks for wine.

I drop my phone into the bowels of my work bag. It's time to go home and stare at information about my ex, for purely professional reasons.

CHAPTER TWENTY-THREE

The next day, for the first time in four years, I pull up outside the Landon estate on the edge of town. It looks the same, behind the gate, sprawling out over seventy acres. The main house is shrouded by trees that line the gravel driveway.

My phone buzzes in the cupholder. The Fates group text once again.

Snap pics of the house! Clara says.

Especially the garden. Do they do weddings? Heather replies.

Don't steal anything! Even if it's shiny, Lucy says. *JK, don't want you to think I'm a racist again.*

It's like she almost had a moment of self-awareness before the cognitive dissonance really took hold.

I roll down my window at the gate and press the buzzer. The wait feels eerily familiar. I've sat outside this gate in this car more times than I could ever count.

After about twenty seconds a voice says, "Name and affiliation?"

"Genevieve Francis with the *Sykeswood Tribune* here for a pre-scheduled interview with Mrs. and Ms. Landon."

"*Genevieve Francis?*" the voice says through the intercom, friendlier now.

"Yes?" I reply. Wait, it can't be . . . "Mr. Jay? You're still here?"

Mr. Jay had been in charge of Landon estate security for twenty years by the time Jude and I started dating. A middle-aged Black man who lived in a house with his wife and daughter on the Landon property, he was one of the few Black people I saw around here when I was dating Jude. He was at every event, every family dinner, and every house party Jude threw when his parents were out of town. He'd always warn me when Jackie was in a mood, or when Julian had just given Jude a lecture on success, five minutes before my arrival. He was my lifeline in a house that I was frequently reminded I was never supposed to belong in.

"Until the day I die," Mr. Jay replies. "Gen, you're back?"

"In a professional capacity," I reply.

"Welcome back," he says. "I, for one, am thrilled to have you."

The gates slowly part, and I forget how much the estate used to take my breath away. The trees lining the drive are meticulously kept up, and more were planted to present the illusion of a forest surrounding the estate. As I begin to drive in, I remember evening picnics by the pond, deep in those trees, our private place. I glance over to see if I can spot it, but it's too far hidden.

Mr. Jay, looking the same as he did at the funeral and wearing the same uniform he always did, blue on blue with a white tag across the breast pocket that reads *Security Officer*, stands in the doorway.

"You're *still* driving that car?" he asks.

I step out of the car and close the door. "It's only been four years, she still runs."

"She barely ran then," he replies. "Come here, girl."

He opens his arms and I gladly jog into them. Losing Jude hurt, but losing the good parts of his world did too. Mr. Jay was always the best part. He and Mrs. Jay took such good care of me and Oliver when we came over. We even had dinners with his family a few times, sans any of the Landons.

"It's good to see you too, Mr. Jay. You look great."

"I got a treadmill desk. Keeping the blood pressure in check."

"I love to hear it," I reply. "How have you been? How are Mrs. Jay and Emily?"

Mr. Jay drops his head for a moment, and when he looks back up at me there are tears in his eyes. He blinks them away. Oh no. God, why didn't I keep in touch? I really cared about him and his family.

"Emily is doing wonderfully, she's graduating college this year," he says. "Mrs. Jay unexpectedly passed last year."

"I'm so sorry, Mr. Jay."

He waves his hand. "She always knew you'd be back. She wrote down her caramel cake recipe at the end for Emily to learn. To bake for your wedding."

My wedding. Can everyone really see something between me and Jude, even after all this time? "Emily's still baking?" I ask.

"Emily wants to open her own line of bakeries inspired by her mother's cooking. She's going to go to business school next year and open her first shop downtown after she graduates."

"That's wonderful," I reply. "I will definitely be first in line when it opens."

Mr. Jay smiles and motions for me to follow him to the side door. He leans in and whispers, "Jackie has been huffing around the living room all morning, Joanna just woke up and is taking her mimosa in the library."

Some things never change. Jackie and Joanna always felt frozen in time, living the same days over and over.

"Thank you."

I inhale, smelling the slightest bit of Jackie's perfume floating in the air. I try not to stare at the giant painting of Julian that now hangs right inside the foyer door. It replaced the family painting, which now hangs on the other wall, paling in both size and quality to the vividly lifelike one of Julian. I swear his eyes are following me.

I pause when I reach the open living room door to see that Mr. Jay wasn't joking. I watch as Jackie paces back and forth, flipping through a magazine. I raise my hand to knock on the door.

"You weren't announced," Jackie says.

Well, we're off to a rollicking start. "I never . . . have been?" I reply.

"Sit." She flits her hand toward the chaise lounge in front of the wall-spanning windows.

I sit and pull out my audio recorder. I set it on the table in front of the chaise lounge where Jackie's morning herbal tea is still set with a plate of half-eaten fruit.

There's a stack of magazines on the table, mostly fashion but a few business ones as well, each with small Post-its sticking out of several pages. The most prominent one is the *People Magazine* Most Eligible Bachelor issue with Jude on the cover. It really isn't the best photo of Jude; his smile is closer to a cringe and he's standing sort of tilted forward with his arms crossed in what I assume was meant to be an imposing position.

Jackie holds her hand out, blocking my view of the magazine, with her palm facing me. "No recording," she says, her tone clipped.

She's always unnecessarily difficult. "It's the best way to make sure that I accurately quote you in the profile," I reply. I chew the inside of my cheek, trying to keep my tone as curt as Jackie's.

Jackie rolls her eyes. "This isn't about the profile in some local paper."

"You previously agreed to be interviewed," I say.

"Yes, and I will, after we talk. *Off* the journalistic record." She glares at me.

I slip the audio recorder into my pocket. What on earth could she want to talk to me about? Whatever it is, I don't want to know. Jackie wanting to speak with me in private has never led to anything good. The last time I told her to "fuck off" because she tried to push me to sign the NDA.

Whatever she wants to say is probably whatever she didn't get to say the other night when Jude and I left dinner early. I'm sure whatever threats she had stored up have been saved, and probably exacerbated now that there are no witnesses. Well, if it's a real threat at least Adam could get the piece he really wants me to write. I can see it now: *Poisoned Ivy, Using Journalists as Fertilizer in the Landon Environmental Empire.*

"I'm all ears," I say. Ears and memory. I want to remember her quotes verbatim so I can scribble them in my notebook while setting up the audio recorder for the real interview.

I try to catch a glimpse out into the hall to see if Joanna is maybe hiding behind a wall, ready to report back to Jude and start another family feud. I know she's not particularly quiet, so when I don't at least hear some shuffling on the floor, I assume Jackie and I are truly alone.

The *People Magazine* is in full view again and I feel like there's a stone sitting in the pit of my stomach. Jude's terrible photo takes that stone and begins turning it into something lighter. I feel a flutter up through my chest. Even in a terrible photo, there's still just something about him that I'm drawn to.

"Girls like you are never willing to make the sacrifice it takes to be with a powerful man. You're too ambitious for your own good. You can't have that and have him," Jackie says.

Oh, of course. Because Jude was born into wealth and a job, I should sacrifice my own life and goals? It's a ridiculous assertion that she's been making since our sophomore year of college. I didn't accept it then, and I won't accept it now.

"What sacrifices should I have made?" I ask. "To my morality or my better judgment?"

Part of me knows that I shouldn't turn this into a competition over who's right and who's wrong. Removing our history from the equation, I don't see why the two of us couldn't make it work. The only thing stopping us is how we ended things four years ago, and the lies that precipitated that.

"I was protecting my son and his reputation. He was a child."

"He was twenty," I reply. "Younger people have faced consequences for less."

Jackie rolls her eyes. "This isn't about race."

"When did I say it was?" I ask.

I was scared for him. For my friend, for my person who I saw spiraling out of control every day. The person who I thought would always be honest with me, and then he wasn't. And I was scared that the privileges his family offered would make him everything I couldn't respect, and a person I could never love.

Jackie's jaw twitches. "You wanted him to fit in with your agenda."

I almost want her to say the quiet part out loud. I know what she means by "agenda" and it's infuriating. Because I wanted him to be a better human, I'm not supportive enough?

"My agenda? You mean using his platform as a Landon to speak out against drunk driving and advocating for resources for addicts? That's wrong?"

"It's not the image we want to project."

"You don't want to project an image of helping people?" I ask.

Jackie slams her hand down on the arm of her chair, the metal from her ring causing the sound to reverberate throughout the room.

"You didn't try," Jackie says.

"You don't know what I tried," I reply. "And I don't have to justify what I did. I chose myself, yes. But I chose him too. He was inconsolable, he was erratic. We'd have eloped the next day and he would have regretted it three hours later. He wasn't himself."

The moments that play in my head almost as much as the proposal itself are the couple of minutes after. Jude was still standing in front of the casket, staring at me along with everyone else at the funeral. Before either of us could say anything else, before I could try to caveat my refusal again, Jackie pulled him away. That was the last time I saw him until the gala. I did him a service by saying no. We wouldn't have been happy. We weren't then, and we wouldn't be now.

"He loved you," she says. "He still does."

I know he did. I know he does, and it's heartbreaking. But I'm so scared to try again.

"I loved him too."

Jackie's face softens and she starts to reach out for my hand. "And? Do you still?" She pulls her hand back before she actually touches me.

Once again, I can't answer. And anyway, if I were going to answer, I should probably tell Jude before I tell his meddling mother.

"Can we please just focus on the profile?"

I don't know the answer to her question, and I don't really want to think about it enough to be able to answer. Compartmentalization is key if I'm ever going to get through the end of this profile without losing my sanity.

"Fine. Ask your little questions," Jackie replies.

I pull my audio recorder out of my pocket and place it on the arm of the seat between us.

Jackie shifts in her armchair and fiddles with her engagement ring, like Jude does with his father's wedding band. She's wearing a forest green, long-sleeved, silk wrap dress, and she adjusts the waist of the dress a couple of times. It's the first time I've ever seen her fidget.

"Mr. Landon, Julian, was pretty universally regarded as a great man both personally and professionally—"

"He was." She smirks, as if interrupting me is some kind of win.

"It's a pretty massive legacy; how do you feel Jude has handled the transition into CEO?"

Jackie exhales for what feels like thirty seconds. "As well as could be expected."

"Meaning?"

Jackie takes a sip of her tea, which must be cold by now. She crinkles her nose and places the cup back on the table.

"Meaning he struggled at first, with grief I presume, from all that he lost. Then he found his footing, and a partnership with someone suitable, before being potentially dragged down again by his past," she replies.

I open my mouth, but anything I wanted to say is cut off by clapping in the doorway. Joanna is wearing a silk pajama set, clapping while balancing a mimosa glass between her index and middle fingers. She always knows how to make an entrance, and this is the one time I didn't want her to. I was actually getting something out of Jackie. Maybe.

Jackie stands and nearly knocks over my audio recorder in the process.

"Naturally, Jude grieved our father," Joanna says. "But he also felt weighed down by the pressure to *be* our father. The change we're seeing now is him realizing that he doesn't have to be Julian Landon."

Jackie holds her hand up and waves it in the air. "No," she says. "That's not accurate, strike it from the record."

Joanna rolls her eyes. "We're not in court, Mother." She moves some of her caramel brown–highlighted hair out of her face and I catch a glimpse of Jackie's first engagement ring on her finger.

I can make lemonade out of lemons here. Joanna will at least give me something real. She's the family wild card.

"So, in both of your opinions, what has been the pinnacle of Jude's professional development thus far?" I ask.

Jackie shoots me a pointed look. "Partnering with our dear family friend Kaitlyn Franklin to truly change the world."

Joanna smiles. "I think that it is, in some way, this profile."

"Could you elaborate?" I ask, before I let my brain really process what she's trying to say.

Joanna takes another swill of her mimosa and holds up her index finger while she wipes her mouth with her other hand.

"Jude has been so private for the last few years because he was afraid that if he was open with his true goals and desires that he wouldn't be taken seriously," she says.

There's my outstanding question. I still don't know Jude's true goals and desires, professionally or personally. He's changed, he's grown, but I still feel like there's something missing. I don't know everything I need to to decide how I feel about him staying in my life.

"And now he is," Jackie replies. "Put that in."

Messing with Jackie must be exhausting. At least with her eyes closed, Joanna can't see Jackie rolling hers repeatedly in her direction. It would be fun if it wasn't keeping me from actually being able to do my job. I could be here all day, as if I don't have other articles.

Joanna sits up again. "This profile will give him the social and professional capital to push forward the agenda he's interested in pursuing."

"Which is?" I ask.

"Actually helping people beyond those in our tax bracket," Joanna says.

Jackie clears her throat. Apparently mentioning taxes is a major faux pas. "I think that's enough for today," Jackie says. "We can send statements to your . . . press email?"

Why does she have to say it like that? I'm a member of the press, I have a press email. God, she's annoying. I definitely haven't missed her.

"Of course," I reply. "Thank you for your time." I pull out one of my few business cards, printed during my first month at the *Tribune*, and lay it on the table.

Jackie slides it underneath the *People Magazine* and turns her head to Julian's bust.

Joanna stands and holds out her arm. "Genevieve, darling, let me walk you out."

"Thank you," I say. "And thank you for the interview, Mrs. Landon."

Jackie rolls her eyes for what must be the seventieth time since I arrived. I consider rolling my eyes back, but that would be petty and unprofessional.

"She'll come around," Joanna whispers in my ear. "As long as you do."

"I have most of what I need for the profile," I say. "So I don't know about that."

"You never answered her question," she replies. "About loving Jude."

So she *was* listening in. Of course. Why does everyone need me to declare my love right now? I'm taking my time. My feelings can wait. They have to, because if they get in the way of this profile, who knows what will happen.

"I'd probably tell him before you."

I still love my Jude, to some degree. But this Jude? I'm still feeling him out. Most of our interactions have been either emotionally charged or professional. Usually both. But now that the profile's wrapping up, maybe I'll actually get to know current Jude. I want to, just a little. But even though it can't be worse than last time, I'm scared I'll still end up broken.

CHAPTER TWENTY-FOUR

Mr. Jay sends me off with a dozen chocolate chip coconut cookies, and I drive toward the *Tribune* offices while nibbling on one. I pull into the parking garage, squeezing between an Escalade that's slightly over the line and a Mercedes that is parked so close to the wall that the front is practically kissing the concrete.

I slip the wrapped cookies into my work bag and jog over into the building. I have a couple of usable tidbits, mostly in what Joanna said, to use for the profile, but overall, the meeting was a bust. Minus Mr. Jay, of course.

Before I can even sit down at my desk, Clara slams a copy of today's paper down, squealing.

"Um. Good morning?" I say.

"You *need* to get a quote about this," she says, opening to the gossip section.

Taking up half the page is a photo of Jude and Kaitlyn, leaning into each other over what looks like a seafood tower.

Jude's allergic to shellfish and Kaitlyn was once quoted as saying she "doesn't do anything that would compromise my French tips." They're just playing into the speculation at this point. And even though I know she isn't interested in him, it still stings. He just gets to be out there with her for everyone to see, not even a little embarrassed. Jackie must be thrilled. And that was something we never had.

He was never embarrassed to be seen with me, but he noticed the looks we got throughout our relationship. *What does she have that I don't,* with the thinly veiled veneer of jealousy, covering up their real reaction: shock and anger that a prominent white man like him would choose someone who didn't look like them. Their bubble always bursts, and I'm the needle that pops it. With someone like Kaitlyn, he'd never have to worry about that.

"They're old friends," I reply. "Nothing quotable there."

"My roommate is a body language expert, and she totally saw something there," Clara says.

A body language expert by day and Fellini's hostess by night. What a double life. I wonder what her expert opinion was when she saw Jude and I leave the restaurant together. Even if we looked cozier than expected, neither she nor Clara would ever think I could land him.

I can't dismantle every system at play here, but I can try to show everyone who doesn't believe I should be associated with Jude Landon that I'm actually an asset to his image, instead of a detriment. I can't wait to write an amazing profile and show all of them that I deserve to be here.

But why do I have to prove that to them? Why do I want to?

Is constantly feeling the need to prove herself why Jennifer left?

I have to choose to write the best profile for *me*. I want to write something I can be proud of, with as few strings attached as possible. Even if I don't agree with how Jude got me the profile, I can appreciate that this is the first article where I don't have Adam breathing down my neck, waiting for me to mess up. Jude made sure of that. And now I can cover Kaitlyn too, once Adam clears it. I imagine she'd have more opinions on her coverage, but I can still do what I want to do.

"I'll investigate," I reply.

"Maybe go undercover on a dating app or something. Would he be on Bumble or Raya?" Clara asks.

"I'm going to guess neither, but who knows."

"I'm just throwing material your way," she replies, winking at me.

There's a squeeze in my chest as I think of Jude on a dating app. Would it be CEO Jude, or the real one? Is his profile picture him in a suit or jeans? Does he pretend to be a regular dude with a mid-level job, or does he fully lean into his untold environmental fortune?

Shit. It's not like his dating impacts me. I'm still technically on apps too, even if I haven't felt compelled to open one since the night of the gala.

"Well, between a few of us we've got all the apps covered, so I'm sure we'd have seen him," I say.

"Ugh. I wish. Would you swipe right or left?" she asks. "For me, right all the way, baby."

"Depends on the day," I reply. "Anyway, I'd better get back to this. Especially if I'm going to have to add a dating apps addendum to the profile."

"If you publish his full dating app profile, I will copyedit every piece you write for the rest of time."

Okay, that might be too good to pass up. If he doesn't have one already, I bet I could get him to make one as a favor.

The second Clara is back at her desk, I whip out my phone and text Jude.

Seafood tower?? What kind of epi pen are you working with now?

I take a deep breath before pressing send. It's a little too familiar, almost. He once thought he'd accidentally eaten a piece of shrimp, and his EpiPen was empty. Oliver talked him down from his panic, and I sprinted through the rain to grab the backup. I didn't even make it back to the dining hall before Oliver figured out that what Jude thought was a piece of shrimp was just an imperfectly cooked piece of fish. We laughed about it later, but in the moment all I could think about was the possibility of losing him. Then I did, sort of, just a few weeks later.

The kind that protects you from photo ops arranged by your mother. Seafood tower was a very niche in-joke.

I hope they at least donated the food, or Landon Energy is about to get blasted in the press. Not his hometown newspaper, of course, but it could definitely get covered the next county over.

Not niche enough, if I figured it out. Gotta figure out your rich guy eccentricities a little better.

Maybe I wanted you to figure it out.

Figure it out because he thought it was funny? Or figure it out so I could be sure he wasn't on a date, if I didn't recognize Kaitlyn? I still haven't figured out if I want to know the answer to that one.

Well, speaking of potential dates . . . , I text. *I've got an offer I can't refuse.*

I am NOT doing that column where you all profile first dates. I would rather choke on a shrimp.

Well, you can't do the column because I'd need it on tape. When you blush, your face is the same color as your hair. ☺

Diving into emojis, it feels like we're moving quickly, but also not at all. It's still a little exciting, like we're dancing around something akin to a friendly acquaintanceship.

So, what about the date? This offer is sounding pretty meh so far.

If you let me put your dating app profile in the Tribune, one of my coworkers will copyedit all of my pieces forever. So, do a girl a solid?

That would require me to actually have a dating profile. Which I've never had. So . . .

So . . . does he just have women in different area codes? How is he meeting anyone in a town of 200,000 that has his last name featured on several landmarks? The idea that he is solely relying on Jackie as his matchmaker is chilling.

Well, I think you should take a gamble for all of us and see who's on Raya in the area. You're definitely famous and eligible enough to be approved, I reply.

Are you TRYING to get me coupled up? What's the angle here? Or is this all for a story?

Before I can answer, a text from Adam interrupts us. He's finally ready to talk about my next project.

Regina is off getting Adam's midmorning tea, so I don't even have her to listen in.

"So, you're already jonesing for a new project. Love to see the ambition," Adam says.

"Yes. I was actually approached for two stories on a local businesswoman, one on her most recent environmental venture and the other on being a queer woman in a heterosexist environment," I reply.

"And how were you approached?" Adam asks.

"She knows Jude Landon and has appreciated some of my recent work."

Adam swallows. Like he's physically uncomfortable with this turn of events.

Why is this a bad thing? I'm bringing in new stories with my renewed personal connections. Shouldn't he be thrilled?

"Well, it's important to keep your objectivity," he says. "Who is the businesswoman?"

"Of course. It's Kaitlyn Franklin. She and I don't have any kind of personal history; she just enjoyed my approach."

"Hmm. Well, we wouldn't want it to look like you're in the pocket of the Landons," he replies.

"What do you mean?"

Clara has written four articles about the founders of a local hedge fund in the last year and a half without being accused of being in anyone's pocket. Heather has covered her now-fiancé's start-up. Even Adam has cultivated long-term professional relationships with prominent businesspeople. He's going to need to spell it out. I want it on the record.

"I'm just saying how it could look to our readership, not what I think," he says. "You've barely had any articles, then you start covering the Landons and get assigned a lot of new pieces? It could look like you're trading something for stories."

"And what exactly would it look like I'm trading?" I ask. Is he seriously implying what I think he is? That I'm sleeping my way into stories?

"Oh, people make up all sorts of things. But this is about your integrity."

My integrity. My integrity should be fucking sparkling since he's never allowed it the opportunity to be tested. And what would Adam know about integrity? He's the one who only let me have this story in an attempt to entrap Jude into an ongoing relationship with the *Tribune*.

"How is this any different than your relationship with the Marks family over in shipping, or Clara's with the Thompsons who own the hedge fund?" I ask.

Adam sighs. "Racism. You're looked at differently, so we have to protect you. Imagine if anyone thought you were currently sleeping with him."

Protecting me? Is that what he thinks he's been doing here with this blatant HR violation? Who I'm sleeping with—or not—is none of his business, and certainly isn't relevant to how I perform my job. I could report him for this. But would they believe me? Would he spin it?

"Why would anyone think I was sleeping with my subject?" I ask. "If our past has been explained."

Adam holds his hands up and looks at me as if I'm the one being irrational.

"Come on, Gen, I'm on your team. If you think you can write a good story, have it on my desk to run in the next Sunday section. But don't be surprised if you get some pretty nasty reactions online. People make assumptions."

So . . . because *racism*, I'm going to get backlash for doing my job? And people will think I can only sleep my way to stories? That sounds about right, from my experience in this field. But Adam's idea of protecting me is just not letting me write? What is the logic in that?

"Well, what are you anticipating?" I ask.

"Look at you, being a real journalist. Asking *all* the questions. I love it!" he replies.

That's not an answer, but okay. I'll bite, despite his condescending tone.

"Well, isn't backlash something that the paper would address? Perhaps through a letter from the editor, or statements of support from my colleagues?" I ask.

"Well, we can't change hearts and minds. Just report the facts."

"I would actually argue that we can do both, *by* reporting the facts," I reply.

Why is he even in journalism if he thinks we're just soulless harbingers of the truth, without a lick of context? Why would he want to take over a local paper founded by immigrants who revealed the inhumane conditions their neighbors were suffering in meatpacking plants in the 1880s? The *Tribune* was created to call out injustices. And now it's just another paper run by white people for white people, without a care in the world for people who look like me.

He's not going to budge. But then again, neither can I. Now that people are actually willing to trust me with their stories, how can I turn away from that? And how can Adam expect me to? Just so I, and by extension the paper, will appear seamless.

As I go back to my desk, I wonder if I just stepped out of line. But then again, where is the line? And why does it only seem to have been drawn for me?

I'm actually excited. About my new opportunities, even about the profile. At the very least, it's allowed me to search for some semblance of closure with Jude, who isn't the boogeyman I've made him out to be over the last four years. Plus, it turns out he's actually doing some groundbreaking work, with people who could also be interested in talking with me.

Jennifer,

I am so happy to hear from you! Thank you for your kind words. I always admired you, and you were a big reason why I came to the Tribune. I would love to catch up—on or off the record as well. In addition, if you're open, I would really like to know why you felt leaving was your best option. I'm weighing my own, and I'm torn between what I always dreamed of accomplishing here versus what might actually be feasible. Thank you for reaching out!

Sincerely,
Gen

I press send.

It's then that I realize I have another message to send, a reply to Jude.

If you make a profile, I'll show you mine? Little quid pro quo situation? I text.

Well, I'd need help. An embarrassing amount of help. Wanna assist over dinner? Maybe tonight? he responds.

I should say I have plans, so I sound less pathetic. He already knows I'm single, and we're still wrapping up the profile. Nothing can happen—not that I want it to. Things are going well with us right now. We're . . . friends. That's good. Safe.

It's not like we'd have the same choice in apps anyway. So who can it hurt? Right?

Sure. Where were you thinking? I respond.

I'll meet you in the Tribune lobby at 6. It's a surprise.

But it's not a date. I'm pretty sure. Though I'm not entirely sure I would mind if it were.

CHAPTER TWENTY-FIVE

Jude has never been the most inconspicuous of men, given that he's taller than a solid number of other guys, and a redhead. It certainly doesn't help that now he's actually fashionable, and in possession of a respectable amount of somewhat flashy men's jewelry, courtesy of his late father. But never has he been more obvious than when he's trying to situate himself just out of view, wearing a beanie he's had since seventh grade, checking his phone behind a pillar in the lobby.

Luckily for him, most people have left already, and no one appears to recognize him.

"You're a real James Bond," I say.

"Suave, handsome, mysterious?" he asks. "I'll take it."

"Oh. You missed my sarcasm."

"I didn't, I just wanted to see if I could get you to call me suave," he replies.

"Oh God, never."

He could have gotten me to call him *handsome*, but I'll keep that to myself. Especially given the beanie. There are kids going to middle school who are younger than that thing. I can't encourage him.

As we leave the lobby, I wonder where he's taking me. Fellini's isn't within walking distance, and I don't see a nondescript black car waiting for us. He nods in the direction of Vernon Square, which leads to the arts district in town. For someone wearing loafers on the wet sidewalk, he's moving pretty quickly, and I have to jog to keep up with him.

Jude stops in front of a staircase that leads down to an underground door. He smiles halfway, as if he's unhappy to have to say whatever he thinks he has to.

"I'm not leading you into any kind of perilous situation," he says.

"To be fair, that's exactly what someone leading you into a perilous situation would say," I reply. "What is this place?"

"A cocktail bar. It has like sixteen seats, very low-key and quiet usually." After he notices my face he adds, "It has excellent food, and an extensive mocktail list with locally sourced ingredients."

The place is dimly lit, but right away I see that the walls are covered in African art. The first wall is full of beautiful works of dark-skinned Black women as literal queens, sitting on thrones, being fawned over by men and women alike. I look at another wall and there are stunning landscapes of civilizations in Africa making their own art, their own inventions. There are only two other people here, sitting at the bar and chatting with the bartender, a Black woman. I'm in awe. This is maybe the most perfect restaurant I've ever stepped foot in.

"The owner, Miss Isis," Jude whispers to me, leading me to a table in the corner of the restaurant.

"It's like a Black speakeasy," I say. "How did *you* find this place?"

"Oh, just because I'm white I can't be attuned to a soul-food restaurant off the beaten path?"

I roll my eyes. "Do you even eat fried food anymore?"

"Only Miss Isis's," he replies.

Miss Isis winks at him and grabs two menus from underneath the bar. She's already mixing something. When she raises her eyebrows, Jude nods at her and cocks his head toward me. He must be a regular. I wonder how often he brings a guest. Though if his dating pool is exclusively determined by Jackie's whims, there's no way he could bring a date here.

I can't believe I've never heard of this place. Each drink is named after a groundbreaking Black woman, and features a complementary mocktail option. The menu is limited but features most of my favorite foods. I never want to leave.

Miss Isis drops off our drinks and a basket of sweet potato biscuits. She squeezes Jude's shoulder and gives me a polite smile.

"Miss Isis, this is Genevieve Francis. We're old friends, and she's profiling me for the *Tribune*. Gen, this is Miss Isis, the owner, mixologist, and chef extraordinaire of Isis's place," Jude says.

"This place is amazing. How long have you been here?" I ask.

"About eight months," she replies.

Something passes between her and Jude that I can't quite quantify. Whatever it is, they're far more familiar than I would expect for a restaurant owner and customer.

"Well, I can't wait to try everything. You have cornered the market on almost all of my comfort foods," I reply, then gesture at my glass. "Which mocktail is this?"

Jude clears his throat. "It's off-menu. I come here most days after work when I'm in town, and get to try Miss Isis's latest creations."

"I'll go grab you all a selection of menu items," Miss Isis says, disappearing back behind the bar.

Jude slides the basket of sweet potato biscuits over to me, his eyebrows raised.

The first bite is brown-buttered perfection, and each subsequent taste leaves me wanting more. I'm going to need a standing order of these, every day for the rest of my life. Oliver is going to get an earful when I get home because, number one, I want him to try and re-create these, and number two, he's supposed to know all of the cool restaurants, especially if they're Black-owned.

"You never mentioned how you found this place," I say.

"Miss Isis worked for Landon Energy. She quit about a year ago to open her dream restaurant."

His humbleness is almost endearing because it's sincere. Opening a restaurant, especially in the middle of town, isn't cheap. "Ah. You're a silent investor," I reply.

"Well, it's not silent when you announce it to the entire restaurant," he says.

The handful of people inside are looking at us, but not like we're rarities in a museum. We're just normal, slightly loud people enjoying a restaurant where Jude is a regular. I've always wanted a local Black-owned restaurant with the kind of foods I ate at summer family reunions. And now there is one, because Jude was willing to put his money where his mouth is and invest in Black entrepreneurs. Here, in this restaurant, there is nothing disjointed about us being together.

"Why this place? I'm sure you get opportunities to invest in local businesses all the time," I ask.

I think I already know the answer, but I want to hear him say it. When we were together and dreaming of our future, I always wanted to use whatever share of the Landon money we had to invest back in the communities that money had been made on the backs of. Jude was tentatively supportive of the idea back then, but he didn't fully understand why I was pushing for it. There are so few ways to ethically make the kind of money the Landons have had for generations. The least I felt he could do was spend some of it trying to make the world a better place.

"I do, and I take a lot of them. Yet another reason why the board doesn't love me, even though it's my money, not the company's." He rubs his forehead.

"But this one?"

"My ancestors founded this town and relegated groups of people, mostly formerly enslaved Black people, to what is now Drier Park. The town council will never agree on formal reparations, so I try to do it informally with local Black-owned businesses. This one was a no-brainer. Honestly, I don't even care if it turns a profit," he says.

I feel a rush of pride that he's finally doing what I always wanted, using his family wealth and connections for good. And then there's that twinge, that spark. My career is finally picking up, and he's using his platform in a way I'm deeply aligned with. This is what I wished for the night of the gala.

"I will personally empty my bank account to make sure this place stays in business," I reply.

He smiles. "I know. That's why I chose it."

I thought . . . I thought he chose it for the overall societal message. Sure, I was a part of his awareness of that, but not the only reason. "What?"

"An Afrocentric, female empowerment–themed, comfort food–filled, Black-owned speakeasy. The moment I read Miss Isis's proposal, I knew it was a place you'd love," he says.

We weren't even speaking, we weren't even in each other's orbit, and he funded a restaurant because he knew that I would love it. He wanted it to exist just so I could find comfort in eating here. He was always on my side, even when it didn't feel like it to me.

"What were you going to do if I showed up one night? If I found it without you?" I ask.

"I'm surprised you didn't, honestly. But, of course, I was planning to hide in a corner with my trusted normal-guy baseball cap on, and work up the courage to beg for your forgiveness. And buy you a drink. Probably a po'boy too for good measure. And some beignets to go if you were still really mad."

He's always known the way to my heart, and more importantly my stomach. Though the idea that he could get past me with a baseball cap on is laughable. I'd know him anywhere.

"What if I never came? Would you still fund it?" I ask.

He shoots me a look, and I realize he's annoyed with the question.

"Of course I would. I'm not as big of an asshole as you think I am. This is a real commitment for me. I would have funded this place anyway, because Miss Isis is fabulous and so many people do and will love this place. But, in my heart, I wanted it here so *you* could love it. So you would have someplace to sneak off to after work. When your articles weren't being published. When you were sick of being around white gatekeepers," he says.

I don't think he's an asshole at all, and now I feel a little guilty. Still, I almost can't believe that he'd do all of this because of me—*for* me. But can I really accept this at face value? How could this gesture be anything other than incredibly romantic? This is basically the biggest declaration of love I could think of.

"You realize that technically you're a white gatekeeper, right?"

His jaw twitches. "Yes, I do. And if seeing me here threatened to ruin this place for you, I'd truly become a silent investor. I'm not intentionally making your life harder; I just really suck at romantic and professional overtures," he says.

There's a flutter in my chest. "Trust me, you don't," I reply. "I love it. I really do. And I love how you're using your platform."

He smiles again, almost sadly this time, and I wonder what he's thinking. Maybe it's the same as what I'm wondering. I don't know if we'd be here, in a restaurant like this, if we'd stayed together. Maybe we needed to break up and grow apart before coming back together, even if it sucked.

Miss Isis whips by the table, almost silently, dropping off a sampler of the entire menu.

If this dinner wasn't designed to absolutely obliterate my stomach, in the best way, I'd think this was a date. A really promising one.

The only thing that seems less promising is Jude's face right now. He should be thrilled, if this is what he wanted. But he's not, and I don't know why. One of the cracks he left in my heart threatens to split open again, a hairline fracture of whatever stability it feels like we're starting to build in this relationship.

As if he can sense that I'm going to pull away, he says, "I'm scared that you're holding back—not because of the profile, but because you're still waiting for me to publicly admit my alcoholism, and the accident."

I almost wish that were the reason. Four years later, I have a better understanding of how difficult that would be for Jude, publicly, given that his recovery has been almost entirely private and insular to only a handful of people. I can't ask him to make that part of himself available for everyone to consume and judge. He's addressed it within himself, he's changed his behavior, and is using his persona in other ways. The only person he hasn't addressed it with is Oliver, and that isn't my apology to accept.

Here, in Isis's Place, I feel at home with him. I could say anything, pop open the top button of my rapidly shrinking work pants while we eat like we would in college, even kiss him across the table. But this bubble of just us two isn't who we are out in the real world. Especially not now. We can't even pretend to be on the same level, and I can't figure out how to reconcile the woman I want to be, the career I want to have, with being the partner or even friend that Jude needs.

"That isn't why," I reply, lowering my voice. "I'm just trying to figure some things out."

"Like?" He doesn't waver in his eye contact, like it's a challenge.

I sigh. "Like whether I really want the pressure of being in your orbit. Even as a friend. It didn't end so well last time."

He swallows, his eyes looking sad. "Well, aren't we different?" he asks.

Are we? I don't feel so different right now. And that's exactly what scares me. I look away, toward the art on the walls.

"I hope so," I reply.

Jude gently touches my arm across the table. "You don't think we could work through this together? Even as friends?"

I turn my head back toward him. "No one would respect me. They'd think I'm only getting articles because of you. Even if that's true," I reply. "Even if it's platonic. No one thinks that I even belong in your orbit."

"You're getting articles because you deserve them. I don't know why it took so long for them to see that, but they finally do. I hate how you put yourself down because a small group of people have told you that you don't matter, or you don't belong." He looks indignant at the idea that I could think I don't deserve any of this.

I hate it too. I hate that racism makes me feel like a burden, even to myself. It's not enough that I have to manage everyone else's reactions to me, I'm the one dealing with the constant guilt of letting it run my life. It's the most profound experience of gaslighting, embedded in my own brain from a life of trying to navigate almost all-white spaces.

I do matter. What I want matters. But what I want doesn't negate the societal circumstances we're in right now.

"I'm sorry, Jude. I can't do this right now," I say. "Thank you for dinner, and for finding this place. But I have to go."

He stands, like he's going to come running after me. But he doesn't. Just like in the graveyard, he doesn't follow.

CHAPTER TWENTY-SIX

The next morning, I'm almost late to work for the first time in three years. I didn't sleep. I couldn't. God, it feels just like it did before. I'm sick to my stomach and my chest feels like it's splitting open. Fuck. But I know I'm doing the right thing. I have to put some distance between us, so I don't end up hurt again. So I'm not completely broken in both my personal and professional lives.

My phone begins to buzz, and I reach into my bag to find it. I stand over to the side of the building door and answer it after eight or nine rings. Before I can even say anything, Regina starts talking at me.

"You need to get up here, now," she says.

"I'm in the parking garage, give me a minute."

"You don't have a minute," she whispers.

My phone buzzes with a text from her.

Adam's giving the Landon profile to Lucy.

My heart stops. What the fuck? One bad moment and they take me off the piece? So much for Jude only wanting to do the profile with me. Well, there it is. He took it away. I don't even get a chance, after everything both Adam and Jude have put me through. It's not fucking fair. I'm the one who put in the work. This was *mine*.

I rush past security, who wave me through toward the elevators. I press the button and fiddle with my watch as I wait for the elevator to come down. It shoots up to the seventh floor instead and I decide to risk the stairs. I sprint up the first two flights and find myself fading by the third. By the time I drag myself up the fourth flight I'm dry heaving and sweating a bit.

I'm not allowed to have a panic attack right now, even though I know it's coming on. I have to stand my ground. This is *my* story, and no one should be able to take it from me except Jude himself.

I've got to hold it together, just for a few minutes. Just until I can figure out what happened and talk to Adam.

The Fates approach me the second I reach the doorway.

"I've done the work," I say. "I've conducted the interviews and research, and Ju . . . Mr. Landon is comfortable with me writing the profile."

"Well, clearly, something's changed," Lucy says. "Come on, I'll still give you some credit. But this is an incredible opportunity. Don't you want that for me?"

"No, actually," I reply. "I want it for myself, because I'm the one who has been drafting it. I brought sources in. I deserve to see it through—wouldn't you want that for *me*?"

"Look, I didn't want to say anything, but rumor has it your relationship got a little less than professional, and that's why Adam wants me to take over. Sorry to be the one to tell you," Lucy says.

She's not sorry. Of course she isn't. They could all play fake nice when they thought I had a lucrative connection. But now I'm back to being no better than the gum underneath their shoes based on some unsubstantiated rumors.

I notice Regina, pretending to take a TikTok, videoing us. She's always taking notes of the microaggressions, saving emails. But now Lucy's nails are digging into my arm in front of the entire newsroom, and it looks like this is moving from micro to just plain aggression.

"You got what you wanted. Just leave me alone," I say.

I put my face in my hands. Even if it wasn't my choice, at first, I was actually excited to write this profile, and maybe change the public perception of someone the world doesn't really know. And it brought me back to Jude. I never knew how much I wanted that until it happened. How much I wanted the world, and myself, to know him. Even though now it really really hurts.

Jude isn't spiteful. He never has been. Sure, he used to be reactionary, sometimes due to the alcohol, but he's never intentionally mean. He wouldn't have taken away the profile. And if he was going to, for some reason, he would have told me. This is all Adam, but why? And does Jude know?

I sniffle and wipe the tear that's formed at the edge of my eye.

With everyone staring at me, I knock on Adam's office door. He's going to have to see me. He's going to have to face me on this.

"Look, I didn't want to do it, but I had to," Adam says as I enter.

"Excuse me? You *had* to after I put in all the work. Why?"

Adam smirks and slides a manila folder over to me. He's reveling in this. He never wanted me to have the profile anyway.

I flip the folder open. It's full of photos. Grainy photos of me and Jude in the car after we left Fellini's. Photos that look like . . .

"Oh come on, do you really believe this?" I ask.

"Photos don't lie. And these really do tell a thousand words. Was this the start, or has the affair been going on this whole time?" He glares at me.

No. Just because it *looks* like we could be kissing in these photos doesn't mean we're having an affair. I don't even remember what happened here. He probably dropped a napkin or something and was leaning over to grab it off my seat. Or he was trying to pick up a tomato from our bruschetta that fell on my shirt. Nothing happened.

I point at the top picture. "He's leaning over, sure, but you can't prove contact."

"This isn't a police investigation, Gen. It doesn't matter if it did or didn't happen. It appears it did, which means that you doing the profile is officially a liability for the paper. Imagine how this would look if you not only dated him before but are currently sleeping with him, *your subject*. Major ethics violation."

I feel angry heat rising up my face. "Is it not a major workplace violation to speculate on your subordinate's sex life without proba- ble cause? What would HR say?"

Adam laughs, his eyes cold. "I'll take my chances. Pretty sure they wouldn't look favorably on you either."

He flips to the last photo in the stack, which is just blurry enough to look like Jude and I are kissing.

"We didn't do anything," I say firmly.

"Frankly, I don't care," he replies. "What matters now is how it looks."

"Does Jude know?"

"No. I'll let you tell him. This is on you and your actions."

This isn't right, on so many levels. There's more to this story, there's got to be.

"I'm going to fight against this, Adam. I earned this profile," I say.

"You're talented, for sure," he says. "But knowing Jude Landon personally gave you a leg up in this instance. You still need to prove yourself here if you want other assignments like this in the future."

Well, there it is. He finally admitted it. That he doesn't think I should have gotten the profile. That he never would have considered me for this kind of opportunity. That wherever I am on the ladder, it's not enough. And even Jude couldn't change that.

CHAPTER TWENTY-SEVEN

Mickey and I decide that it's in our best interest to do Thirsty Thursday from the safety of my apartment, so I can avoid running into anyone from the *Tribune*. I spent the rest of the day working in a conference room, trying to avoid making eye contact with anyone who might have seen the pictures.

Oliver stops shaking the margaritas when I lay my keys on the kitchen counter.

"Hey guys," I say. "You're both home? At six?"

"A once in a blue moon occurrence," Eva says. "Mickey texted about Thirsty Thursday. She just left school fifteen minutes ago."

"Ah," I reply. "It's a party."

Mickey texting a friend group-wide Thirsty Thursday message means that she knows something is super wrong. All I told her was that I had a bad day and didn't want to chance seeing any of my coworkers at Tía Rosa's.

"Mickey's picking up pizzas and cheesy garlic knots from Sal's," Oliver replies.

"You got dinner with Jude? I need you to spill," Eva says. She takes a deep breath and pats herself on the chest. "I've been holding that in this whole time."

I was shocked she didn't text me earlier, given that we've been on opposite schedules for the past couple of nights. We're not the closest of friends, but she's been heavily invested in the will they/won't they of this Jude situation. I think it's a fun distraction for her from spreadsheets and budget projections. Plus, when you're the one in a stable, healthy relationship, I bet a front row seat to the Gen and Jude saga is like witnessing a psychological experiment in real time.

Eva has legitimately told me that she believes in past lives, and that she senses that Jude and I have been together throughout history. I don't know what other storylines she's come up with, but she may have to write a novel.

I could just leave it here. I could say dinner with Jude was fine, mostly business. Pretend I never walked out, that I never told him I didn't want to be in his orbit anymore. Act like the profile got taken away for some other reason than the nature of our now nonexistent relationship.

There's an urgent knock at our door. It's Mickey, who is balancing three big pizza boxes, and three smaller boxes on top of those, in one hand.

She moves the knocking hand back under the biggest boxes and speed-walks over to the kitchen counter even though there's no way she can see. When she catches me watching her, she snorts.

"It's called sense memory," she says. "My friends' home is like my home, so I just feel the kitchen counter in my bones."

"It's totally a thing," Eva replies.

Oliver and I exchange a glance before he pulls four plates down from our cabinet. Eva catches us and I see her purse her lips together instead of calling us out.

Mickey opens one of the containers of garlic knots and takes a full seven-second inhale. She picks one up, turns it over in her hand, and then holds it close to her face and smells it. She takes a bite, and the cheese inside stretches out as she pulls the remains away from her.

"It's perfect," she says. "This is a work of art."

Eva puts one of the garlic knots on a plate and cuts into it with a fork and knife. She ignores the look of bewilderment that Mickey shoots her as she tastes a small piece, using her fork to put it in her mouth. "Mmm," she says.

"With a *fork*?" Mickey asks.

"You say this every time," Eva says. "I don't like getting my hands covered in garlic and oil. Hence why *Oliver* is the chef."

"You don't get to stretch the cheese if you use a fork," Mickey adds. "Which is a critical part." She hands me a plate with a garlic knot.

The knot almost melts in my mouth, and I feel myself beginning to salivate as I pull the second half of it away and the cheese stretches out several inches. No sooner do I finish the knot than I notice that everyone is watching me, even though Mickey has pushed open the pizza boxes.

"Mickey's here, so you have to tell us now," Eva says.

"Spare not a single detail," Mickey says.

"Especially if you're back together—like you secretly made up?" Eva says.

I may need Eva to make a conspiracy board, bits of string and all, because I am absolutely not following her logic train. Is that what it's like to be optimistic? You just invent good out of a situation that is decidedly negative? It absolutely couldn't be me; I'll stick it out in my negativity and try to turn it around with concrete results. Plus, after those pictures, anyone thinking that we secretly made up is just another dig of the knife.

Oliver shakes his head and grabs another slice of pizza. "Have you talked to him since the speakeasy?"

"No. And I don't really have a reason to now," I reply.

"It couldn't have been *that* bad," Eva says. "Surely you two can figure it out before the profile comes out?"

Forgiveness can be good, I suppose. My heart is already tugging me in that direction, even if my brain still wants to fight against it. I have valid reasons for not wanting to be enmeshed in the Landon world anymore. But I actually enjoyed the time I got to spend with him. I missed my friend. I missed the love we shared.

"Adam took the profile away because someone took photos of us where it looks like we're kissing," I say.

Oliver's eyes widen. "Are you kidding?"

"No. Apparently there's some evidence of impropriety, even though we haven't done anything. The pictures are grainy but they can be misinterpreted."

"Are you serious?" Mickey replies. "I *know* they're not fucking with a Black woman's success. Hell no. Are we finally picketing outside the building? Hell, *both* buildings?"

Mickey has wanted to incite a protest about the *Tribune*'s treatment of me for the last two years. She's come up with a series of poster slogans and hashtags that I've never found the courage to whip out. Maybe now, if I link up with Jennifer, we can do it. I've never participated in a protest, only reported from the front lines. Maybe now is my time.

"You okay?" Oliver asks.

"No. Even though being able to write about anything and anyone other than Jude would have thrilled me a few days ago, now I don't feel the same way," I reply.

We've never been great at endings, but how we left things in the speakeasy, and now with the profile, is just exceptionally bad. We were just starting to find our rhythm together after all this time. Now we're just a sad song, stuck on repeat, and I don't want to listen anymore.

"Well, maybe you should reach out, either way," Oliver says.

"What about you, Oliver? Ready to rekindle that friendship?" I ask.

Oliver shrugs. "Maybe. He's been texting me since the gala. Wanting to talk, apologizing. He voided the NDA, apparently. I haven't texted him back."

"Forgiveness lets your soul breathe easier," Eva says.

"My soul's been fine. Though he does seem different. Better," Oliver says.

He is. But maybe I'm not. Jude may be the one who engineered the circumstances of our breakup, but *I'm* the one keeping us stuck.

CHAPTER TWENTY-EIGHT

Jude must have called or texted me a thousand times over the weekend. I never answered; I even considered blocking his number entirely. He's the one who dragged me into this, and look where it's gotten me. Nothing happens to him, but I'm the one who's going to get shit about it at work on this fine Monday morning.

I don't want to think about whatever revenge fantasy the Fates have cooked up. They've already stolen my profile, my big chance to put my name on the map. I can't imagine what else they could take.

I could keep driving, past the office, past downtown, off into the upstate New York countryside. There's got to be a cabin somewhere for me to live out the rest of an idyllic reclusive life. If I can get Wi-Fi installed.

I pull into the parking garage and whip into the first spot I see. Ten minutes early; maybe I can slip in a brief meditation session. I need to be centered in something other than anger right now. I've been angry for so long, crying before and after work. Ranting to whoever will listen.

My phone rings and I accept the call on reflex. Fingers crossed it's not Jude. So much for coming in relaxed.

"Hi, Gen, I can tell you've answered, I hear your breathing," a voice says. "It's Lauren, by the way."

"Hi, Lauren, what's up?" I ask.

"You were supposed to interview Kaitlyn Franklin tomorrow, in the other timeline, but she's apparently in your office right now, like at your desk, in the newsroom. She refuses to let your colleague talk to her. I know it's early—"

"I'll be up in a couple of minutes, and I'll handle it. Thank you, Lauren."

I don't know what I'd do without Lauren giving me the heads-up that almost all the significant women in Jude's life have an agenda surrounding this profile. Even me, I guess.

The elevator doors open on the fourth floor, and I contemplate just hitting the button for the lobby and taking a sick day. Regina catches my eye from the newsroom and cocks her head toward Kaitlyn. I step out of the elevator, questioning every life decision I've made up to now.

I wipe the sweat off my forehead and take a deep breath before pushing open the door. Kaitlyn is sitting at my desk, staring at her phone, while everyone else in the office is staring at her.

The group chat, which I've been ignoring since yesterday, keeps pinging. I glance at my phone and see text after text.

Lucy says: *SOS*. Followed by Clara: *Kaitlyn. Franklin. Is. Here.* Then Heather: *Where are you?* Then Lucy again: *She won't let me talk to her?? It's MY profile. What a b.* Then they descend into a full inventory of her outfit and every makeup brand they think she's wearing. Are her earrings Tiffany's or Van Cleef & Arpels? The world may never know.

Kaitlyn looks up from her phone screen and spins around in my chair. She locks in on me and stands. She's wearing the same dress as in her picture from last night, but it's paired with a jacket and tights. If she did stay out all night, she had time to make sure her hair, which is wrapped into a tight bun that pulls the skin of her forehead back, and dewy morning makeup were impeccable before showing up here.

"I'm doing my interview today. Now. With you, not one of them." Kaitlyn waves her hand vaguely in the direction of the Fates.

"Well, another reporter is doing the profile on Jude now. I can introduce you—" I say.

"No. You're doing it." She turns to the Fates. "Any of you have an issue with that?"

Lucy starts to raise her hand, but Clara smacks it down. Jesus, how bad was it before I got here? I've never seen the Fates turn on each other, or shut each other down. It gives me a deeply petty sense of satisfaction.

"How did you know?" I whisper to Kaitlyn.

"Jude called me, livid over the pictures and Adam's actions. I know you didn't do anything, and I hate that they're perpetuating the same agenda against you that I've been a victim of," Kaitlyn says, then makes her voice louder. "And we can use that office." She points to Adam's door.

Her upper lip curls as she accidentally clocks Heather's heart-shaped diamond. Heather's hand flies to her chest, not realizing that Kaitlyn's expression is fully one of disdain.

"That's the editor's office," I reply.

"I can read," she says. "It's your office now. At least for right now."

Regina stares at me like she's witnessing a horror movie in real time and pushes open Adam's door without knocking.

Adam stands up and adjusts his belt. "Ms. Franklin, hello again," he says.

"Adam," she replies. "Genevieve and I will be using this office for our interview for the Jude Landon profile. Please vacate."

At least she said please, I guess. I feel myself heating up to at least four different body temperatures, all of them well beyond anything my body has ever felt before. I wonder who will call HR now that I have an aggressive friend.

"I'm sure Gen would be happy to take you to one of our conference rooms," Adam replies, not skipping a beat either.

Kaitlyn starts with his shoes, and her eyes slowly move up, gazing for a few seconds at each section of his body, until she reaches his face. When he begins turning red, she smiles with the caution that rich women usually use to smile at someone much poorer than they are before asking for a photo op at a charity event.

"I'm sure that a conference room is acceptable to *Genevieve*, but this office is acceptable to me. Barely. Think of it as reparations for going against Jude's wishes and taking this profile away from a supremely qualified Black woman," she replies.

Oh, Jesus, not reparations. Kaitlyn Franklin should not be making me struggle to hold in a laugh right now. Maybe she's not as bad as I thought. She certainly isn't Jackie "slavery ended centuries ago, and you should get over it" Landon.

"Plus," she continues, "you're the editor of a paper that has tried to get more than one upskirt shot of me. The least you can offer is this office."

I've never seen anyone use their gaze as a weapon of war so effectively, and I'm definitely going to practice mine in the mirror. My quality of life is going to improve so much if my face just says, "Don't fuck with me, I know what I'm doing and you'll find out about it later" from nine to five.

"I'll keep out of the way," Adam says. "Gen, go ahead."

Damn. He caved quickly. There's definitely more going on here. Who's really pulling the strings?

We switch positions, me sitting in his chair, which I have to raise several inches to put myself at eye level with Kaitlyn, and him standing in the back of the room, still darker than his usual shade of pink.

I pull the audio recorder from my pocket and place it in the middle of Adam's desk. Before I can turn it on, Kaitlyn takes my hand, and I almost find myself blushing too. Kaitlyn starts the recording herself.

"Jude has really had a transformative year as CEO," she says, without waiting for me to ask her a question. "I've known him since we were both children, and he's really come into himself."

"How—" I begin.

"I studied mechanical engineering in college with a minor in climate science," she continues. "When I graduated, he had been CEO for two years, and none of his proposals to the board had been accepted."

I nod and pretend to take notes on my lap, but it doesn't matter. She's looking above my head anyway.

"I always knew that Landon Energy was the right partnership for me, but I thought I'd just start on staff and work my way up. You know, like a normal person. But Jude had other ideas."

"Which were?" I ask.

"Like I *said*, the board had turned down all of his ideas. And he was pitching the projects of Black and Brown creators, many looking to help their own communities. So, as an experiment, I pitched the same project—a water system. But the initial proposal was . . . questionable," she replies. "The numbers were slightly off."

"Deliberately," I say.

She smiles, genuinely this time, and tips her head toward me. "The board accepted my proposal with no hesitation. So now I'm building a company, with family capital, and trying to hire as many of the innovators that Landon Energy's board rejected as possible. I was supposed to be a silent partner, with one of the creators as CEO. But word got out that I was working on this project, so I've had to become the face, at least temporarily. It seems as though one of the Landon Energy board members leaked the news to Adam here, and he published it without hesitation, without even getting a quote from me."

Adam coughs behind me. Kaitlyn's like an alien come to earth in his office.

"So, if I have this right, you started a side company, specifically comprised of Black and Brown engineers whose projects were rejected by the Landon Energy board, in your opinion unjustly. You planned to keep your involvement private, until someone leaked it to the *Tribune*, and now you're publicly the face, but you plan to turn the company over. What has been your motivation behind that, and how do you feel about coming across as the 'white savior'?"

Kaitlyn's face looks sad for a moment, before she composes herself back into neutral.

"I hate it, honestly, and I'm insecure about it. I'm a good engineer. I have some ideas that are pretty cool, but they're nothing compared to those of the people I've partnered with. Now I get the credit for their work, because a bunch of white men don't want to recognize them? I feel like a fraud," she says.

It's a remarkably vulnerable answer from someone who has largely eschewed being in the public eye. She's much cooler than I ever thought. She seems like the kind of person I'd be friends with; maybe in another life I would have found a way to fit in Jude's world with people like Kaitlyn.

"How does the Landon Energy board come into it?" I ask.

"One of the members leaked the information to Adam. They don't believe in Jude's vision, so we're out to prove them wrong. Success is the best revenge, right? Once my company is safely acquired, I plan to publicly reveal the board's racist actions with verified accounts from thirty of the engineers."

Now *that's* a story I'd want to write. That's the kind of story that gets national traction and potentially causes real change. It's the kind of story that makes careers. That wins Pulitzers.

"I imagine Jude would be wary of angering the board," I say.

"Precisely," she replies. "Jude was hesitant because he's noble. He's like his father in that way. They were and are both business purists; they *genuinely* think you can get ahead by working harder than everyone else and networking."

"You don't agree."

"I think that sometimes you have to play the game. Jude doesn't like to play games. He's quite direct, which I respect," she says.

"Some people don't like to be direct. They make decisions for others without having the courage to actually stand by their convictions. Without the moxie to actually tell the people they're screwing over that they're being fucked."

The last four years are almost worth it, now that I've seen Adam forced to feel as uncomfortable as I am on a daily basis. *Almost.*

"What else can you tell us about Jude's style as CEO?" I ask.

She sighs. "He holds himself to a higher standard than anyone I've ever met, including myself. He wants to be great, but never thinks he is."

"What do you attribute that to?" I ask.

"He walks in bigger shoes. Julian built the company from just about nothing besides a million-dollar bank loan and a few hundred thousand dollars of family capital. He made a legacy and Jude doesn't know what his legacy will be yet."

I bite my tongue, quite literally, to keep from pushing back on the "just about nothing" and million-dollar loan plus hundreds of thousands of family money.

"What do you think his legacy will be?" I ask.

"Whatever he decides," she replies. "He's an extraordinary man. Something I never thought I could give a straight white man in the one percent credit for. Certainly not any currently in this room."

Adam opens his mouth to speak, but Kaitlyn waves her hand in front of his face.

"Jude's extraordinary in his vision, limited in his execution. If you're looking for a romance, look casket-side at Genevieve here. I've heard a grotesque amount about her, and apparently, she's grossly underappreciated by this publication. Until you can't exist without her. Like now, when one of your favorite sources refuse to speak to anyone else."

"We have plenty of sources," Adam replies.

"Yeah, but I'd be a killer one. I know where the bodies are buried. And I'll only speak to her," Kaitlyn says. She turns to me. "You're a career woman in your own right who has completely blown away one of the most successful men under thirty in this country. Don't let *him* tell you who you are and what you can write. Your pieces are actually well-written and balanced, unlike the saccharine, racist dribble I see from the likes of the cackling hyenas in those cubicles."

Adam stares at me, completely dumbfounded, and I can't find it in myself to do anything besides shrug.

CHAPTER TWENTY-NINE

I wake up Tuesday morning to six texts from Jude apologizing for Kaitlyn's intrusion and asking me to call him to discuss what really happened with the profile. His texts seem to convey a mounting horror as he, in real time, processed what Kaitlyn did and realized I wasn't planning to answer immediately.

I still don't answer. And I hold back tears the whole drive to work.

When I walk into the newsroom, everyone goes quiet. The Fates are gathered in the back, and they all turn away from me as I move past them, noses upturned. As if Kaitlyn storming the office was my fault. As if they didn't already steal the profile from me. If even a fraction of this happened to any of them, we'd never hear the end of it.

No sooner do I get a few feet inside than Regina pulls me off to the side.

"Adam's out with an investor. Go into his office and pull the curtain," she whispers.

"Wha—"

"Do it."

Kaitlyn has probably made a repeat appearance and decided to be editor-in-chief for a day. She really *is* a situation, consistently, but I suppose that's what makes her an actual boss.

I follow Regina's instructions and try not to make eye contact with anyone as I pull the curtain closed. Kaitlyn isn't in here; no one is.

Regina follows me inside a few seconds later and shoves the door closed behind her.

"What is going on?" I ask. "Are you okay?"

Regina sighs. "The photos of you and Jude Landon were sent out to the entire office and the subscribers listserv."

Fuck them. Truly, fuck them. It's not about ethics or being fair. They wanted revenge because I got something they didn't. And now they have it and still want to ruin me completely.

Regina continues, "My totally off-the-record guess is that Adam sent them. Because the owner of the paper is investigating him for racism, based on an anonymous tip."

"But I didn't tell Jennifer anything. We haven't set up a time to talk," I say.

"You aren't the only Black woman who works here," she replies.

Oh shit. Regina's racism journal. She really blew it up. And potentially took Adam's career with her. What a badass move.

In an alternate universe, I could scream. I could literally banshee-screech at the top of my lungs and take a swing at the Fates' careers. I could go on a full tirade around the newsroom, exposing what each and every person here has done to me over the last four years. But I don't get that luxury. If I even cry, I lose. I have to be the strong one, the one who keeps her composure, otherwise my career is truly over. Maybe they'd even call the cops for good measure. That seems right up their alleys. Absolute fucking Karens. I hate them right now, I really do.

Every experience I've had, any boost this paper could give me, it's not worth it. It's not worth the cruelty, the mistreatment, and flat-out bullying Regina and I, and every other Black woman at the paper, have endured. And throughout it all I know that they probably wouldn't even think it's racist, because they don't have to notice. Why would you notice racism happening if it has never affected you?

"What do I do?" I ask. "Regina, please tell me what to do. Tell me who to talk to."

"You've got a meeting with the lawyers in thirty minutes. Until then, hold your head high, and don't engage. You can't afford to be labeled aggressive again too, especially not while they're sussing out whether you'll sue. Let's go."

Regina opens the door and we both step out. She sits down at her desk.

I keep my eyes on my desktop and pull up my email, where I'm included on a twenty-message thread and counting. I open the first message in the thread, from Lucy to the entire newsroom. The email has no subject; it's just the three grainy photos of Jude and me in my car outside the library.

The next message is from Clara: *Ethics????*

Then Heather: *I hate to say this but . . . what about integrity?*

Evelyn rounds out the first few messages with a simple: *Grossly unprofessional.*

They all knew about the pictures before they came out. Why now? They've had days to try and ruin my career.

The next seventeen messages are a mix of forwards that I'm cc'ed on: to human resources, to our ethics department, to the owner of the newspaper, the National Association of Black Journalists, as well as other professional organizations. They even tried to forward the photos to the *New York Times*.

I feel bile rising up in my throat.

"I didn't know there was affirmative action for car sex," Lucy whispers, loudly enough so that everyone across the nearest three cubicles can hear.

Regina digs her hand into my shoulder before I can say anything.

"Nothing is ever an affront when it's you all gaming the system. It's not even an affront when one of you actually steals an article," Regina says. "I'm certainly not going to let you take this out on someone who was just trying to do her job. The job she was asked to do over all of you until you cried fake tears about objectivity because you can't imagine writing a story about a non-white person that doesn't start with a sentence about how sad it is to not look like you."

Regina positions herself between me and the Fates, who all look various degrees of offended, as if *they're* the ones being called whores around the newsroom by their colleagues.

"Well, Adam . . . ," Heather begins.

"Well Adam, what?" While all of us were going back and forth, no one heard the newsroom door open. Adam stares down at Heather. "Don't stop on my account, Heather."

"It's unfair that she gets to sleep her way to a front-page article," Lucy says.

Adam nods. "Well, she doesn't get the front-page article, now does she? Speaking of, shouldn't you be writing?"

That's it? That's my whole defense from Adam? How did he even get this job? He's an HR nightmare hiding in plain sight. There have got to be some skeletons in his closet. If he won't defend me, if he's going to insist on letting them drag me through the mud, I'm taking him down with me. Regina already got the ball rolling.

Adam leans in toward me so only I can hear him. "It'll blow over," he says. "But maybe work from home for the rest of the week."

If I make eye contact with him, I think I might actually scream.

My cell phone begins to buzz on the desk and Jude's personal cell phone number flashes across the screen. I grab it, trying to blink back the tears that threaten to spill out.

Regina hands me my bag and pats me on the back. "We'll get through this," she whispers. "HR is already investigating, NABJ is assigning a representative to our case."

I lean into her for a moment and a tear spills over onto her shoulder. I wipe the water line off my face and hurry out of the newsroom. I wait until I'm in the hallway and there is a closed door between me and newsroom to answer the phone.

"Can this wait?" I say.

"I am so sorry that someone took pictures of us and are trying to misconstrue what was going on. I've released a statement . . ."

"It's fine."

"It's not. You're not, I can hear it," he says.

He's right, I'm not. And I'm scared to let him see me like this. I don't want to be the girl who's about to lose her job over him. The girl who's involved in several ethical investigations over a profile he wanted her to write. This doesn't feel good. Having him in my life does not feel good right now. I may have enjoyed parts of this profile but it was officially never worth it.

I hang up before either of us can say anything else. I don't know what to do, but right now, I need to think about my moves beyond Jude. My entire career depends on it.

CHAPTER THIRTY

I smell grilled cheese wafting from the kitchen less than a minute after I submit my final draft of tomorrow's article to Adam. He may be mired in an HR investigation, but I'm still the only Black woman in the office, so here I am covering a shooting in Drier Park. I open my bedroom door, my shirt maybe irrevocably wrinkled from the slouched position I typed in for five hours straight with tears streaming onto it.

Oliver is standing alone in the kitchen, sprinkling extra parmesan over the sandwich on the skillet. He came home as soon as he could after I called him from the car on my way back from the newsroom.

"My stomach is in knots," I say.

"I already made you a ginger tea," Oliver replies. "Mickey's recommendation. Though I'd maybe make a different drink choice to go with cheese."

"Where is Mickey? And Eva?" I ask.

"They figured you wanted to be alone-ish."

Alone-ish has been our code since I became editor of our college paper. Alone while writing, but near someone who can debrief with me after.

"They're at the salad place on Fifth," Oliver says. "Apparently, Helena told someone named Francine who told Rachel who told Mickey that she was going to be lesson planning there with a group of friends and anyone was welcome."

"I feel like they should just ask each other out . . . ," I say.

"Where's the fun in that?" Oliver asks. "Plus, you know Eva loves rom-coms and thought it was a sign or something."

He flips the grilled cheese onto a plate and slides it across the counter to me.

"I'm not hungry," I say. "But thank you."

"Gen code for freaking out," he replies. "I know you probably haven't eaten since breakfast. You left the Eggo wrapper out."

"What if her article is good? Like what if it's really fucking good and she gets all the credit?"

"Then she'll get a lot of attention and more articles. And have to meet the higher standards *you* set."

"Oh, of course. It'll be hard for *her*. As if tomorrow isn't going to be my last byline at the *Tribune*."

I wanted to leave, but not like this. The profile was supposed to be my way out, but now it's truly tanking my career—and I didn't even get to write it.

"You have a portfolio now. If you quit, you can still come out on top," he says.

"When my colleagues are spreading rumors that I slept my way to a story? They tried to cc the *New York Times* but the email bounced back. Like . . . what am I supposed to do here?"

"I don't know."

"Well, it's just us, so you'll have to play the Greek chorus."

Oliver shimmies his shoulders a bit and straightens up, channeling Eva's excitement and Mickey's spontaneous serious side.

"Well, Eva would say you should ask Jude for help, and that maybe it'll lead to you and Jude getting back together, the true rom-com experience. Mickey would say that you should write the profile anyway with what you have and publish it somewhere else tomorrow. Like your blog in college."

"Pretty sure I could get in trouble for that one."

"Worse trouble than you're in right now?"

"Who knows. Is this that legacy thing people talk about? Like, my children are someday going to be like, 'Wow, Mom, you write articles. So what happened to that guy who the Twitter archive says gave you your entire career?'"

"This hasn't made it to Twitter yet," Oliver says. "Eva combed through it on her lunch break. Only the newsroom seems to know."

What kind of paparazzo would only send pictures to a local newspaper staff? They were never going to run them. Unless . . . of course. One of the Fates somehow saw me outside of Fellini's and showed Adam the photos so he would take the profile away. But the photos were innocuous and Adam practically admitted as much to me . . .

Something is up. Just because some pictures went marginally public, everyone is freaking out? Either those aren't the only pictures someone found, or there's someone else involved here. But who else would try to get the profile taken away?

I blink back tears just as a knock reverberates throughout the apartment. Eva has, in the past, made some very convincing flow-charts of current people who she thinks were historical figures in a previous life. Maybe she has a theory on this too and how it can all turn out okay. I'd like to hear that theory.

Oliver motions for me to finish my grilled cheese and turns the stove off.

"Who is it?" I ask.

He opens the door and takes a few steps back, his eyes apologetic. There are footsteps behind him.

Jude follows Oliver inside, looking around the room until he spots me. He smiles, and turns back to Oliver.

My heart stops. He's here. He didn't let me just walk away again. Jude is keeping his promises. But what does that mean now that everything has officially blown up in our faces? Again.

I should have been honest on the phone. But I couldn't. I needed a second to process without him muddying everything. I had to figure out if I still wanted to fight for the profile, for my job, or if I wanted to hand in my resignation tomorrow. And if I talked to him, I knew I'd fight for the profile despite myself. Because my stupid heart doesn't want to stay consistent with my head. Or my frustration.

"I'd love to catch up," Jude says to Oliver.

"Give me time. I'll give you two the room," Oliver replies.

I don't get a chance to respond before he's back in his and Eva's bedroom with the door closed. I can almost swear I hear him turn the lock.

Jude puts a good four feet between us. He leans forward onto the counter, balancing on his elbows.

I never even imagined him being here, in this apartment. It feels like the room is constricting as we're standing in it. Like there's only us, in a single room, separated by nothing.

"He'll come around. With some effort. You'll have to send some pretty high-quality wine. Maybe some cheese pairings. And a French chef," I say.

"Someone from the Sorbonne?"

"I'll allow it!" Oliver calls out from his bedroom.

"I assume you didn't come here to negotiate friendship with Oliver through the bedroom door?" I say.

Maybe he did. Maybe, after a few too many times of me walking away, he's done with me and wants me to know about it. And that would be a good thing, right?

No. I have to stop doing this. I have to stop doubting him when this Jude hasn't given me a reason to. He isn't the Jude from our past, he's better. He's open, he's laying it all out there with me. I need to do the same. Even if it means being vulnerable with him for what could be the last time.

Jude lays his phone between us, showing the pictures from Fellini's. They're out, fully, on social media. I imagine whichever outlet leaked the photos received a thorough dressing down from the Landon Energy head of public relations.

His face is a little red, like he's been crying too. He'd never want anyone to know, but he sometimes cries when he's frustrated.

"My mother had the photos taken," he says.

I feel frozen in the moment, like all the air has suddenly been sucked into a black hole in the middle of the room. We're standing in open space, surrounded by darkness.

"What?" I say.

"My mother had us followed out of Fellini's that night thinking the pictures would make the newspaper shelve the profile. She didn't want our past to get out but wanted it to look unprofessional in the current moment on your part."

"Seriously? What the *fuck*, Jude?"

I didn't think she hated me *that* much. Enough to want me out of Jude's life but not enough to completely tank my reputation. What have I ever done to her besides being too Black, too opinionated, and too ambitious to be her daughter-in-law?

"I know. I just wanted to be the one to tell you. She doesn't know that the profile will still be front-page news tomorrow, without you as the writer."

"Why?" I ask.

"She assumed the photos would be compromising. She sent them to an editor at the *Tribune*—Evelyn Jacobs?"

But why Evelyn? Do they know each other? Or was she just the most convenient messenger?

"They *were* compromising," I say. "For me anyway. For you I'm sure it'd just be another blip in the news cycle. Eligible bachelor Jude Landon seen with lowly newspaper writer, gives her perks for not raking him over the coals in the press."

"Lowly newspaper writer," he repeats, staring at me like I've completely lost my mind.

"I've been told to work from home this week because everyone thinks I'm too big of a whore. My colleagues are spreading rumors that I slept with you to get the profile and Adam won't defend me, even though I'm not even writing it," I reply.

"I'll fix it. I've been such an idiot getting you involved in my mess again."

It's been a long time since I've seen him this vulnerable, and I feel my stomach twisting in a way it hasn't since the funeral. With concern. With sadness. Hate is the last thing I feel.

"You *can't* fix it. And you're not an idiot. At least not completely," I reply. "How was the draft of Lucy's profile? I'm sure she's sent it to you by now."

"I read it in the parking lot."

I hear it in his voice, and I almost sigh with relief. He hates it. Whatever she wrote, it was exactly what he didn't want. The Fates haven't won yet.

"I wanted something honest, and I knew you'd be the person to give me that. You'd make me human, like you do in all the stories you tell, instead of like some larger-than-life figure. It felt like I paid for a puff piece. I'm handsome, understanding, an ideal boss, kind, woke. Like bribery. My board is going to be even more livid."

He pulls a piece of paper from his jacket pocket. As he unfolds it, I realize that it's from the Landon Energy website. The blank space where his bio is supposed to be.

"I want you to write your profile, if you're still interested, so I can publish it on the Landon Energy website as my official bio."

"You just want to know what I was going to say about you," I reply.

"Desperately. But if I'm going to truly put myself out into the world, I want to be presented as I am, good and bad. I don't care if the investors or the board are mad about it. The least I can do is have principles. The absolute bare minimum. You taught me that."

"It might be a conflict of interest. Even though it's not another publication."

He smiles. "Thank you."

"I didn't take it."

"Eh, your eyes tell me otherwise."

Our faces are less than an inch away from each other and his eyes are dancing back and forth between my irises and my lips. I think I may turn to liquid right here if he doesn't just kiss me.

Wait, no.

I step back and almost slam my hip into the edge of the counter. I'm not ready yet. There are still a few more things that need figuring out.

"When did you buy the ring?" I ask. "It's still on your mantel. It's the one I told you I wanted. I was with you 24/7 that whole week after your father died."

He didn't even know my ring size, there's no guarantee the ring would have fit. It might have been poetic if he'd put it on my finger and it immediately slid off into the ground with Julian.

"We're really rehashing this again? Right now?" he asks.

"Isn't it better than giving in and making out?"

"Not at all. Wait. Was there a chance we were going to—"

"Answer . . . the question," I reply, trying to catch my breath back into my body, so it can't linger in the air between us.

"I bought the ring before my father died, just to have it. And I carried it with me everywhere for three weeks. I didn't plan to propose at the funeral; I just did. I barely remember what happened. I thought I'd wait until graduation, like in a movie. But then Dad died, I was out of control, and I felt like you were all I had."

Those days after Julian's death are still mostly a blur for me, and probably for him too. I spent every day and night with Jude, who barely spoke until that moment at the funeral. He had visitors at the Landon estate almost every hour from nine AM to seven PM, mostly from board members or fellow businessmen. They all started with condolences and pivoted to their latest projects or ideas within the first ten minutes. He went from a locally famous trust fund kid to an international multimillionaire overnight at twenty-one. No one cared if he was okay; he was just a human dollar sign.

For a moment it's like we're back at the grave site, Jude in his gray suit and me in a black dress that I haven't worn since. I can almost feel the sapphire earrings swinging from my ears. I reach up to touch them and am spun back into reality. We're in my apartment, Jude's in a blue suit, and I couldn't even say if that black dress is in my closet right now.

"I still don't think I did anything wrong," I say.

"You didn't," he replies. "I did. I put you in a no-win, uncomfortable situation in front of several hundred people and I felt entitled to your endless love and support because I was grieving."

"Insightful."

"Well, I've had four years to ruminate about it in therapy, so . . ."

I can't believe he's still going. Another check in the "Jude Landon has evolved" column. But have I evolved enough to meet him where he now is?

"We're dancing in circles of our own making, huh?" I say. "It's like we never broke up."

"If only."

I almost don't want the silence to break. If it breaks, then he'll probably excuse himself and I don't know that I'll see him again. Will we still stay in touch? Does he even want to?

My phone buzzes on the counter, an unlisted number. Maybe a source? When I answer, I wish that for once I could be right about something.

I head to my bedroom and close the door for privacy.

"Oh, thank goodness," Adam says. "We have an emergency."

"Why are you calling me from an unlisted number?"

"I wanted to make sure you'd answer. Since you probably feel like I've thrown you under the bus."

"Countless times in the last few weeks alone."

"Well, we have different perspectives. You still have all of your information for the profile?" he asks.

Oh, Jesus, now what? Before I can answer he continues.

"I need you to write it. You'll be front-page news tomorrow. Plus, if the profile is well-received, I'll consider you for an assistant editor role. Do you want Features? Local News? I'll give it to you if you come through here."

"I thought Lucy was writing it."

"Well, she's not. The owner is concerned that I was too reactionary in pulling the profile from you. Apparently the optics . . . aren't good."

Adam sucks in air so hard that when he breathes out, I hear a whistle ringing in my eardrum.

So now he's giving it back, only because he looks bad. Because he's under investigation.

"So I'm getting jerked around on a career-making story at the last minute to cover up your mistakes?" I ask.

As soon as it's out of my mouth, I want to pull it back. I've stepped too far, again. I can't pretend I didn't say it. But I needed to. I needed to say it to him. To someone. Especially him. I take a deep breath and try to channel my inner Kaitlyn Franklin. I'm right, and it's high time I stood up for the people the *Tribune* constantly puts down.

"What? That's not relevant. Just get me the profile and I'll make your dreams come true, Jennifer."

"It's Gen*evieve*. Again. And no. I will be working with Jude directly, as a freelancer, on a piece he can be proud of."

"You'd rather be a freelancer for Jude Landon than an editor for me?" he asks.

"Until you adequately address what happened in that newsroom today, what's happened for my last four years, hell, what happened between Evelyn and Regina, then yes. If you don't, then this is my two weeks' notice."

The phone clicks off.

I let out a breath, and my stomach unclenches itself for the first time in years.

I'm getting out, and I'm going to move forward on my own terms. With Jude, maybe in more ways than one.

When I go back to the kitchen, Jude is gone, but this time he's left a note.

I don't want to be a distraction. Thank you for writing it. A box of coffee is on its way. Betting you're about to have a long night. Yours, Jude.

A long night, indeed.

I haven't been in a writing flow in what feels like forever. But I spend most of the night with an illustration of Jude, his life and career forming in front of me into a profile I actually feel proud of. I email it to Jude in the early hours of the morning.

Even if it only ends up on a business website, it's one of my best. I wonder if I can put it on my CV.

CHAPTER THIRTY-ONE

The next morning, I wake up to four missed calls from Regina and a bouquet of red roses on my bedside table. I pull a card off of one of the stems as I sit up. *It was perfect. Thank you. Please don't be mad. I promise it will work out. Yours, Jude*

Why would I be mad? What did he do, and why is Regina blowing up my phone before work has even started?

Still half asleep, I hit Regina's cell phone number.

"*Finally*," she says, picking up before the first ring even finishes.

"What's going on?" I ask.

"You don't sound awake," she says.

"I am. Sort of. What's up?"

"How fast can you get to WSYS?" she asks.

"The TV studio? Why?"

"They want to interview you and Jude Landon together during the ten o'clock hour. The profile is already trending on Twitter, and there have been nonstop calls about it for the last two hours."

What I assume is the desk phone next to her rings as if for extra emphasis. Why would a website bio be trending? The local news definitely has other stories to cover; I know for a fact that there was a contentious school board meeting last night.

"Oh. Wow."

Regina snorts. "So, you haven't read this morning's paper."

"What do you mean?"

"Adam was on the phone with Jude right up until we went to print. Jude agreed to a cross posting, updating his bio with the most prescient information, but allowing the *Tribune* to publish your profile, with his letter explaining why he chose you originally and why he objected to the unpublished profile Lucy wrote."

What? I stop breathing for a moment. He did what? The paper . . . I need to see today's paper. I rush over to my laptop. This can't be happening.

Oh my God. It's right there on the homepage. Part of me is thrilled that people will get to read my piece, but the other part, a deeper part, is horrified that he went behind my back all over again.

"He didn't tell me any of this. He just . . . I'm going to kill him. Seriously."

"Adam threatened him with a lawsuit against both of you. He promised to blackball you if Jude didn't agree."

What on earth could Adam even sue me for? It's not my fault if the profile he originally promised didn't fit in with his later agenda. And Jude. Making huge decisions without me once again. Even if this one is a boon to my career, it's still a huge slap in the face that he didn't even call me before it happened. I thought we were moving forward.

"Regina, what am I supposed to do?"

The phone rings again. "I've got to get this," she says. "Be at the studio in forty-five minutes, and bring foundation, because they most likely won't have your shade." Before I can respond she hangs up.

I throw the comforter off and nearly knock over the roses in the process. Jogging across the kitchen to the bathroom, I hear footsteps behind me. Oliver is holding his tablet, waving my story in the air.

"Did he tell you? What he was doing?" I ask.

"Nope. But I should have known when he dropped off the flowers at three AM. You okay?"

"I'm pissed. But there's some larger plan at work, maybe. It just feels a little too familiar. Him deciding my life for me in late night machinations."

Oliver hands me the tablet, holding the front page out in front of me. There's my byline: *Genevieve Francis*, written in bold type on the front page.

I wanted to do this on my own, and here I am, reaching one of my biggest goals because of Jude Landon. I can't bring myself to read whatever they chose to publish right now. So I scroll through my texts instead. Mom and Dad sent me at least fifty hearts each, Eva said she loved it, and Mickey texted 100 exclamation points. Jude texted, *I know I operated outside of your consent, and I'm sorry. I'll explain everything when I can. Thank you for a beautiful piece.*

I nearly throw the phone across the room. What could the explanation be? What kind of lawsuit would hurt Landon Energy? He could crush Adam. Something deeper has to be happening. Jude *has* grown, he's shown me that. But this is college Jude behavior, it's reactionary, but to what? And now I have to go in, uninformed, to a live television interview. Fuck, what am I sup-posed do here? Besides bring my own foundation.

Oliver waves his phone in the air. "Eva says you should wear the navy blue skirt-suit and cross your ankles, not your legs, like a royal. And try to see if you can get Jude to match his suit."

I spot the time on my phone. Shit. Now I have to squeeze myself into a skirt-suit I bought twenty pounds ago. Plus, now that she knows I'm awake, Eva is texting me: *FLESH-COLORED PANTYHOSE!!!!*

I ignore the squeeze in my heart when I remember that I'm almost definitely fired. I wanted to leave on my own terms, having maybe made the paper a better place for the next Black girl. Now I can't. But I can try to make a good impression on TV and put that on my résumé for the next publication. I'm going to figure this out.

The pockets of the skirt are too shallow to hold my keys or wallet, so I grab my work bag and phone and throw my newest foundation bottle inside. I try to run out the door, but it ends up being more of a shuffle to the parking lot in three-inch heels.

When I pull into the TV station with barely five minutes to spare, there are already cameras outside, pointed at the door. All this can't be for Jude; someone else has to be here.

I park toward the middle of the lot and tug my skirt down as I step out of the car. I don't think I've worn this since I interviewed for my current job at the *Tribune*, and I don't remember it clinging quite so tightly around my hips at twenty-two.

As I approach the door, I realize that Jude is standing in front of the cameras, trying to quell the crowd. He spots me and his eyes widen.

"I should be getting inside," he says to the reporters. "I'm sure I'll see some of you at Landon Energy later. I'll give you an hour head start."

When I take a step toward the crowd, Jude shakes his head. *Wait*, he mouths. He holds my gaze as he backs inside the studio.

The reporters begin to disperse back into their respective vans. One of them passes me and gives me a once-over but shakes his head.

Another reporter stares me dead in the face. "You're the reporter," she says.

"Aren't we all reporters?" I ask.

"No, you're the one who wrote the profile. His ex," she says.

A few of the other reporters overhear and within five seconds six cameras and at least fifteen phones are pointed at my face.

"I should head in," I say.

"Are you and Jude dating?" someone shouts.

"No," I reply.

"Hooking up?" someone else asks.

"No."

"Is it true that you were fired from your job for mixing business and *pleasure*?" someone asks.

"No."

"Is it true you stole the article from another woman? Feminism, huh?" someone yells.

I feel someone tugging my arm. It's a security guard. I try not to struggle because I don't want any of this to be on camera. I'd rather be the girl with the profile than the girl on video kicking a security officer in the balls.

"No more questions," he says, pulling me out of the crowd and toward the door.

When we get inside, I pull away from him and he stumbles back in surprise.

"Who the hell are you?" I ask.

"My private security," Jude says, coming out from the shadow of the hallway nearby. "I told you to wait."

"I didn't think I'd be mobbed," I reply. "Jesus, you have private security?"

"Of course," he says, his voice dropping into CEO Jude mode.

"Of course?"

"Not all the time, obviously, but for public stuff, yeah."

"Great."

"You look nice," he says. "Was I with you when you bought that?"

He gestures to my outfit and isn't exactly shy in the once-over he gives me, his eyes loitering around my hip area.

I ignore what I start to feel in the direct line of his gaze and hike the skirt down again.

"You said it looked like something your mom would wear to, and I quote, 'a casual Friday book club meeting at the country club,'" I reply.

"That's the one."

"Are you planning to explain now or later? Still deciding on the vibe I want to bring to what I assume is a fluff piece for you," I say.

All this time I've wondered if I'm the one struggling to move past who I was, who *we* were. Maybe it's him. Since he keeps repeating the things that made us break up in the first place.

"I know you're pissed. And that all that's standing between me and an absolutely devastating verbal takedown is the fact that we're literally surrounded by cameras and people. But please give me a chance to explain after the interview," he says.

"Why should I? Why do you deserve a chance?" I ask.

"Because I had a really good reason. And this is going to turn out really well, even if it doesn't feel like it right now."

I can't wait to hear it, but I know we don't have time. I only have fifteen minutes to let a makeup artist who will pretend to have never seen a Black person before try to pick an eyeshadow.

"Did you do a pre-interview?" I ask.

"Lauren got a primer on the interview questions and all of yours are about our relationship. They only let me nix one topic, and I thought you'd want to avoid questions about the *Tribune* more."

I hate that I feel surprised, as if anyone actually wanted to hear from me about the process of researching the profile. I'm going to have to channel my inner Kaitlyn Franklin again and force my way into this unexpected boys' club.

"You weren't wrong."

"Thank God. Something I'm right about."

I roll my eyes.

CHAPTER THIRTY-TWO

When the lights go on at *WSYS in the Morning*, Isabel Nelson, the anchor across from us who hasn't said anything in the five minutes we spent sitting on set off-air, smiles at us. Her smile is mostly directed at Jude, but she spares me a brief glance every now and again.

"Thank you both for being here," Isabel says.

Jude turns to me and gently taps me on the side. Before we went live, he told me that he wanted me to control the narrative today. As if I'll get a single question that allows me to do that.

"Thank you for having us," I reply.

"Of course," Isabel says, giving me a small nod. She turns to Jude. "Jude, you became CEO of a major corporation at twenty-one after the death of your father, the great Julian Landon. How did you cope with the grief while learning a new trade?"

"Yes, I did. Well, to be honest with you and the WSYS viewers, it took a fair amount of therapy. I talked with someone twice a week for at least a year after my father died. I was also fortunate to have incredible investors and a strong board who helped get me up to speed, and have given me room to grow, both as a person and as a CEO, over the past four years."

I glance down at my shoes and back up at Isabel, whose gaze is entirely with Jude. It's like I'm not even here. A familiar feeling.

"Amazing. A man who goes to therapy—what a catch, ladies! Speaking of, throughout your tenure you've been very well known for promoting the projects of women," Isabel says.

"I promote great projects," Jude says. "And, frankly, women are doing some of the best innovation right now, across many fields. I'm incredibly aware that women are underrepresented in corporations, and I do my best to seek them out when trying to expand the company's interests."

"Speaking of women you've helped promote, Genevieve Francis," Isabel says.

Jesus, what an introduction. I feel Jude tense up next to me. I can predict exactly how this moment will play out in the newsroom. The Fates are definitely snickering while watching on the TV in Evelyn's office, feeling vindicated that the entire ten o'clock audience is being told I owe everything to Jude. Exactly what I tried to avoid by working at the *Tribune* in the first place.

"Yes," I reply.

"You wrote the first major, authorized profile of Jude for the *Sykeswood Tribune*," Isabel says.

"I did," I reply. "It was an exciting opportunity, especially given—"

"And, more interestingly, you're his ex," Isabel interrupts.

"I am," I reply.

More interestingly bounces around in my head. More interestingly than breaking the story of a major public figure in environmental technology is the idea that I dated him in high school. But I'm holding it together. I'm about to be the most media-savvy accidental morning show guest there ever was.

"Did your relationship give you any pause when you were writing the article?" Isabel asks.

"Of course," I reply. "I hesitated when I was first approached about the piece. But in speaking with Jude, I saw his perspective and reasoning for wanting me specifically to do the profile. I feel as though I was able to offer a unique viewpoint on his success."

"How long did the two of you date?" Isabel asks.

"Six years," I say. "We saw each other through the transition from high school to college, so it's been illuminating to see the man he's become since."

"Why did you break up?" she asks.

"I messed up a good thing," Jude interrupts. "After my father died, I pushed her away as much as I could, and I didn't give her the opportunity to be there for me."

I look over at him and smile, and he squeezes my hand quickly enough that I don't think Isabel, or the camera people, notice. He's fading out of CEO Jude mode, trying to make me the star of this story. It's sweet of him, but I'm growing angrier and angrier that I'm even in this position. I shouldn't have to defend a four-year-old breakup when talking about a story I wrote for my job. I wouldn't have to if people like Isabel Nelson didn't already think I don't deserve to breathe the same air as him. But none of that is Jude's fault. So can I really keep blaming him for the way other people are treating me? He's trying to make it better. Even though he's the one who made it worse.

"Did you try to be there for him?" Isabel asks me.

"Of course, but there's only so much you can do while keeping in line with the other person's wishes. But in working on the profile—"

"You didn't try to force the issue?" she asks, making her voice louder to drown me out. "Your boyfriend of six years was going through grief and his whole life was thrown on a new course."

Oh, no she's not. She is not out here trying to make it seem like I'm the bad guy here. Both of us were right, and both of us were wrong, but that's between me and Jude. Not Isabel fucking Nelson of *WSYS in the Morning*. She doesn't even have a journalism degree; I checked. But she gets to question me like she's some sort of authority on integrity and my relationship.

Rein it in, Gen. It's morning television.

"There's only so much you can force," I reply. "As I said, grief isn't always rational, and trying to force someone to do something they're not open to in that moment can be particularly harmful. However—"

"Interesting," Isabel replies. She turns back to Jude. "So, at twenty-one, you felt abandoned, not only because your father died unexpectedly, but because you lost your longtime partner at the same time . . ."

What gives her the right to do this? As if our breakup was easy for me? As if I would be so callous and unfeeling that I'd just let him suffer in silence? Fuck this. Fuck people like her treating me like I don't have feelings too. Like I'm not important.

"I understand how you're setting this up," I say. "Like my longtime boyfriend became CEO of a major company after the death of his father, I couldn't handle the pressure, and I bolted. But that isn't what happened, and I think this line of questioning is inherently problematic and pretty sexist."

The segment director begins giving Isabel signals to wrap the interview up, and I notice that her earpiece is glowing blue.

"I think we need to wrap up and go to commercial," Isabel says.

Jude squeezes my hand again and clears his throat. I notice the segment producer stop giving the wrap-up sign. Of course, everyone wants to listen to what *Jude* has to say. He's trying, but he really could buck up a little more and call out the story Isabel is trying to spin.

"I proposed to Gen at my father's funeral and broke up with her when she asked if grief was perhaps coloring the moment," Jude interrupts. "We were twenty-one and had never seriously discussed marriage. I blindsided her in front of three hundred people, then refused to speak to her after she—rightfully—wouldn't say yes in the moment."

"Jude," I whisper, but he shakes his head at me.

He's made the wrong play. In losing his professional veneer, he's thrown a wrench in our entire narrative. Publicly, I can move past just being his ex. But a proposal? I'm going to be portrayed as his betraying wife in the media, without any of the perks of actually having been his wife. I'm the deceitful temptress who seduced him into letting me write the profile after I left him at his father's grave.

I've officially lost control of this narrative. If I ever had control in the first place.

"I messed up. I was unfair. I was inherently problematic. I took a situation I didn't have control over and tried to exert control in a way that took away Gen's agency in that moment. This profile wasn't a consolation prize for a jilted ex-girlfriend, or a play to get back together. I didn't feel comfortable having anyone write about my accomplishments until I felt like I had some, and I didn't feel comfortable having someone who only knew the Jude Landon of the tabloids, of the public eye, write the first major profile of me," he finishes. "Especially not when the attempt of a fan was, well, unpublished."

I have to cover my near choke with my hand. A *fan*. I know Lucy is seething and I can't help but revel in it for a moment.

"You . . . *proposed*?" Isabel repeats.

"I did," he replies. "And Genevieve has tried to be beyond respectful in not disclosing that to the public to maintain my image. I wanted to give a junior staff member at a local publication the opportunity to boost their credentials. Of those at the *Tribune*, Genevieve was the only one I felt I could trust, personal history aside."

"We have to go to commercial," Isabel says. "But major news here that Jude Landon was almost off the market. I'm Isabel Nelson and this is *WSYS in the Morning*. We'll be back with Helen Underwood."

The camera cuts away from all of us, and both Jude and I are slightly slack-jawed at the turn of events.

Isabel pulls off her microphone pack and smiles at me. She hands the mic pack to the nearest production assistant.

"Sorry about that," she says.

"Sorry?" I ask.

"Viewers are here for him," she says. "They love the romantic angle."

"The romantic angle between exes," I reply.

"Imagine if he'd proposed again on TV," she says. "Incredible television."

I almost throw my mic pack on the floor. "Seriously?" I say to no one in particular, once Isabel is gone.

"I'm so sorry," Jude says. "I messed up. I messed up big time. I got caught up and I just . . . Oh my God. I shouldn't have said any of that."

He does look like he's seen a ghost, and a little like he might be sick behind the couch. Of the two of us, he seems to be the more surprised that this interview devolved so immediately.

"We're replaying the same scenarios here," I reply. "You make an attempt at saving me and then actually make things worse. And you took away my agency here, just like you said."

"Was this worse for you and your career?" he asks. "Should I have just accepted the lesser profile to keep you out of this? And I don't mean to, I just . . . I'm trying and I'm probably not doing the best job here."

"Yes. It was. But you could have proposed to Isabel. *Incredible television.*"

"It would have been a great red herring. No one would even be thinking about you," he says. "Well, I always do."

God, why does he have to be like this? Sweet and earnest. Honest to a complete fault. He's finally becoming the best version of himself. And here I am, just trying to hold it together.

"I wish," I reply. "But I guess we'll just have to wait it out. Unless you have another grand plan I'm not in on."

"My grand plans, however well-intentioned, never seem to actually work, so I'm going to officially retire them. And beg for tolerance, since I'm sure forgiveness is a step too far," he says.

I hate how he can be so self-aware. Even when he makes mistakes, however bad, he can own up to them now. He didn't do that before.

"Tolerance. I can work with that," I reply. "If you swear to never keep anything from me again."

He raises his right hand and crosses in front of his chest. "I spent so long lying to myself and everyone else. I'm just trying to be honest, but I also made you uncomfortable, and fuck, I'm a typical rich white dude," he says.

I snort. "The F-bomb. Thought you were too classy."

"Ah, you like the less camera-ready version of me," he replies.

He ruffles his hair, and it sticks up at six different angles across his head, making him look like a red porcupine.

I like both, a lot. Camera-ready Jude is just devastatingly good-looking. Like, I want him to absolutely decimate my life good-looking. Actually, he maybe has already decimated the life I've been barely living for the past four years. I just hope it's for the better. But the less camera-ready Jude . . . that's the guy I could love. The one I could come home to. The one I would want to.

"Takes me right back to Knight Hall Room 2302," I say. "You had a six-pack of warm beer, we lay on your twin bed, and you told me that someday I'd be Mrs. Francis-Landon, and I'd have the . . ."

"Biggest, gaudiest designer ring I could find. So big you couldn't lift your hand up," he finishes.

"And I could wear it to our five-year reunion with my *New York Times* press pass to show everyone that we were the best of the best."

It was a cute dream. Two kids who thought that a relationship could subsist on coffee, French fries, four-carat diamonds, and easy career success. We thought it would be easy to keep loving each other, keep fighting for each other, until we were actually tested.

And, as it turns out, it was really fucking hard. Because we weren't ready to give each other what we needed.

He follows me into the dark corridor on the side of the studio. I hear the clacking of his loafers stop behind me just before we hit the light.

"You still are. The best of the best," he says. "I know that. And recognize it even though I keep fucking up."

I turn around and he's right behind me, less than a foot away. Close enough to grab and tell him that I think we could maybe be ready now.

"I know you're trying."

"Thank you for saying no," he says. "You didn't do it for me, I know. But thank you. Thank you for always knowing what to do when I never do. I should have used my platform after the DUI, but I was a coward. I still am."

I don't think he's a coward. Deep down, I never did. Putting yourself out in the world, at your best and at your worst, is terrifying. His worst was lower than a lot of people's, and he's turned it around. I think he's brave, but I don't know how to tell him. I'm the one who's afraid now.

We're no more than two inches away from each other and I can barely see the outline of his face.

"At least you made an otherwise terrible interview exciting for the viewing audience," I say.

"Ugh, I should have proposed again," he says. "You rejecting me a second time would have been ratings gold."

I roll my eyes. "You'd end up on *People Magazine* dramatically recounting how no one loves you."

"And I'd *really* sell it," he replies.

And I'd probably have a copy hidden under my mattress, so I could stare at his tragic face. The picture couldn't be worse than the other one, and I still have a copy of that one.

"I know you would."

I know he's smiling even though I can't see it. He takes my hands and holds them close to his chest for a moment.

"I love you," he says. His voice reverberates around the walls, so that I hear him say love three times.

"Jude . . ."

"I just needed to say it. In the dark, where I can't see your face. Since I can never tell you again."

When we started the profile, this was the exact moment I was afraid of. That he'd love the artifact I was, instead of the person I am. But he's seen me, truly seen me in my best moments and my worst over these last weeks. So even if he doesn't fully know me now, I know that he means it. And him wanting to love me, in all my cynical, barely employed glory, feels like a moment I don't want to deny. Because I feel it too.

I sigh and say exactly what I know I shouldn't. "You can say it in the light."

"No, I can't," he replies.

He can, though. He can say it in the light, and I can watch his lips as he says it. I can watch the way his eyes crinkle if he smiles after it comes out. But I know if he does, I'll say it back. I never could resist that eye crinkle and it's even harder now that he has a little more character behind those crystalline eyes. I loved the boy, who was idealistic to the point of delusion, who saw good in the world and his family that I didn't think was there. And here I am, faced with the man who is still optimistic and hopeful about his impact, but grounded in a realism I thought he'd never find in his penthouse apartment. He's becoming the Jude I always wanted.

"I should go," I say.

And I should. I should run out of here and never say another word. If I don't, I'll open a door that I'm not sure I'm ready to go through. Not when my life is completely upended.

"Thank you for the profile," he says. "I didn't think you could get better, but you did. As a writer and as a person."

"Eh. Haven't gotten too much practice at either," I reply.

"I assume this is it," he says. "We're done? No contact?"

"Probably," I reply. "Maybe you'll save me from an irate chef somewhere else. Or I'll answer that voice mail you left after the gala."

I'm pretty sure I will. When I figure out my next move, delete my Indeed profile, and get my name on the front page of a respectable newspaper without Jude Landon anywhere nearby, I think I'll call him.

"I'll wait for that day."

His shoes start to click-clack away and I feel like the regret is going to choke me. It's clawing at my throat, and I think I might burst right at this moment. If I want him to stay around, maybe answer my call, I have to say it.

"I love you too," I say. "I never stopped."

The word love echoes back at me, and the clacking of Jude's shoes stops. For a moment it's like nothing ever changed. Neither of us says anything else. We just stand together in the corridor in the dark for what feels like an hour, staring at shadows.

CHAPTER THIRTY-THREE

"You *left*?" Mickey says. "You said I love you to each other and then left?"

Mickey came over right after school, with a full verbal essay prepared on how awful the interview was. She and Helena watched it together during lunch in the teachers' lounge, and there was apparently a moment of eye contact between them so steamy, she can't even get into it without blushing.

"Yep," I say, sipping my glass of wine.

"You're in love," she says. "You're in *love*. With Jude Landon."

"To be fair, you've maintained that I never fell out of love with Jude Landon."

"But you've *grown*, you're both successful, and that love is still there." Mickey taps the crook of her index finger to her eye, and I think I may actually see a tear there.

"Yeah," I say. "It is. It's been four years and I'm still hung up on my high school boyfriend. How pathetic is that?"

"At least your high school boyfriend is now a multimillionaire CEO. There are worse people to be hung up on. Like someone who may not even like Black women?"

She's not wrong. At least Jude is a big shot now, and generally considered to be a catch. Not that he wasn't a catch when we were together before.

"You don't know Helena isn't into black women."

"I know that she grew up in an area that's sixty percent POC and she's only dated white women. Like, you grew up surrounded by Black women just as or more interesting than me, more beautiful than me, and you never considered any of them seriously as romantic partners? By your mid to late twenties? Red fucking flag. And I'm running right into it like a bull."

Mickey leans her head back into the couch and downs the rest of her glass of wine.

"She hasn't told you she just has 'certain preferences,' right?"

"Not yet, but my senses are tingling. Don't get me wrong, after that *look* today, I wanted a summer wedding. But I can't be a token. Not again."

"You shouldn't have to justify why someone should date you. You're the best, she should be falling all over herself to do whatever she has to to get a shot at dating you."

She reaches over to the wine bottle next to me and refills her glass. Then she hands the bottle to me, and I do the same.

My phone buzzes next to me. I lean back on the couch and turn the phone over. For the first time in a long time, I have no desire to jump at whoever is trying to contact me, even if it's another paper. They can wait until morning,

Mickey is searching the cabinets. "Where do you keep the wine?"

"Third cabinet on the left," I reply.

My phone buzzes again. I slide across the couch to pick it up and see alerts across all of my social media profiles. I open the first notification and see that my name is trending on Twitter.

"Um . . . ," I begin.

Mickey leans over my shoulder and nearly drops the bottle of rosé she's holding. She grabs my phone. "Your interview went viral," she says, scrolling.

"Shit."

"No, I think it's . . . good?" she replies. "People are pissed at the questions that reporter asked, calling it sexist. They want both her and Jude to apologize . . . and . . . they want you recognized by name, not association, for the profile! Ooh, an unnamed source from the *Tribune* is claiming you've been put on leave because of the paparazzi photos of you and Jude. And that some of your coworkers are racist, hard r."

I'm willing to bet a pretty hefty portion of my final *Tribune* paycheck that the unnamed source is Regina. She specifically has several social media accounts to just lurk.

I grab the phone.

She even leaked the email thread that the Fates sent out with the pictures. And are those chat records?

Mickey snatches the phone back before I can read much of it.

"Oh hell no, you're not reading that. Avoid avoid avoid," Mickey replies.

"Come on."

"The overview was that Clara wanted to hook up with Jude and was jealous. She said you don't deserve him, and he'd never want to actually be with someone like you. Heather said that you should have been more supportive of Clara and Lucy's careers, and let one of them have the profile, but you were selfish, probably because of your background. Lucy called you a Black whore, and said you deserved to get fired."

"Okay, that overview is enough. Jesus."

She scrolls to show me the pretty creative roasts of Jude's powder blue prom suit, photos of which have somehow also made it onto the web. He was trying to match my dress, but I can agree it wasn't the best choice for his skin tone.

I pour myself a steep glass of rosé, and try not to read everything over Mickey's shoulder. I know she'll sanitize everything for me in case some trolls are trying to tweet racial slurs about me or something. Some of the trolls might even be my coworkers, which is always fun.

"This is amazing. People are really rallying and . . ." She trails off.

"And what?"

She hands my phone back to me. Twitter is still open and the first tweet I see is a photo of me and Jude. But this time it isn't one of the car photos from the other night. I squint and enlarge the photo. It takes me a moment to realize what this is a picture of.

Someone somehow has found and leaked a photo of Jude down on one knee at his father's funeral. It's grainy, but it's clear that it's Jude and me in front of his father's casket.

"People fucking suck. Why would anyone upload this? Do you think he's okay?" I ask.

"I'm sure he's fine."

"I should go check on him, right? Since things are heating up online? Just to make sure he's good."

Mickey rolls her eyes. She knows I just want to see him again, and a bit of wine was just the liquid courage I needed.

"Well, you can't drive; you've been drinking," Mickey replies. "And do you even know where Jude lives?"

"I drove him home the other night. It's the penthouse in that sky-rise downtown. And I'll be fine. I just need to talk to him."

She nods and orders the Uber.

CHAPTER THIRTY-FOUR

Thirty minutes later my Uber is pulling up to Jude's building. I take a deep breath; this is going to be Jude in his element, in his home. This is going to be Jude after I told him I love him. A Jude I haven't seen in what feels like a lifetime.

The driver bypasses the front entrance and I open my mouth to protest. Before I can say anything, he pulls up in front of a side door.

"What is this?" I ask. It doesn't look like the door tenants would go through; it's almost hidden at the side, and you need what seems like a key card to get in.

"Service entrance," he replies.

"I'm visiting someone," I say. I'm just buzzed enough that I want to tell him off, but I'm too stunned to actually execute whatever would pop into my head.

"Oh." He doesn't move.

I push open the door. "Have a good night," I say. I try not to notice that he drives right past me when I'm standing at the front entrance.

I clock four security guards and a front desk worker. The front desk worker looks me up and down as I approach her. I'm wearing leggings, but they're the nice pair that are supposed to look like professional pants. I even tucked in my T-shirt.

"Hi," I say.

"Delivery?" she asks.

"No, I'm here to see Jude Landon."

Her eyes scan my outfit again. "Is he . . . expecting you?" she asks.

"I'm Genevieve Francis. I wrote the profile about him that came out today," I say.

She has today's *Tribune* in front of her on the desk, turned to the second page of the profile. There's a small picture of Jude in the center of the page that I can see from where I'm standing.

"Sorry, we can't let you in unless he's expecting you and has left your name at the desk," she says, closing the newspaper.

Four hundred retorts pop into my head, but I bite my tongue. "That's fine; I'll give him a call." I pull my phone out and click Jude's number.

He answers on the first ring. "Gen, hey," he says. "I didn't expect . . ."

"I'm downstairs."

"Downstairs where?" he asks.

"In your building."

"Seriously?" he says.

"Seriously."

"I'm on my way down."

He appears a minute later, slightly out of breath, having, apparently, sprinted down the stairs. His hair is a little all over the place like the way it used to stick out in all directions after he showered.

He waves at the front desk attendant. "Hey, Erin, this is Gen. If she ever comes in for me, send her up, no questions asked, even if I'm not here," he says. "She can have an extra key, use any of the amenities. It's hers too, all of it."

"Of course, Mr. Landon," Erin replies. She gives me yet another once-over and turns her nose up.

I follow Jude into the elevator. He's wearing silk pajama pants that cling to every angle of his lower body and a white T-shirt that's almost sheer. I try my best not to stare, but I already feel my face heating up and my desire for the elevator to stop suddenly inches higher and higher.

"So, what are you doing here?" he asks. "Not that I'm not happy to see you. I just didn't expect . . . I'm glad you're here."

"I'm trending," I reply.

"For the profile?" he asks. "Congratulations."

"You haven't seen?" I ask.

"I've been taking a phone break tonight. I'm sure everyone loves it, though. Did you just come to brag?"

"You answered my call on the first ring," I reply.

"Hmm?"

"You said you're on a phone break, but you answered my call on the first ring."

"I'm not looking for a break from *you*," he says.

I imagine he's been fielding calls not only from other media outlets and the board, but from his mother pretty much all day. Maybe even Joanna, asking him if she needs to throw together a weekend wedding in six days.

"A photo from the funeral leaked. Of you proposing," I say.

He closes his eyes for a few seconds. "Surprised it took this long, honestly."

"There weren't supposed to be cameras or phones," I reply.

He pulls out his phone and finds the picture on Twitter pretty quickly. He zooms in and nods, sucking on his teeth.

"That's never stopped anyone before," he says. He points to the photo. "See the quality? Long-range camera, taken from probably fifty or sixty feet away." He shrugs. "I'm guessing the photo wasn't worth anything until now, after everything I said on the show earlier."

"Either you're taking this remarkably well, or you're a pro at repressing your feelings," I reply.

"Both, darling. I sort of have to be about this stuff. I'm a public figure, and a lot of my worst moments have been in private. I've had time to process all of that, and I'm adjusting."

My heart lurches when he calls me darling. But I also hate that he feels like he has to hold it together when someone does something shitty just because he's a public figure. He signed up for a public professional life, and he's starting to share the personal, but can't some things just stay between us? Privately, what's here is good. Or at least it could be. But publicly, the interest of those around us is making us both miserable.

"Just say it sucks," I say. "I don't want the pretense, Jude. You can be vulnerable."

He sighs. "I've been really fucking vulnerable recently and I'm a little tired to be honest. So can you let me be cool for a second? Let me try and impress you with how well-adjusted I am."

I roll my eyes. "Eh, you can't really impress me," I say, playfully swatting his arm.

He smiles. "Is that the only reason why you came over here? Or did you just want to see me?"

His breath tickles my nose and every sinew in my body wants to wrap myself in him.

"Okay, yes, maybe it was an excuse. A check-in, as you would say," I reply.

The elevator stops but the doors take a moment to open and we're standing in silence. I put my hand on his arm and feel his muscle flex as he leans into me. We walk out into the hall almost arm in arm.

There are no other apartments on this floor, since Jude has the penthouse, so it's not like we're bound to run into anyone unless Jackie has paid a paparazzo to stake him out from the inside.

"I'm not mad at you about the interview, by the way," I say. "In case you were wondering. Or about any of it, right now."

He raises his eyebrows. "Really? Or is that just the wine talking?"

"How can you tell? Should I go? Is this compromising for you?" I ask.

"You smell like wine and you have the flush you used to get after our Franzia dinner parties in college," he replies. "And no. I've been around tipsy people before."

"As soon as I saw that tweet, I just wanted to tell you," I say. "And I now realize that was probably dumb and I could have just texted it. I can go."

We stand across from a nondescript wooden door with a P on it. Jude pulls out a key from his pajama pocket and I move my hand off of his arm.

Jude reaches out for my hand instead, and when I nod, he takes it in his. "Do you want me to show you around instead?" he asks.

"Sure, since I'm apparently co-owner. When do I get added to the lease?"

Jude opens the door. "Whenever you want. Not kidding on that, by the way." He doesn't let go of my hand and I don't pull it away. "This is the foyer, obviously."

I guess if I can't have a job, property in the city isn't a terrible consolation prize. As long as I don't have to contribute to the taxes. Splitting bills on a salary of $0 would be a little unfair, given all I've gone through for this man.

The floor is entirely made of light brown wood, and with the exception of a small mirror to the left of the door, the walls are covered in family photos. Most of the pictures are of Jude and his father alone, but there are a few of the entire Landon family, and a smattering of ones of just Jude and Joanna, mostly as kids. There's only one of Jude and Jackie alone, and it looks like it's from one of his early days as CEO. The suit he was wearing was a little too big for him; he lost a fair amount of weight right after Julian died, and he was wearing Julian's watch, which hung off of his wrist. Attached to the photo, glinting inside the frame, is a twenty-four-hour sober chip. I wonder why he chose to hang that photo, but I don't ask.

He leads me into the living room, which is the first room off the foyer. He has a huge brown sectional and several leather armchairs surrounding an eighty-inch television screen with a surround-sound system, and a fireplace. The walls around the room are covered in pencil sketches.

"The designs on the wall," he says, pointing to the sketches, "were my father's. He had all sorts of ideas about wind turbines and more efficient solar panels, and I found all of these in his . . . my office after he died. Everyone else wanted to throw them away; they're not particularly feasible, but I couldn't get rid of them."

"I think it's a beautiful way to remember him."

"I wish I were more like him," he says. "If he were in my shoes, he would have handled it perfectly. He was barely thirty when he started the company."

"I'm sure he made mistakes along the way," I reply. "He did with you. And he had more time."

"And yet still not enough," he replies.

There would be worse places to live. Worse people to love. This Jude is somehow so different from the old one in all the best ways. But he's the same in some of the ways I wish he could see.

"Jude," I say, searching for his gaze.

"Yeah?" He looks at me.

"You're enough." I squeeze his hand.

He kicks at a piece of plastic on the floor before picking it up to drop into his recycling bin. "I want to be."

"You are. I mean it." I hold his gaze.

"Am I enough for you?" he asks, still staring at that piece of plastic now sitting at the bottom of his recycle bin.

"It's not about you being enough for me. *You* have always been enough," I reply. "It's about whether or not, despite everything we've been through, we can be enough to make this work without sacrificing all of ourselves."

Is it even worth it to try again? Or will we fall back into the same pattern we did then? Love is something, but it's not enough. We both learned that four years ago.

He reaches out for my hand, and instead of squeezing it, he holds it up to his chest.

"That's a mutual decision. To me, yes, always. But I'm also the one who messed up in the first place," he replies. "And also the second. And the third. I'm not doing well with you."

I lay my palm flat against his chest. "You did. But you were also grieving for some of it. And I didn't know how grief could impact every moment and every action you took back then. I didn't understand."

"That doesn't make what happened okay," he replies. His hand is still on mine.

"I didn't say it was okay. It will never be okay, but I just understand now." I drop my hand, and he picks it up, his palm sweaty.

Holding my hand against his hip, he leads me back into a dining room that looks like it's never been touched. There's a chandelier, of course, and a fifteen-foot-long dark wood dining table without a scratch on it. A navy blue tablecloth is folded up into a square at the center of the table.

An empty golden portrait frame hangs on the wall. It doesn't even look like there's even been a portrait there.

He sighs. "Mom says it's for my family portrait when I have a wife and kids. A wedding photo, a tasteful one, is acceptable in the interim. An engagement photo can be used in a pinch if hosting a formal holiday like Thanksgiving. But the frame itself must hang as a reminder to guests that I'm searching."

It takes a fair amount of energy to not laugh. As if anyone who made it to Jude's penthouse would have no idea whether or not he was single. It looks like the frame was specially commissioned; it's engraved with Jude's initials. Or maybe Julian's.

"When does she think you'll find this wife?" I ask. Jackie's commitment to marrying off only her youngest child is amusing.

He's a man, he could wait another twenty years to settle down and no one would bat an eye. It's not like she's feeling the urge to chase a grandchild in her red bottoms.

"She's been throwing matches at me seriously for the last couple of years. Obviously, it hasn't worked. She's really tried with Kaitlyn, despite Kaitlyn's clear lack of interest in men overall." He sounds amused too, though there's a hint of annoyance in his voice.

"She's just trying to keep the redhead gene alive."

"It would make an incredible family portrait, for sure," he says. "But that's not my top priority in picking a partner."

I lean against the dining table, extracting my hand from his. To be the one in that portrait, would I have to keep losing? I try not to stare at the empty frame and imagine myself there. I fit with Jude, with who he is at his core, but I don't fit with his life or his family. The way every single person who realizes I'm associated with him has looked at me over the last twenty-four hours just reinforces it. Even if Jude doesn't see me that way, how can I rely on only his view to get me through all of the parties, all of the fundraisers? I'm not that evolved. I'm not that confident. Not yet.

He ducks his head, and I wonder if he's ruminating on me pulling my hand away.

I follow Jude as he leads me through the back of the living room into the wine cellar, which is the size of my bedroom. I could do worse, I suppose, than someone who has non-boxed wine and an entire wine cellar. In my dating experience, most guys in this age bracket barely have furniture.

"We partner with a sustainable vineyard," Jude says. "They've sent cases of wine and I just leave it in there. Easy to grab something as a gift for dinner parties."

"Should you even have this in your house? Given . . ."

"It's a gray area. But since no one outside of my immediate family, Kaitlyn, and you, know I don't drink . . . it's there. At the end of the day, my sobriety is my responsibility. And I hated wine anyway, so don't worry."

"You don't have to joke about it," I say. "It kind of sucks that you think you need to have that here to feel normal in your circles."

"It does. Let's go back to the living room." He listened. He can at least admit that the public pressure sucks, even if he won't fully address it.

He has a full wooden bar back against the wall of the living room, with no bottles surrounding it, just an array of different colored glasses, iridescent in the light of the chandelier above them.

"Is there even anything over there?" I ask.

"Martinelli's fulfills most of my needs. Plus, all of the ingredients for some killer mocktails. Lots of juices. Lots of maraschino cherries." He smiles.

"I should probably ask you to make me your favorite," I say, leaning my head toward him.

"Ms. Francis, are you flirting?"

"It's the wine. Gone straight to my head."

He grins. I'm tempted to tell him it was the wine he sent, but that would definitely be flirting.

"You still a tequila girl?" he asks.

"After this past week? For sure."

Jude ducks his head for a moment. "Because of me?" he asks, not looking up at me.

"Because of racism. And because of your mom and those photos." I reply. "It wasn't that overt, at first. Just a lot of little things.

It starts with being excluded from their conversations. Getting called the wrong name and they laugh. Being denied the same opportunities. But they build up. A million little paper cuts accumulated over years."

"I'm sorry," he says.

"They tell you that we're all family and when one of us succeeds all of us succeed, but that's just not true. They get page three and I get to proofread their pieces without getting the opportunity to write my own," I reply. "And the time I get to write my own, it's because I happened to have a connection, not because anyone considered me for it."

The way Jude's looking at me, I know Adam never gave him the full picture. I'm sure Adam said a lot of nothing to him. Just like he told me that if I just showed my potential and worked hard, something would happen. But it never did. It's been three years with him as editor-in-chief and I had to fight for him to remember my *name*. And now that I've called him racist, I'm done.

I wipe a tear that's begun forming in the corner of my eye. I haven't cried in front of him in so long, but it feels oddly familiar. So does talking about racism, even if he still doesn't fully get it.

"I feel like if I hadn't fucked things up at the funeral, we'd still be together, and my connections could have made things easier for you earlier." He blushes, like he's admitting some deeply embarrassing secret.

"You did use your connections." He never sabotaged me or anything. I made a choice, and sure, it was reactionary, but it was my choice to make.

"And you didn't take them, because of what happened? If you had, do you think maybe you wouldn't have had to go through all of this?" His voice is pleading, and part of me feels a pang of sadness that he's taking such internal responsibility for my experiences. The other part feels a bit taken aback. As if me staying with him would have saved me from systemic racism.

"Oh, don't worry, I would have just been called a whore earlier. We'd probably have two heirs to Landon Energy, four nannies, and a pending divorce." I make my tone joking while I try to sort out my feelings about the turn of this conversation.

Jude takes a step back from me. "You really think we'd be divorced?" He's genuinely hurt by the idea.

"I'll never know," I reply, winking at him.

His face relaxes. He's so tightly wound, so visibly concerned with every signal I'm giving, every move that I'm making. I can see how much he truly cares about saying the right thing, and while I appreciate it, I also don't want it. I don't need him to be right, I just need him to be willing to grow with me, to hear me even when he doesn't understand. I need him to be better than he was, so we can be better together. And he is better. But are we better together?

I follow him out into the hall, and he leads me farther back into the apartment. We stop outside one of the three bathrooms as we pass.

"Since I know wine makes you pee," he says, sticking his tongue out at me.

"Of all the things to remember about me."

"I can't believe I was so attuned to another person's bladder patterns. I didn't think that'd happen until we had kids. If we did. If you wanted." He bites his lip and looks at the ground.

I do want kids. Not right now, since I can barely remember to drink enough water to keep myself alive, but someday. And I wanted them with Jude. But that's a whole other level of partnership, and we'd really need to be able to talk about anything and everything. I'd need to feel more comfortable about our conversations, about the ways his privilege and my life intersect, before bringing another person into the dynamic.

"If we had a kid, would you give them the company?" I ask.

Jude's upper lip twitches. "Well, first I'd check and see if they wanted it. I'm hoping not to die prematurely, so I'd hope that they'd want to do it and they'd have already established themselves and their families if they wanted their own family. I'd love to stipulate a minimum age of thirty-five. Like a president."

We pass another photo of Jude and Julian in the hallway. This one is of the two of them on a golf course, wearing matching yellow golf polos and grinning from ear to ear. I do wonder what would have happened if Jude had inherited the company later. Would he have gotten sober? Would he be the party boy the tabloids wanted him to be while he waited to ascend?

Jude at thirty-five makes me smile. But would thirty-five-year-old me be ready for the life that comes with being Mrs. Landon? Could I ever be ready for that?

"Wealth wouldn't protect them from everything," I reply. Just like his wealth wouldn't have protected me from what's happened at the *Tribune*. It didn't protect me at all. All of this has happened despite his wealth, despite his influence, despite his standing up for me. This is just how it is. Wealth can just make it a little cushier in between.

"No, it wouldn't," he says. "And I'm realizing I've been a bit of an idiot thinking I could have saved you from racism."

I tip my head toward him. It took him a minute but he got there, without too much of my prodding. He's trying. Maybe I can give a little grace.

But should I have to? Would it be easier to just be with someone who gets it right away?

We keep walking, and I try not to get lost in the idea of this apartment, this life. The cushy parts.

His home office is pretty empty, with the exception of a fifteen-foot mahogany desk and office chair. The bookshelves that line the walls are almost completely empty.

"Are you going to frame the article in there?" I ask. "For posterity, of course." I point inside the office.

"I'd decorate an entire wall with your articles. Oh God, that was too intense." His face flushes.

It's funny though. "Fully. I've been drinking and *I'm* not even being that intense."

"Wine does make you intense. Now, should we talk about the elephant in the room?" he asks.

There's a painting on the wall of an elephant, adorned in jewels. It stands in contrast to every other piece of décor, so I know it's a gift from Joanna.

"That was a horrific dad joke, how dare you," I say.

"That's for fertility," he replies. "Joanna wants to be an aunt."

"Well, that can be thrown away," I reply, only half kidding.

"Don't worry, I haven't figured out the sustainability behind getting someone pregnant with just a look."

"Thank goodness, because I think we'd be having triplets."

We stare at each other, neither of us able to break the gaze. Both of our eyes go to the other's lips.

I don't know which one of us leans in first. It doesn't matter, because before I know it, we're both leaning in and our lips have touched for the first time in four years.

There are fireworks in my chest. Somehow not a day has passed since our last kiss, except this kiss is better than any we've ever had.

I never want this moment to end—but I know I have to be the one to end it. I turn my head away so that his lips graze my cheek, which is almost sweeter.

I straighten up and smooth the bit of sawdust off of my leggings.

His face visibly falls. "I feel like you're always looking for an excuse to go," he says.

"I feel like you're always looking for an excuse not to let me."

"Yes, absolutely," he says. "Because we love each other."

"I know," I reply.

I take a long look at the Landon family photo wall. Do I want to be there? Am I up to the challenge? I think I finally know the answer, but I have to find the right time to tell him. Though I may know a place.

CHAPTER THIRTY-FIVE

I wake up the next morning with a throbbing headache that radiates up the bridge of my nose into my forehead and a case of dry mouth. I reach toward the nightstand and realize that Mickey left me a bottle of water and a note covered in hearts. On the bottom of the note she scrawled "Genevieve Landon" so small that I almost miss it.

I drink the entire water bottle and dry heave a bit as some of the water goes down the wrong pipe. I pick up my phone and scroll through to my text thread with Regina. She hasn't texted me since yesterday, and I'm tempted to ask her how it seems in the office.

I shake my head and put the phone on the bed. Regina can't fix this for me, and she can't do anything about the Fates. I don't know who can, frankly, except Adam, but he's turned away from all of it.

I grab the nearest pair of clean jeans and a red blouse. I tuck the blouse into the jeans and grab my brown ankle-high boots.

Oliver has left me a plate of avocado toast and coffee brewing in the pot.

I pour the coffee into my to-go tumbler while eating a piece of the avocado toast over the sink. I get through about half before my stomach begins to sour. I retch over the kitchen trash can, and nothing comes out. Wine hangovers are the worst.

I've had my resignation letter written for two years. With a couple of updates, hastily typed after the interview yesterday, it's ready. But I'm not going to be afraid anymore. I'm going to stand up to all of them. Which means I have to do this in person.

I hit peak rush hour traffic downtown and end up sitting two blocks away from the building for fifteen minutes, giving me plenty of time to finish my coffee while contemplating buying a second cup. I'm going to need to be a little wired for this.

I tap my fingers on the elevator handrail the whole way up while I rock back and forth on and off of my toes. I was always a horrible ballerina, but I found comfort in being able to go up on my tiptoes. A repetitive motion to calm me down.

The elevator doors open, and I try to blink away the dark spots that are starting to cloud my eyes. I step out of the elevator and take stock of my surroundings. I still taste the faintest whiff of coffee on my own breath, I hear the elevator chime and close behind me, and I smell air freshener so thick in the air that I almost choke. I dig my fingernails into my palm and the black spots begin to fade so that I see my desk through the glass window.

Regina is the first person to look up. She shakes her head and motions for me to go back out to the elevator.

Adam, who is talking into his phone, follows her gaze to me. He says something into the phone and hangs up. He pushes his chair away from the desk and stands up.

All three Fates turn in tandem and Clara gasps when she sees me. Lucy's eyes narrow and Heather's hand flies to her mouth. Heather is the first to acknowledge me with a wave and a plastered-on smile.

Adam opens the door to his office and motions for me to come inside. His forehead is furrowed.

I lay my work bag on my desk and begin taking out my usual work materials. When I pull out my audio recorder the newsroom goes so silent that you could hear a piece of copy paper hit the floor. I take out my laptop.

No one has ever given me as much attention in my four years here as the entire newsroom is right now. It's like the entire ecosystem will rise or fall based on which direction I decide to go.

I stop in front of Regina's desk, just a few feet away from Adam.

"Gen, just go," Regina whispers. "It hasn't died down yet."

"Thank you for everything," I reply. "I couldn't have survived here without you."

"Gen," Adam says.

I nod at Regina and follow Adam into his office.

The moment I step inside he pulls the curtains, though I'm certain everyone is still watching, hoping to get some glimpse of what is happening through the shadows.

I sit down before Adam invites me to.

"So, it looks like the profile was well received," I say.

Adam sits down across from me and puts his elbows on the table. "It was a great profile," he replies. "I couldn't have expected more."

I hand him my letter.

"I have strong feelings," I begin. "About how you should have handled several situations here. About the kind of journalist and leader I want to be. And how I can't do any of that here. About how I made sure to detail all of my experiences in a message to the NABJ, and HR here."

"Gen, there's no need for you to make this nasty."

"I didn't make this nasty. You allowed the nastiness to percolate and looked away when it became untenable for your one Black reporter," I reply. "I encourage you to take stock of the culture here, and the behavior of some of your employees while in the newsroom. Otherwise, their *objectivity* when writing about matters of race may be questioned."

Regina pushes open Adam's door so quietly I don't realize that she's standing behind me. I jump a bit when I see her out of the corner of my eye.

"Regina, now is not the time," Adam says.

"I just received a call from publicity," she replies. "Gen is being courted by three different magazines and another paper for an exposé on racism in local news media."

"That's great." Adam's facial expression doesn't change. Apparently, it's not *that* great.

"They're also calling because we're being inundated with social media posts from former staffers about a toxic workplace, and media backlash from both local and national mediums about Gen potentially being let go from the paper," Regina says.

Adam slams his hand into the desk and I jump back.

Regina stands in front of me, her arms out, blocking access to me. "Walk it off, Adam," she says.

He stands up and straightens the bottom of his shirt.

Something hits the floor outside of the office and we all move toward the shuttered windows. Regina continues to stand in front of me, and Adam has to squeeze past her to get to the door.

He pushes the door open, steps out, but immediately takes a few steps back.

I turn to Regina. "Can you see?" I whisper.

She shakes her head and stands on her tiptoes to try and see past Adam.

Lucy bursts in, her eyes wide. "The *Times*. There are reporters from the *Times* here, and they want quotes."

Well, looks like shit is finally hitting the fan for Adam. I'm glad to see it.

CHAPTER THIRTY-SIX

Eva whistles as I recount the events of last night with Jude and this morning with the newsroom to her and Oliver over Indian food at our kitchen table. She leans her head back.

"Can you pass the naan?" Oliver asks.

Eva snaps her head up. "*Oliver*, how can you eat? Are you not completely taken by this tale of love and retribution?" she asks.

"I'm taken by the naan," he replies. "But I'll admit the Jackie bit threw me. Not that she orchestrated the photos but that she'd actually cop to it and try to be helpful by leaking the story to the *Times*? Little late, but still a big step."

He finally reaches over Eva to grab the naan himself.

Eva groans. "But the *love*. He loves you; you love him? This is poetry."

Oliver breaks off a piece of naan and begins chewing. He chews for several seconds, while staring at the nearest chicken dish.

Once he swallows, he says, "So, what are you going to do about your job?"

The eternal question. Besides being successful in my own right, part of my goal as a journalist has been to raise other Black women up. I did presentations for the rising freshmen when I was in high school, and specifically recruited junior reporters from Black sororities when I was in college. I had such a great experience when I interned at the *Tribune*, with Jennifer Warren, the editor that Adam mixes me up with, as my mentor. I wanted to give that experience to someone else, especially in my sometimes oppressively white hometown.

"I'm taking a call with one of the magazines tomorrow, one specifically targeted toward Black women, and I accepted the opportunity to write my Black women at work article with *Essence*. Otherwise, I'm just sending my résumé out, waiting to hear," I reply.

"I'm sorry," Oliver says. "I know you wanted this to be different, to be the place you could really start to create a legacy away from the Landons."

I nod. "I think I did. I just don't know what will happen to it."

"You started your legacy there, but it certainly won't have to end there," Eva replies. "You'll be a hot ticket for so many publications."

Eva picks up the container of samosas and drops two on her plate and two on Oliver's. She hands me the last two.

A text from Regina pops up on my phone telling me to turn on the local news. I slide the phone over to Oliver, who gets up to turn on the TV in the living room.

Eva lays down some of our extra towels across the couch in case we spill sauce. She brought the couch in for all of us and has been reliably concerned for its integrity since. We're the only twenty-somethings I've heard of with a dedicated living room towel basket, specifically for eating.

When we turn to the local news, Jude is just sitting down with the evening anchor, Rachel Jenkins. Rachel Jenkins is a Black woman, and our collective favorite anchor for her brightly colored pantsuits and treatment of every local news story like it's an international espionage case involving three heads of state. Tonight, Rachel's wearing a canary yellow suit with a matching set of chunky earrings.

Eva turns to me. "This outfit is a ten out of ten," she says.

"I'd rate it a twelve. Incredible color," I reply.

Onscreen, Rachel turns to the camera. "Welcome to *WSYS in the Evening*. I'm Rachel Jenkins, and I'm here with a story of love, recovery, and corporate misbehavior. Sitting across from me is Jude Landon, local business owner. Hi, Jude."

"Hi, Rachel, thank you for having me," Jude says.

"Viewers may also recognize Jude for his appearance on our morning show yesterday, with his profiler from the *Tribune*, Genevieve Francis," Rachel says. "They participated in a very talked-about interview, where they were asked questions that some called sexist. Let's see a clip."

The video of Jude and me on the morning show begins to play and I cover my eyes. Even through my fingers I'm analyzing my posture, whether my skirt rode up too much, and if my earrings are swinging an excessive amount in my ears.

When the clip ends, I put my hands back on the couch.

Onscreen, Rachel leans in toward Jude. "What do you think, seeing that clip back?" she asks.

"It's not great," Jude says. "I knew that the line of questioning was sexist in the moment, but I was caught off guard. Seeing it back is just . . ." He hangs his head for a moment. "It's upsetting to see."

"You weren't the only one who thought so," Rachel says.

"I know. I am ashamed, though, that I allowed that to happen."

"Many women, particularly Black women, seemed to feel as though those questions were reducing Ms. Francis to her personal connection to you, without emphasizing her professional accomplishments."

"That's exactly right," Jude replies. "That's what it did, Rachel. Gen and I dated, but that's not the most interesting thing about either of us, certainly not her. Maybe it is for me." He laughs a bit.

"I hear a lot of emotion in your voice," Rachel says.

"There is," Jude replies. "I have many feelings for and about Gen Francis."

I feel my heart skip a beat and realize that both Oliver and Eva are watching me instead of the interview.

"How was her profile received at your company?" Rachel asks.

"Quite well by most," Jude replies. "Employees were really pleased with how our initiatives were received and seemed to appreciate my being more open than I have been in the past."

"Let's talk about your father, renowned entrepreneur and philanthropist Julian Landon," Rachel says. "He left you big shoes to fill, and in the profile you talked about how difficult it was to be in his shadow."

"It was," Jude replies. "Especially since I was given his shoes when they were still several sizes too big. I didn't know how to run a company when I inherited Landon Energy. I'm just now really starting to learn how to maximize my effectiveness as a leader. And I'm hoping that more of the proposals I bring will be seriously considered."

"Will Genevieve Francis be given a seat at the table?" Rachel asks. "Professionally, of course."

I haven't even figured out composting, I certainly wouldn't want to be on the board of Landon Energy. Not that I have qualifications to sit on any board. What is she getting at?

Jude smiles. "Well, she's not an expert in environmental technology or policy, or business, so I'm not sure that'd be appropriate. But I would love for her to have a seat at many other tables. She has an exciting career ahead of her."

"Let's talk about the *Tribune*," Rachel says. "It's come out just a few hours ago that there were some pretty severe instances of racist and sexist behavior directed at Ms. Francis in the wake of the profile."

Several of the chat logs, names redacted of course, appear on screen, and I turn my head. They don't get any less brutal the longer I stare at them.

"Yes," Jude replies. "Gen herself expressed some of her experiences to me recently, and I've spoken to Adam Cartman, the editor-in-chief, today to express my disappointment as a member of the community and someone who trusted the *Tribune* with my story."

"Would you have trusted the *Tribune*, knowing what you know now?" Rachel asks.

"I would have trusted Gen," Jude replies. "It was never the publication that mattered, it was the writer."

I realize that I'm smiling and that I've begun to tear up a bit. I dab the corner of my eye with the crook of my finger.

Eva squeezes my hand, and even Oliver looks a little swept up in the moment; he's staring at Jude, and the corners of his mouth are starting to curl up.

"What's Jude Landon's next move?" Rachel asks.

"Find new board members, preferably women, and women of color in particular," he replies. "And to find more projects moving forward that will help the people who need it most."

"Is there a motto you'll take forward with you?" Rachel asks.

"Driving an electric car doesn't make you a good person and solar panels on your roof doesn't actually mean you care about the legacy you leave for your children," Jude replies. "It's something Gen and I used to say to each other."

A tear falls down my cheek and I'm grinning at the television. I could swear he winked at the camera when he said it, knowing I'd be watching.

"What would you like your legacy to be?" Rachel asks.

"Making whatever parts of the world better that I can. I'm a cis, rich, white, heterosexual man—it's the *least* I can do with the privileges I have. I want my children to not cringe in twenty years when they read the profile for the first time. I want to deserve the words that Gen wrote."

He already does. He deserves every single thing I've said about him. Good and bad. He's the person I always wanted him to be.

"Is there anything else you'd like to add? Something the profile didn't cover?" Rachel asks.

Jude stares directly into the camera. "Actually . . . d . . . do we have time?"

Rachel looks off-screen and nods at, I assume, a producer. "Is three minutes enough?"

"Yes."

"You have the floor."

Oh God. Tell me this isn't the televised proposal they wanted.

"Part of my legacy has to involve addressing all my past mistakes. Not just the ones that look splashy on a m . . . m . . . magazine cover."

Eva gasps.

"No way," Oliver says.

Back onscreen Jude takes a deep breath. "Sorry. I have a stutter. Always have, but I mostly outgrew it. Speech therapy. Money. All that." He's slipped from CEO Jude voice.

"That's okay, take your time. Well, not too much," Rachel says, giving a small laugh.

"When I was twenty, three months before my father died, I went to a party with Gen and one of our friends. Gen got a ride home with someone else, and I told her that our friend and I were going to get an Uber back to our apartment.

"And then I didn't. I'd had three beers, several shots. I couldn't walk in a straight line. I got behind the wheel with our friend and crashed into a tree in someone's backyard. The owners called the police, and long story short, I failed a sobriety test and blew a .18 on the Breathalyzer."

"You're here today, saying that you drove drunk with a friend . . . Where is your friend today?" Rachel looks up at the ceiling like she's looking into the annals of heaven.

Oliver reaches over Eva and grips my hand. Neither of us can believe he's actually doing this.

On TV, a tear splashes down Jude's face. He holds his right hand out, and Julian's ring causes a camera glare as it hits the studio lights. "He's fine. He had a concussion afterward, but he was generous with me. He told me he shouldn't have gotten in the car, when in reality I shouldn't have thought it was okay in the first place."

"And the police, what did they do after you failed the sobriety tests?" Rachel asks.

"I got a DUI. Fully booked as an adult. I spent the night in jail. And afterward, my parents, with love, but misguidedly, used their wealth and resources to bury it."

"Our producers are looking in their databases right now and there's not a single record of your arrest."

"Exactly. I lied to Gen after. I lied to our friends. I had a drinking problem, and I pretended that it was just a one-time thing. I've never driven drunk since, but I had before."

I turn to Oliver, my eyes searching his face. We both knew it wasn't the first time, but we'd never talked about it, to Jude or each other.

Oliver turns toward the nearest wall and nods. His eyes start to fill with tears. "I thought he was just tipsy. Until we hit that tree, I always thought he was just tipsy. Not . . . not as bad as he was."

I reach over to turn off the TV, but Oliver shakes his head. He reaches for the remote and turns the volume up.

"What's your relationship to alcohol now?" Rachel asks onscreen.

"I don't drink. I haven't since the day of my father's funeral. I attend AA meetings twice a week. I go to therapy, like I mentioned in the interview. And a whole bunch of other stuff that won't be particularly interesting to the audience."

"Why come clean now?" Rachel asks.

"Because part of recovery is making amends. The first part actually. And I never did. To my friend, O, I'm sorry. I'm so sorry for putting you in danger and asking you to lie to our friends and families for me. And to everyone who has been or knows someone whose life has been impacted by a drunk driver, I will never be able to properly give my regrets and my condolences."

"This will be a big headline," Rachel says.

Jude takes a deep breath. "I hope so. I have this platform, made bigger by Gen's profile. And part of living up to her words is living up to her ideals. In that vein, I plan to donate to clinics and non-profits for addicts, as well as homeless shelters. As well as dedicate sixty percent of Landon Energy's profits toward specifically address-ing the environmental conditions that help contribute to addiction in lower-income populations. My board has already approved the initiative."

A link to the Landon Energy website pops up on the chyron, as well as a list of local resources and activists.

"Thank you for having me. And letting me tell my story."

"Jude Landon, everyone," Rachel says. "When we come back, we'll be checking in with Jason Voss and tomorrow's weather. Is there a storm coming? Hurricane watch is on."

I lay my head into my hands, which Oliver is still holding. I'm even more sure about my choice now. I just hope Jude will be on board.

CHAPTER THIRTY-SEVEN

It never occurred to me that anyone would care about the politics of a local newspaper in a town of a few hundred thousand people. It looks like my profile of Jude has made national news, so the sudden resignation of the editor that published said profile is now everywhere in the major media outlets. Apparently, Jude's interview last night made a real splash, and now I'm being asked for a statement by almost every outlet I've ever really cared about.

I pick up my phone and press Regina's contact.

She answers on the second ring.

"He really resigned?" I ask.

"With a commitment to teach himself to be anti-racist before ever stepping into a newsroom again. Publicly."

"Did he say anything?" I ask.

"Nope. Walked out without a word. The unholy trinity is in tears. Their mentor is practically dead, they say."

"Are you going to stay?" I ask.

"Without you? Nah. Handed in my resignation on floral stationery this morning."

Thank goodness. Regina has always been too talented, too incredible for that place. I hope I can follow her somewhere, really get to learn from her. She's a rock star.

Oliver has left me a J-shaped pancake, the closest he can get to admitting he might actually text Jude back. Eva has left me a handwritten note with four hearts surrounding the message: *Go get him! (And also a new job, which is equally as important or more whatever your priorities. HUGS.)*

I have a phone screening with a magazine in half an hour. I've fantasized about the moment I'd walk into the *Tribune* with another opportunity in my back pocket; scrolling through Indeed looking for other jobs on my lunch break was my most consistent form of self-care. At this point, I don't think I'll ever walk in there again, and it's bittersweet.

I eat the pancake while scrolling through social media responses to Jude's interview last night. I'm not the only one who was swooning and in awe over what he said. Several mental health organizations are reporting that Landon Energy has been in contact with them since the interview, searching for resources and potential partnerships. A good number of strangers are openly musing on whether or not we'll get back together.

I try to make my eyes glaze over the less supportive posts; the ones that say I'm not worthy of him, or that I'm just a gold-digger trying to trap him and drive him away from his family. Several of them seem to be coming from burner accounts, created in the last twenty-four hours, and I wonder which one of my coworkers figured out that strategy.

A text from Mickey pops up. *Don't read social media*, she says. *I can tell you the highlights.*

Too late, I reply.

She sends several eye rolling faces.

I call Mickey, and she answers after five rings.

"You didn't come over last night, were you with Helena?" I ask.

She snorts. "I was supposed to be, but she didn't show up. So I was sitting at Isis's Place, you know, the new Black-owned bar you told me about, and who shows up but my date from last week. The medical resident with the 4c curls."

"Okay, I'm intrigued."

"She was grabbing drinks with some of the other residents, but when she saw me at the bar, she asked if I wanted to chat."

"And?" I ask.

"And we grabbed a table. And I left her apartment this morning in one of her sweaters," she replies.

Damn. When Mickey is on, she's on. I need to take notes.

"Incredible."

"Okay, got to go, there's a ten-year-old giving me side-eye and I absolutely can't allow this to continue," she says. Before she hangs up, I hear her say, "I *know* you're not giving me that look, when you're *supposed* to be putting your homework in the bin."

I smile to myself and make a mental note to find out what happens with Helena in school today from Mickey later.

My phone begins to buzz. A New York City number. *Here we go, first job interview in four long years.*

I take a couple of deep breaths.

"Hello?" I say into the phone.

"Is this Genevieve Francis?"

"Yes, it is."

"Hi, it's Ursula from *Cocoa Butter* magazine. We loved your piece on Jude Landon."

"Thank you," I reply. "I love what you all are doing for young Black women with your platform."

"We love what you're doing with yours, and I'm sure there's something we could collaborate on."

I realize that I'm almost being courted for the first time in my professional life, and my eyes well up. Maybe I can still get to where I want to be in my career, as well as my personal life.

"I would love to hear more about what you're working on, and any positions you may have available," I reply.

"Fantastic. What would be your dream article to write?"

"A series of in-depth pieces of Black women's experiences in journalism, from interns to editors-in-chief."

"That sounds like something we could get behind. Anything else?"

I silently wipe away tears as I answer the rest of Ursula's questions. For the first time, I feel seen professionally. I can't go back to the way things were under Adam, but I can't let the next person go through this either.

Barely five minutes after the interview ends, I see that my prom photo has once again popped up on my phone.

"Hey," Jude says. "How are you?"

"Hanging in there," I reply. "There have been ups and downs."

"Can you meet me at my father's grave when you get off of work?" he asks.

"Don't bring the ring."

"I will not bring the ring, but it's important that we meet there. I promise it's nothing creepy," he says.

"Okay." I hang up before I can second-guess myself.

CHAPTER THIRTY-EIGHT

I try not to shudder as I walk past the tombstones of dead people I'll never know. I recognize the exact spots where I felt like I'd left some part of myself. By the formerly bejeweled gravestone for a shipping magnate, I left the feeling of Jude's hand in mine. In front of the collection of six-foot-tall tombstones I left feelings of romantic security. Next to the family crypt I left one of the shards in my chest, and literally, a nail, when I clutched onto one of the walls to stay upright on the way out of the graveyard.

I look ahead and try not to remember looking through these same monuments for Jude four years ago. I try to forget that he didn't come after me.

This time, I see him. He's sitting on the ground inside the fenced area dedicated to the Landon family. Jude looks over in my direction, and when he spots me he waves. I almost smile, thinking he's going to get his suit dirty before I remember the grass stains on his pant legs at Julian's funeral. I feel myself begin shaking.

I don't want to be that girl again, the one that he left. I can't be her. She got her heart broken, by Jude, by her job, by her own hopes for the future. Even if Jude's different, even if he wouldn't hurt me like that again, he's only half of the equation. I still have something else to repair, for the new woman I want to be.

He waves again. After a few seconds of me not moving toward him, he stands up.

I shake my head and take a couple of steps back. I reach up to my ears; I can almost feel the earrings dangling against my neck, even though I'm wearing studs. I put my head in my hands and try to block out the memories flooding back.

Oliver had to drag me out of here last time, because I couldn't stand on my own legs. Mickey kept me alive for weeks by practically spoon-feeding me soup and small bits of toast. I couldn't fathom the idea of being without Jude, and I became a shell of myself waiting for him to come back to me.

I hear squishing mud coming closer and closer, until someone gently taps my knuckle. I lower my hands and see Jude standing in front of me.

He extends his hand to me. I nod, and he takes mine.

Just like last time, I'm not alone. Jude takes the lead, always a few steps ahead of me, but looking back every few seconds as though I'll have disappeared. Like my own personal Orpheus, he doesn't trust that I'll stay with him. I don't know that I trust it either. There's something here, like the sunflowers I see in the corner of the Landon family plot. But, like those flowers, it hasn't fully bloomed, and if we pick at it too soon, it won't grow.

He steers until we hit the golden fence surrounding the Landon family plot. He holds the gate open, still not letting go of my hand.

I immediately lock eyes with Jackie Landon's future grave site, which lies next to Julian's. Theirs are the only two monuments in the plot.

Jude has lain down a picnic blanket on the ground in front of Julian's pillar. His messenger bag is set on the furthest left corner of the blanket.

I pull my hand away from his and sit down in the center of the blanket, hoping he'll sit a few feet away.

He sits down next to me, so that our arms are almost touching, and unbuttons his suit jacket. He pulls off the jacket and lays it on the blanket beside him.

"So, you're maybe wondering why I asked you to meet me here, of all places," he says. "I promise there's a good reason for that part." He motions to his briefcase.

"Ah, this is a working meeting," I reply.

He laughs, the slightly high-pitched, throaty laugh I remember from so many of our moments together.

I raise my eyebrows and adjust my position on the blanket. I clasp my hands together in my lap, digging my fingernails into the palms of my hands.

Jude reaches into his briefcase again and pulls out a small bottle of Martinelli's apple cider with two metal cups. He nods his head to the bottle in question.

"Please," I reply, and he pours. I take a sip. It's perfectly carbonated and somehow just tastes expensive. "Are we celebrating?"

Jude takes a sip of his cider instead of answering. He pulls a file folder out of his briefcase.

He opens the folder and I see a clipped stack of papers. Jude slides the clip off, pulls out several of the papers, and then re-clips the rest. He lays the clipped documents to the side.

"May I move closer?" he asks.

I nod.

He slides over until our hips are touching. He lays the papers across his lap and points to the top sheet, which reads: *Julian Landon's Last Will and Testament.*

"I don't know that this is my business," I reply. "The profile is over. And we're not—"

"It's not about that," he says. "Is it okay if I read something he enclosed in the will?"

"If you feel comfortable sharing it, then of course," I reply.

He clears his throat. "To my son Jude Alexander, I bequeath all of my shares in Landon Energy, my title, and the penthouse apartment. I also bequeath to Jude $70 million in liquid assets, and $20 million of other investments, to be detailed below."

"Okay, this seems like a bit of a not-so-humble brag," I interrupt.

"We're getting there. I want to be totally transparent with the information I was given," he says.

"Okay."

He turns the page and takes a deep breath. He has begun to sweat a bit and dabs his forehead with the sleeve of his dress shirt, leaving a small wet spot right below his emerald green cuff link.

"To my son Jude Alexander, I also leave words I hope he takes to heart moving forward. As CEO, my life often gets very lonely. My biggest regret, if I die prematurely, is how little time I spent with my family. I risked my parents' reputation when I married your mother," he says.

Julian came from money that Jackie didn't, even if she's appropriated wealth seamlessly. His girlfriend before Jackie was the person his parents, who owned a series of manufacturing companies, wanted him to marry. When he brought Jackie home, it's rumored his father left the room the moment he saw her. He started Landon Energy right after they cut him off, with money he had slowly hoarded from them over years.

"You will not be doing the same," Jude continues, "if you marry Genevieve Francis. I've watched the two of you over these years, and in you, I see the love your mother and I had. So, to you, and to Genevieve, I bequeath my blessing that, when you both deem it appropriate, you get married."

I wipe away a tear that's begun to creep down my cheek. Julian was always kind to me, even when Jackie made her disdain known.

Jude continues, "Jude, I formally ask that you do not ruin your relationship with Genevieve. Your mother has a list of suitable replacements and I find each one of them insufferable. I therefore emphasize my blessing for your marriage to Genevieve, and I bequeath to you half of my mother's jewelry collection, the specific items listed inset. The other half of the collection will be left to my daughter, Joanna Rebecca Landon."

"You're not really putting my mind at ease that this isn't a proposal," I reply. "Though it'd certainly be unique in both a romantic and morbid way."

"I'm getting to the point, I swear," he says. "But there are beautiful loose gems and diamonds in that collection that can be used to create a custom ring for my future wife, hence why he left them to me. I got all of the loose jewels and Joanna got all of the pre-set jewelry."

I definitely didn't get to whatever room those are in in Jude's apartment. I'm sure that Joanna's collection is set up like a museum in the Landon family home, with cases of jewelry adorning what was once a bedroom.

"Your dad wanted you to make your own custom jewelry collection?" I ask.

"It seems like it," he replies. "He was really convinced I'd marry someone with much better taste than me."

"No idea who that could be. He was quite vague," I say.

Jude smiles and gently elbows me in the side. "I'll keep going," he says. "Finally, to my presumed future daughter-in-law, Genevieve Elizabeth Francis, regardless of your relationship with my son, I bequeath you first rights at any protracted form of media about myself and Landon Energy. I have enjoyed the pieces of yours that I've read, and you are the person I want to tell our story."

I try to blink back more tears, but they begin to flow down my face. Jude may have wanted me to write the profile, but Julian is the one who made sure that opportunity would be there, no matter what happened.

"I can't believe he said all of that. I'm moved, I truly am," I say.

Jude holds the paper up in front of him for a moment. "Hold on, there's a bit more," he says. "In the event of the dissolution of Genevieve and Jude's relationship, all stated in this will still stands. I wish the best for Genevieve, whether that is with or without my son." Jude places the paper down on the file folder.

"So that's why . . . the profile."

"Yes," he replies. "And no. I wanted you to write the profile, regardless of the will. He wanted you to write the book."

"The book? The Landon family truly will not let me *rest*."

"If you've got some free time, it might be fun. Imagine reading another three decades of financials!"

"Ha. Ha. I'll consider that proposal."

"Ah, so numbers instead of diamonds get consideration. Got it."

I laugh, even though it still stings. We're within three feet of where I left my heart, last time.

"May I ask how you reacted?" I ask.

"We did the will reading the day after the funeral. I was so furious at him for dying in the first place, and you know the rest. Him telling me that I should marry you made me want to distance myself even more. So I did.

"Oliver described the aftermath of that day to me in breathtaking detail. Every word you said. What your sobs felt like. He really lit me up, and I couldn't take it, so I pushed him out too. I'd like to say grief made me fragile, but that was all me. I can't blame a transient state. Oliver said as much then, and yesterday when he texted me about the interview."

Oliver never really has known when to take a step back and avoid a confrontation. I don't know that I've ever been more grateful for it than now, when he insisted on standing up for me when he knew it could cost him his other best friend.

"So, what happened with the profile?" I ask.

"Things were in a really bad place with the board, and the company was getting a lot of reports from consumers and potential investors that my extreme privacy was essentially a turn-off. I was barely seen in public, I stopped using social media, and the only things people saw were that horrible *People* cover and the occasional paparazzi shot if I went to New York or LA for business."

"So, the profile was designed to be a boost."

"Yes and no," he says. "It was designed to be my coming out, essentially. Good or bad, it was something more than people were getting. So I floated the idea by Adam over several months."

"That explains the office rumors about a mystery CEO wanting an article."

"Exactly. I thought maybe you'd figure it out, but Adam apparently kept it pretty close to the belt. I insisted that it be a lower-level staff member to avoid the typical hierarchy. And my own blind spots led me to believe that there was no way you weren't the top junior employee. Adam gave me every name besides yours when telling me who could write the piece."

Of course he did. Another lie from Adam about how I would have gotten the profile either way.

"Adam told me I was guaranteed for the profile because he didn't think I'd try to hit on you," I say.

Jude snorts. "He didn't mention you at all until he'd raved about every single other junior and senior writer, and I directly mentioned your name as someone I knew worked there."

"Screw him," I say.

"Truly. When I brought you up, he framed it as if I was doing an act of charity by *letting* you try and write the profile. When I pointed out that you'd written several profiles in college that were well received, while none of the other junior employees had done a profile before, he was absolutely shocked."

"I'm shocked he knew who you were talking about, since he didn't know my name."

Jude squeezes my hand and takes another sip of apple cider. He pushes Julian's will back into the file folder just as a gust of wind comes. He holds the folder closed and then slips it back into his briefcase.

"So, to conclude," he says. "I asked Mom and Joanna to start selling some of their stock. I didn't tell them why, so they assumed it was just to help pay off some of the family expenses."

"I'm sure you didn't have to ask Joanna twice," I reply, smiling.

"Once it became clear to me that I was potentially in danger of being bought out and ousted by the board, I agreed to the profile to try and get Landon Energy in the media before anything went down. If the profile was favorable, there'd be backlash for kicking me out of the company. If it wasn't, then the board looked smart but still too calculated in ousting essentially a kid who never found his footing."

"You're twenty-five," I say.

"But, as a young white man, I knew how the media would portray me. A boy king of sorts, so even if you framed the profile honestly, and it came across as negative, the vast majority of people would view me as a kid in over his head."

He gamed the system. Deliberately this time, and maybe for the best. Maybe he did get something good from his father.

"A regular vigilante," I reply.

"When Adam tried to waver on giving you the profile, I let him know it was required in my father's will, and subsequent company bylines which are binding. Which was, yes, a lie since that's not exactly legal, but he didn't ask very many questions. He used a morality clause to take the profile away after the photos came out."

"Why are you telling me all of this now?" I ask.

"Because I wanted to lay everything bare, in the place where both of us left parts of ourselves four years ago, to see if there was anything we could repair. I needed to be honest to ask if there's any chance you could want to be with me."

I want to be with him, so badly. But not like this. Not when both of us have blown up our lives in the media over the last few days, both intentionally and inadvertently. We're not ready to make it work yet. So, where we broke apart, I intend to give us what I think is our best chance to come back together, in hopefully a little while.

"No."

His hand, which is holding the Martinelli's bottle, slacks. His face falls in an eerily similar way to how it did when we were last in front of this plot.

I hold out my hand.

"Is this revenge? For . . . God, no. How can I accuse you of that? That's so messed up of me. I trust you. I trust this. I'm sorry."

I take his hands. "Stand up," I say.

He stands up, still holding onto my hands. "Okay. I'm standing."

I push myself onto my knees, and kick one of my legs out. "And breathe, geez. It's not like I can dump you."

Jude's eyes widen. He scans the outside of my pockets, presumably trying to see if there's anything inside. "Is this . . . ?" he asks. "You don't even know my size."

"Oh my God, no. Did you really think I was going to turn this around into *that* kind of proposal?" I ask.

"You're the one down on one knee."

"I am. Not to propose marriage, because that would be ridiculous. No offense. Mostly. Maybe a little offense."

Jude takes a gulp of his cider and starts to cough. He waves off my attempt to reach out to him and I try not to flash back to our last time here.

When he catches his breath, he croaks out, "So you're on one knee because . . ."

"I need to figure out what I'm doing next. And I need to do that without the pressure of being directly in your family's orbit. So I *propose*, in this place where we ended our romantic relationship, that we get to know each other again, and maybe go on some dates. We try to rebuild some of the communication we're sorely lacking.

We stop having the same fights, and when I'm ready, if you're still here, we can see if we can take it to that next level. Maybe be in that portrait together someday."

Jude raises his glass. "To seeing. And flexible thinking." In one swift motion he kisses me, and I melt into his lips.

I've never been happier to take my time and see where something goes. We're already starting to reclaim this place, taking the cemetery where we ended one phase of our relationship and turning it into the cemetery where we started the next one.

Another gust of wind blows by, ruffling the trees behind us, and nearly knocking over my cup. I don't believe in ghosts, but I wonder if it's Julian, nodding his approval.

Jude reaches out and scoops up the cup with the hand that isn't still holding mine.

"Let's try. For the rest, we'll just have to wait," I say.

"Well, I'll have you know I'm fantastic at waiting. Apparently, I stayed really hung up on my high school girlfriend."

"I wouldn't know what that's like, I'm excellent at moving on. Haven't thought about my high school boyfriend at all."

Thunder booms above us, as if calling me out on the lie, and rain begins to fall.

Jude takes his blazer and holds it over me. "Race you to my car?"

We both stand and I scrunch the blanket up while Jude chugs the rest of his cider. We drop the empty glasses into his briefcase and start to run toward the street.

This time he doesn't look back; instead, he slows down so we can run side by side, both of us looking toward whatever lies beyond these gravestones.

CHAPTER THIRTY-NINE

Four Years Later

Regina leans into my eye with a mascara wand.

"There are literally people who are trained to do this," I reply. "And they have our shades."

"I'm building intimacy," she replies. "So we can go out there and really sell the mentorship angle. Since *someone* refused the matching outfits."

She gestures to her purple pantsuit paired with a silver shirt and heels.

"You're ridiculous, you know. We can sell the mentorship angle in our sleep because it's the *truth*."

I kick out the new purple heels I bought, as if for emphasis. At least I matched something.

"Did you break them in?" she asks.

"Nope."

"Have I taught you nothing?" Joanna asks, matching Regina in purple chiffon.

"Our favorite investor," Regina says.

"Kisses," Joanna says. "In the air. Can't touch the face."

I take a deep breath. Rachel Jenkins has taken her talents to daytime for us to appear on *WSYS in the Morning* and talk about our latest project. I feel a little self-conscious in my slim-fitting gray suit. I caught a glimpse of Rachel and she's wearing magenta, contrasting Regina's purple.

"It's time," a producer says, cocking her head toward the studio.

Joanna gives us both a thumbs-up and follows us toward the stage. She takes her place behind the camera, and I can hear her whispering lighting instructions to one of the PAs.

Regina holds my hand as we walk out onto the stage, smiling at Rachel, who reaches out to hug both of us just as someone says, "We're on!"

Rachel sits down as we wave to the camera.

"I know, I know. I'm not your usual pop of blonde in the morning. Rachel Jenkins here, with a story I just *had* to tell." She smiles. "Please welcome Regina Carson and Genevieve Francis from the *Drier Park Gazette*."

"Thank you, Rachel, we're thrilled to be here," Regina says.

"I'll do my best to not get us trending for any scandals," Rachel says, winking at the camera.

I know that somewhere behind the scenes Isabel Nelson is seething at that almost-forgotten reference.

"That would be appreciated," I reply.

"So, for anyone who doesn't know, can you tell us about the *Gazette* and how you two got started?" Rachel asks, her finger balanced under her chin as she leans forward.

I nod at Regina.

"Well, we were both underappreciated Black women at a white publication. I was working as an assistant to the editor and Gen was working as a staff writer, without the stories to prove it. Most people know what happened next with the Landon profile and the very public racial reckoning at that paper. Anyway, afterward, we both handed in our resignations and decided to pursue other avenues together," Regina says.

"With one avenue being reviving the *Gazette*, a local Black-owned newspaper that went under seven years ago," Rachel says.

"Yes," I reply. "We wanted to write the stories that spoke to us, and we figured the best way to do that would be to be the ones in charge."

"With a generous donation of . . . exactly how much, from one of our most famous families?" Rachel asks.

"You know we'll never give a number, as that investor has asked us to keep specifics quiet. And she'd like to remain behind the scenes."

Joanna covers her face with her hands, revealing her perfect French tips and an emerald from the Landon family jewelry vault.

"So, tell us about your current initiative," Rachel says.

"Since we were at the former paper, we've both wanted to write a series about Black women in the workplace. I did a trial run of some stories in *Cocoa Butter* a few years ago, but we're expanding it in a bigger way by writing some stories ourselves but also inviting

Black women across journalism, including high school and college publications, to pen their own pieces as part of a Black women in the workplace series," I say.

"And will you be expanding that initiative to other industries?" Rachel asks.

"We'd love to," Regina replies. "Are you interested in turning the tables and being interviewed?"

"Girl, I could give you a book," Rachel says.

Regina and I both laugh. What I wouldn't give for just a fraction of the stories that Rachel could tell.

Rachel holds up an advance reader copy of *The Landons: From Private to Public Energy*.

"Rachel, you know I wasn't supposed to disclose anything," I say, smiling at her.

Rachel shrugs. "I couldn't resist! After the turmoil of your last piece on the Landons, what made you want to go back?" Rachel asks.

"I was asked to and given quite a bit of creative license in how I wanted to approach the story," I reply. "I'm also allowed to handle all publicity for the book in ways I feel comfortable with."

"A big change from last time. What do you attribute that to?" Rachel asks.

I glance off-screen toward Joanna, who is trying, rather unsuccessfully, to quietly usher someone over to her. I smile as he comes into view.

Jude accepted my graveyard proposal, and, after two years of genuine friendship with a hefty side of benefits, I accepted a proper date. Now I get to love the man he is instead of the boy he was.

"A lot of communication, a bit of therapy, and a lifetime's worth of groveling," I reply.

Rachel laughs. "Anything you'd like to say to your former colleagues at the *Tribune*? You refer to them as the Fates frequently in your pieces about the toxic workplace culture."

"Your pieces lack objectivity," Regina says. "Perhaps you should open your perspectives and not come forward with such a bent slant."

"You did your best to make sure we'd never work in this town again," I reply. "So we went to another one and made something better, and more inclusive. We made our own fate."

"Gen Francis and Regina Carson, everyone. I'm Rachel Jenkins, tune in tonight when I get to the bottom of the meat at one local elementary cafeteria. Is it beef, or is it fake? Hold your forks. This one is going to be a doozy."

"Cut! Five minutes until we're back," someone says off-screen.

Joanna runs up, her purple Louboutins making her at least five inches taller than me. She leans down to hug me.

"You were both perfect," she says.

"It went better than last time," I say.

"Much," Jude says from behind the camera, the heels of his dress shoes clicking against the floor.

"How was your speech?"

"Great. Really great. I'll tell you about it over breakfast? I may have already gotten muffins and coffee for you from Emily Jay's bakery. I was thinking we could eat in your car? Sit by the pond?"

"If you spill decaf coffee in Miss Minnie Cooper the Second, I will dump you right on tomorrow's morning show."

"That would kill in the ratings," he replies. "I'm in. I might have to do it on purpose."

I smile up at him, and his eyes crinkle as he smiles back.

He spins his father's ring around his finger and leans his head against my shoulder for a moment.

I pull his head back toward me until our lips fully dissolve into each other. My eyes close, and his fingers dance down my neck toward my back.

His tongue flits into my mouth for a moment before he decides to drop his lips from my mouth to my neck.

"Seriously, get a room. Call training or something," Joanna says.

"Seconded. Eat your muffins and let some things be private," Regina teases, shaking her head at us.

We walk into the unlit corridor on the side of the studio, and hearing his shoes clack against the floor almost makes me flash back to our last time here. Where we said I love you in the darkness.

He must have the same idea, because he stays beside me, holding my hand until we get out into the light.

We both turn to each other, and the words tumble out simultaneously.

"Jinx," we say in unison.

The light flickers for a moment, and I look back down the corridor. Joanna and Regina are standing in the darkness, both of them holding their phones out. I turn to Jude and see that, once again, he's on one knee.

The ring is different this time, and so is my answer.

ACKNOWLEDGMENTS

It takes a village, truly, to write a book, and mine is truly the best. Thank you to all of the people who have made this possible, I am truly so grateful. To my readers, I started writing books when I was eleven, and sharing my work with the world has been my dream ever since. Thank you to everyone who has (and will) engage with my work. You're making my dreams come true.

To all of my friends, thank you for your excitement and encouragement. You all have bragged about me and this book from before it was even a fully formed project, and have cheered me on all the way. I appreciate all of you more than you can ever know.

To my agent, Dorian Maffei, you are an absolute rock star. We've had quite a journey together, and you have fought for my stories and vision every step of the way. I am so lucky that you saw and liked my #PitMad tweet, and that I've gotten the opportunity to have you in my corner. You're the best, and I hope we can

Acknowledgments

continue to work together for many years to come. Thank you, thank you, thank you.

To my editor, Jess Verdi, you give such thoughtful and detailed feedback, and truly understood what I was trying to do with this story. You offer sensitivity and humor in your comments, and I'm thrilled that you gravitated toward this book and advocated for me. Thank you for believing in this project.

To the team at Alcove/Crooked Lane: Thai Perez, Rebecca Nelson, and everyone else who has worked on this project, you have done such wonderful work. Thank you for your care and dedication.

To my family, Mom, Dad, Adrienne, thank you for always believing in me. Mom and Dad, thank you for buying me notebooks every Christmas, and always encouraging my love of reading and writing. Thank you for fighting for me and alongside me, and always reminding me that I can do anything. To Mom, you have frequently been the only Black girl in the room, and you have taught me so much about what it means to be a Black woman in this world, and how imperative it is to always raise others up with you. You are my role model, and I am so fortunate that I had you as my example.

To Sean, you are my constant, my touchstone, my home. I love you, and thank you for being there on the best and worst days of this process. You may not always understand my experiences, but you always empathize and seek to learn and grow. Every day with you is the best, and I could not imagine a better partner. Thank you for reminding me that I can do this, and for keeping me hydrated. I'm the luckiest person to have you by my side.

Finally, to all the Black girls who've made sure I wasn't the only Black girl in the room, thank you. Ruqayyah, Ciara, Briana, Ebony, Natasha, Mattie, Scherly, and IBK, to name just a few. We have

Acknowledgments

been through so much together, and you all have helped support me and hold me down in PWIs. You have stood up for me and with me when we've faced injustice. You've laughed with me over Starbucks runs and office politics. You've gone out of your way to be there for me, both when I'm in the room and when I'm out of it. I could not have gotten through so many of these situations without you. This book is dedicated to you all. I am so eternally appreciative of everything you have done for me. Thank you. Let's keep thriving together.